Praise for the Max Brown Tetralogy (+1)

"*How I Made $3,200,000 from My Hobby* is a sharp, witty debut from a deeply talented and engaging humorist."
—*Self-Publishing Review*

"Michael Bernhart draws you in page after page."
—Sarah Jean Alexander, author of *Wildlives*

"*How Speleology Restored My Sex Drive* by Michael Bernhart is just right. It hit hard and there was hope. It bounced back and reflected brilliantly."
—Stephanie Barber, author of *All the People*

"Bernhart's is a funny and engaging voice . . . sharp, witty . . . talented."
—*The Independent Review of Books*

"*How I Made $3,200,000 from My Hobby* is a big-hearted and resplendent book."
—Adrian Van Young, author of *The Man Who Noticed Everything*

"*How Moral Philosophy Failed* is a small miracle of hope and desperation. With unexpected grace, Bernhart's characters love, hate, and cope from page to beautiful page."
—Jonny Diamond, editor of *LitHub*

"What if a book upended everything you thought you knew about our world? *How Existentialism Almost Killed Me* by Michael Bernhart could absolutely do that."
—Gabe Durham, author of *Fun Camp*

"*How I Made $3,200,000 from My Hobby* pre-chews a charmingly irascible post-millennial W*eltanschauung* and gently funnels its essence back to esurient readers."
—Molly Brodak, author of *A Little Middle of the Night*

"A must-read final chapter in the action-thriller series, *How Moral Philosophy Failed* is a one-of-a-kind tale of crimes against humanity, and the few people willing to step up to fight against it. By the book's final pages readers will be left in shock as the final events begin winding down. This . . . captivating read is filled with action, suspense, and fantastic character development that readers will absolutely love. Be sure to grab your copy today!"

—Anthony Avina, author of *I Was an Evil Teenager: Remastered* and *Identity*

"This book is very similar to art."

—Sommer Browning, author of *Backup Singers*

"Make no mistake about it, Dr. Bernhart knows how to write. Really write."

—Matt DeBenedictis, author of *Congratulations! There's No Last Place if Everyone Is Dead*

"This book (*How Moral Philosophy Failed*) is a spark in a dark place, a light in a desolate landscape. Unweaving the threads of love, family, loss, and disrepair, this novel pounds at the heart of humanity.'"

—Sarah Rose Etter, author of *Tongue Party*

"I always felt Dr. Bernhart was too good-looking to write something this brilliant."

—Michael Fitzgerald, CEO of Submittable and author of *Radiant Days*

"Move over, *The Crying Game*. This is the new best art."

—Amelia Gray, author of *Gutshot*

"I read *How Existentialism Almost Killed Me* by Michael Bernhart with great initial intensity and then, as I kept reading, with increasing self-loathing, for I became surer, with every page, that I would never write a book as lovely, as true, or as pure, as this."

—Karl Taro Greenfeld, author of *The Subprimes* and *Triburbia*

"*How I Made $3,200,000 from My Hobby* . . . is a great book for people who hate literature."

—Lindsay Hunter, author of *Ugly Girls*

"If Stephen King read this (*How Existentialism Almost Killed Me*), he'd regret the eight or nine times he's said, 'If you miss so-and-so, you're missing a treat.' Yes, this is the one that truly deserves those words."

—Gabino Iglesias, author of *Hungry Darkness*

"This book (*How Moral Philosophy Failed*) is GOOD."

—Jamie Iredell, author of *Last Mass* and *I Was a Fat Drunk Catholic-School Insomniac*

"Reading this book is like reading the hush of the crowd right before a Criss Angel performance."

—Kristen Iskandrian, author of *Mother, Motherer, Motherest*

"Who wouldn't want to read this book?"

—Michael Kimball, author *of Us* and *Big Ray.*

"Brave…. Stunning . . . A Triumph."

—Samuel Ligon, author of *Among the Dead and Dreaming*

"When it gets rolling Bernhart's text feels like one of those old carny rides at county fairs, when you're not sure it's supposed to be moving that fast but there's nothing you can do about it."

—Megan McShea, author of *A Mountain City of Toad Splendor*

"Are you ready for these words to live inside of you? The novel (*How Moral Philosophy Failed*) has no point of no return. Its labyrinthine narrative and rhythm will make your heart race and your palms sweat. Bernhart is ruthless in his execution . . . and grants no mercy to the faint of heart."

—Sade Murphy, author of *Dream Machine*

"*The Max Brown Tetralogy (+1)* is a significant contribution to literature. Bernhart's is the voice we all have been waiting for."

—Gina Myers, author of *Hold It Down*

How Speleology Restored My Sex Drive

The
Max
Brown
Tetralogy (+1)
#3

This is a work of fiction. Names, characters, events, organizations, places and incidents are either products of the author's imagination or are used fictitiously. Any similarity to real persons, living or dead, is coincidental and not intended by the author.

Correspondence concerning this book – or the others in the series – may be sent to <u>MaxBrown@HoughPublishing.com</u>. Constructive criticism is always welcome and, given that revisions can be incorporated immediately, will be acted on. Trolls, flamers and other dipshits whose aim is to hurt, not help? Keep your sad little thoughts to yourselves. If you can't, be forewarned that your emails may be published, with full attribution to their authors. Every effort will be made to portray you as pathetic and illiterate as you are. Seems fair.

Published by Hough Publishing, LLC at Jewell Mountain, GA.

Inquiries to Hough Publishing, PO Box 811, Hiawassee, GA 30546, USA. Or, <u>contact@HoughPublishing.com</u>.

www.houghpublishing.com

Published in the United States of America

ISBN   978-0-9976160-3-3

How
Speleology
Restored My Sex Drive

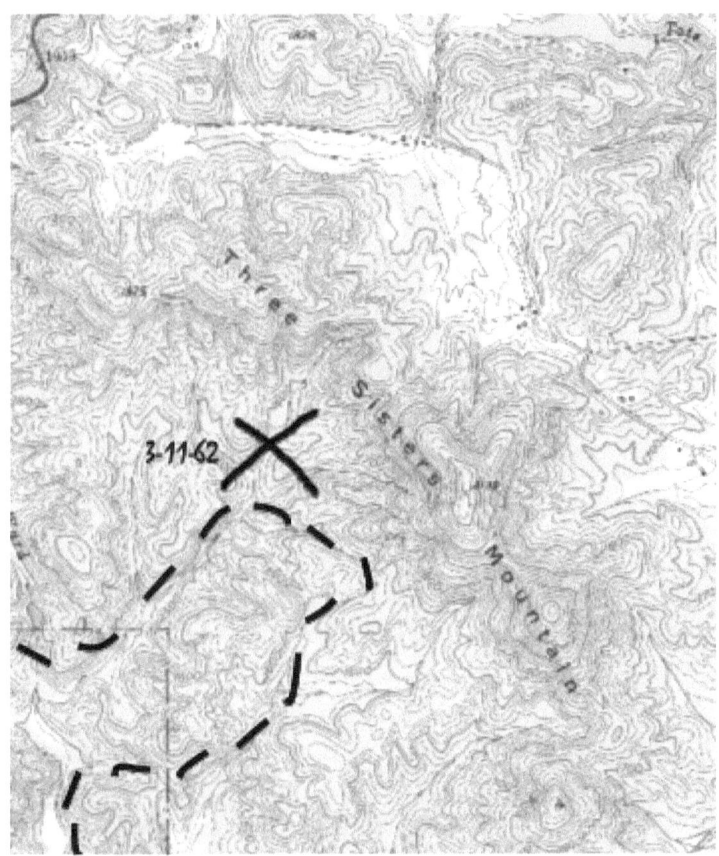

Michael Bernhart

HOUGH PUBLISHING JEWELL MOUNTAIN, GA

How to get away with murder

Does the name Eric Rudolph ring a bell? If not, don't worry about it. Rudolph, personally, doesn't deserve to be remembered, but his career as an American terrorist and the ease with which he evaded capture are instructive.

The crimes. Rudolph blew up abortion clinics in Birmingham, Alabama and Sandy Springs, Georgia, a lesbian bar in Atlanta, Georgia, and, most famously, planted the bomb at the 1996 Olympic Games in Atlanta. The blasts killed two, including a policeman, and injured 123 others. His weapon of choice was dynamite, surrounded by nails.

The politics. Rudolph's professed motives included a desire to embarrass the federal government, make America safe for whites (those of northern European descent), halt abortion, and reverse growing acceptance of homosexuality.

The evasion. The Olympic Games bombing catapulted Rudolph onto the FBI's most wanted list and a reward of $1 million was offered for information leading to his capture. Despite this incentive, he lived for more than five years in the Appalachian Mountains of western North Carolina and northern Georgia; no member of the public came forward with actionable information to assist law enforcement. It was only through blind luck that a rookie policeman stumbled onto Rudolph dumpster-diving behind a grocery store in Murphy, North Carolina. At the time of his arrest he had 250 pounds of dynamite and one completed bomb, ready for use.

But, back to the salient point: a murderer roamed free for five years and no one said a word. Not even for a million dollars.

1

"But why can't we?"

Every parent has heard that question. It's the plaintive whine of a child who's being denied something she feels is perfectly reasonable and within her rights. With the unassailable logic employed by nine-year olds, the child has concluded that the only obstacle standing between her and fulfillment of her deepest desire is the irrational obduracy or laziness of the parent being addressed.

"Because, sweetheart, we just can't. I really don't want to talk about it any further." Does this response work? Of course not. It only confirms what the child already suspected: the parent being addressed – in this case the father – has no defensible arguments to put forward.

"But 'just can't' isn't a reason. Mommy doesn't mind."

The activity that 'Mommy doesn't mind' – a claim that needed checking – was a harebrained excursion to the depths of the ocean or the darkest interior of a cave in search of lost treasure. Here's the background:

Mary and Margaret, the cutest little redheads you'll ever clap eyes on, had been introduced to treasure hunts via the nonstop birthday parties they'd attended that year. The parents of other eight to ten-year-olds seemed unable to devise any entertainment other than to send the party attendees off in search of treasure, either with a map in hand, or written instructions, or guided by notes on trees. The host parents' motives were transparent: the search for treasure kept the kids occupied and out of the house for two hours or longer; of course they liked it. Our girls loved it.

And there was more. The twins' favorite movie was *Treasure Island* which we had watched countless times on videotape. Their father, me, Max Brown, further fueled their enthusiasm with a foolish blunder. I told them about my own treasure hunting in Bangladesh which had yielded a tidy nest egg for the family to live off of in perpetuity. In the telling I minimized the dangers – I'd come within a gnat's ass of being tortured to death

– and inflated my cleverness and resolve. I made it sound exciting.

The upshot? The twins would never again know happiness until they had gone on their own, real, treasure hunt.

I was disinclined. Real treasure hunts are hard, people suffer, people die, and the closer you get to the treasure the more competitors show up, some of whom don't play by the rules. It sounded like a terrible idea.

A united parental front was required to stem this.

———

"Hey, babe, I'm getting heavy pressure to convert this summer's vacation into a treasure hunt – a real one. Your thoughts?" The question was poorly timed. Sally was squinting at a recipe card while a pot on the stove boiled over behind her. She could shoot a gun with alarming accuracy; she could disable professional killers with a few well-placed blows. But she struggled to put edible food on the table. Some primal instinct, perhaps inherited from her mother, left her unable to cede the kitchen to someone else, or to me, anyway. And, in all fairness, my rotation of five dishes (mac & cheese, peanut butter and banana sandwich, spaghetti, canned chili, and pancakes) fell short of haut cuisine. But you could eat it.

"I don't care. Whatever they want," with a dismissive wave of her hand, punctuated by a cry of alarm as the boiling liquid cascaded onto the floor.

Her indifference signaled it was going to be difficult to forge a strong and unified parental alliance; meanwhile, our adversaries, our children, were preparing.

———

"Max, you and Sally are so fortunate. Your daughters get along so well! Our two kids fight all the time. Just last week I thought we could hike up Mont Salève, and . . ."

My attention drifted off. These were never interesting stories – unless a capital crime figured in somewhere – but our host's comments set me to thinking about how well Mary and Margaret got along. They got along beautifully! More than that, they didn't just get along, they colluded in perfect synchrony against their slow-witted parents. Only nine years old, and already they played us like cheap ukuleles.

". . . so you see how it is in other homes. Count your blessings, Max."

Sally and I were at a cocktail party for the parents of children at Ecole Internationale in Geneva. We'd embraced the conventional middle-class logic that only through enrollment in the very snootiest schools did a child have a shot at survival in today's world. We'd said a difficult goodbye to our dear friends on Ameland Island, off the Dutch coast, and moved to Geneva where, six months later, we were still settling in. I'd been looking, half-heartedly, for a part-time university teaching job and Sally was dismally homesick for Holland, although she's a corn-fed mid-western American.

I hear that it's common for many couples' social circle to be made up of only the parents of their children's friends. While the people at the cocktail party were not yet friends, they were the only acquaintances we had in Geneva, aside from our landlady, and they were proving themselves a resoundingly pedestrian bunch. Perhaps because they were so much younger? I excused myself to refresh my drink, again, hoping that Sally would be able to drive us home, when I was intercepted by the twins' teacher.

"Dr. Brown, Dr. Brown. How nice to see you. Your girls are fitting in so well. At their age it is sometimes difficult to adjust, but they have made the move from their little school on that island in Holland to, shall we say . . . the 'big time'?"

"Well, yes, Dr. Piaget, I believe they have. No small thanks to your inspiring tutelage."

This conversation was starting off better than my first encounter with the priggish Piaget. On that occasion he'd appeared unwilling to accept that I was the children's father and that the young and scrumptious Sally had voluntarily consented to wed me. He'd been transparently appalled that she would – grotesque to picture – submit to conjugal relations and bear my offspring. Approaching 52, I had a trace of distinguished grey at the temples, but people were quick to assure me that I looked much younger than my years. These assurances, no matter how well-intentioned, were only reminders of the advanced and re-lentless march of those years. Now Piaget appeared to have come to terms with the aberration that was my marriage. At least he didn't glance back and forth questioningly between Sal-ly and me as he and I talked.

"Very inquiring minds, as you know, Dr. Brown." He sipped his drink as he considered how to extend the conversa-tion. "I understand the family will hunt for treasure this sum-mer." I hadn't understood that at all. "How exquisitely exciting. You know they've requested every book in the Geneva library system on lost treasures and made lists and drawn their own maps, and everything!"

The little schemers. Of course they had. "Ah yes, Dr. Piaget. They're great little planners." I was planning something for them right then and there. "Excuse me, sir. I just caught my wife's eye and there's something we need to discuss."

"Sal, did you know any of this was going on?"

"Kind of."

"Kind of?"

"Well, yes, I did hear them talking about Yamashita's treas-ure in the Philippines."

"God's teeth! Yamashita? Has their research gotten to the part where the last guy who found some of that treasure was imprisoned and tortured?"

"I don't keep up on those things." She sounded defensive.

"I can't say I track these things either, but the poor bastard who seems to have found part of the loot never enjoyed any of it. A court finally supported him, but he died, mysteriously, before the verdict was handed down. I believe he checked out rather young. Not surprising, since the life-expectancy of a fortune-hunter tends to be short."

"The girls say there's still a huge amount of that treasure unaccounted for." She *was* defending them. Sally was part of a cabal to dupe old dad.

"There might be. There're the usual conspiracy stories floating around about how the treasure was found and used for many different – and nefarious – purposes. But I'm straying from the point. Have you three been talking this up?"

Of course they had. Guilt spread across Sally's face, quickly replaced by anger. No one likes to be caught behaving badly. "They just asked my advice on a few things," she sniffed.

It was clear that the little connivers had sought their mother's counsel on how to maneuver dumb old dad into agreeing to this adventure. To point that out was to escalate the argument with Sally. "Well, you and I should talk about this when we get home."

———

You veteran fathers know how it plays out so we won't waste time and paper detailing the discussions, the empty ultimatums, the sullen silences, the strategic retreats, the reconsiderations, and, at the end, a negotiated surrender wherein the children and their complicit mother get what they want, but with some minor conditions set by the father in order to preserve the remaining shreds of his tattered dignity. We would not go to the Philippines. We would go to Georgia (the U.S. state) and look for Confederate gold. I envisioned the following:

The girls would spend a few days plodding along dusty paths in eastern Georgia, waving metal detectors in front of them, until the wilting heat and lack of positive results scuppered their enthusiasm for the project. Then we would go down to Orlando and join thousands of our countrymen who were throwing vast sums of money at the Disney Corporation for the privilege of standing in endless lines. A normal, sane family vacation.

This seemed an acceptable outcome. Never keen on amusement parks, it was one of those things that you had to do or your children would be social pariahs. We had survived Euro Disney; why not Disney World?

Yamashitas gold

How much? Nobody knows. It used to be a lot, like billions of dollars. But there are many stories about different governments like America taking the gold and spending it secretly. Maybe there are still millions left.

What is it? During World War Two the Japanese soldiers stole all the valuable things they could find. A general named Yamashita was put in charge of hiding the gold that they could not get back to Japan and he hid it in tunnels made in a Philippine island. Yamashita did a terrible thing. After the treasure was all hidden he threw a big party for the engineers and diggers that had made the tunnels. He got everyone drunk then he and his friends snuck out and blew up the tunnels.

Where is it? North of the city of Manila.

Proof it exists. Mr. Roxas found a golden Buddha and some gold bars near a town called Baguio but they were taken away from him by the president of the Philippines.

2

According to the in-flight tracking information our KLM 1011 was cruising at 39,000' against moderate headwinds toward Atlanta and I was playing my usual in-flight fantasy: The pilots had been struck down by food poisoning or some other affliction that took them out of the game. Responding to the flight attendant's panicked plea, I would arise magisterially from my seat, wave reassuringly to the passengers, and enter the cockpit where I would . . . The rest of the fantasy is hazy. What did a Lockheed L-1011 cockpit look like? Not like the RF-101C I flew in Vietnam. Would I recognize anything? Then there are fleeting images of me guiding the giant aircraft down the glide slope to a firm, but safe, touchdown. I chop the power, and the fantasy skips ahead to plane-side interviews which I handle with modesty and grace.

I moved on to my other favorite in-flight fantasy, inveigling Sally into the bathroom where we would join the 7.39 miles-high club (39,000/5,280). But would we? There had been a few bedroom failures in recent months, often due to an overload of alcohol, but sometimes without an easy explanation. Would I fail to rise to the occasion? I worried as much about the effect this had on Sally as it had on me.

Positive visualization. *Think how wonderful it will be to screw in the loo, Sally's perfect ass up on the narrow counter, her knickers around her ankles, me thrust . . .* Her voice pierced my reveries.

"Max, have you seen the girls?" Sally looked alarmed. No mile-high club today. The twins had set off to explore the plane – when you're nine years old and endearingly winsome the cabin staff will allow you great leeway – and Sally couldn't locate them.

"In the john?" Negative headshake.

"Have the stews seen them?" Another negative headshake.

"Maybe they wormed their way into the cockpit."

The steward confirmed with the flight deck that there were no nine-year old redheads pulling circuit breakers, throwing switches, extending flaps, or doing any of the other things those two were capable of. He paged them on the plane's PA. "Will Mary and Margaret Taylor-Brown please return to their seats." This produced nothing.

"It's been a long day. They may have just curled up somewhere and they're snoozing." This was said with no conviction. M&M were not the curl up and snooze type in the midst of this much stimulation.

Sally and I worked methodically back through the plane, peering under seats – to the alarm of the occupants – pulling down the doors of the overhead bins – it was possible for those two to climb up there and hide – and asking if anyone had seen them. Well of course everyone had seen them. They're a presence wherever they go.

"Let's think about this logically, babe." She was long beyond logical thought. Sally had succumbed to every parent's worst nightmare: a child that disappears without a trace. Tears appeared in my wife's large green eyes. "Steady, babe, there's no way out of the plane. There've been repeated sightings (although none recent), and the cabin crew have been alerted."

Dark specters invaded my own thinking. Had the relatives of the six Indian thugs we'd dispatched years earlier resumed our blood feud by kidnapping the children? And in a situation where we'd least expect it?

Ridiculous. But then . . . the girls could have been drugged and put into empty duffel bags. U.S. customs never opens baggage.

"C'mon, Sal, let's check front to back again."

We did, with the same result. I was especially alert to any bag in the overhead bins that might hold a 70-pound child.

"Is there a sleep cabin for crew rest?" I was talking to the senior flight attendant. No, there wasn't. "Is there any way to leave the main cabins and descend to the luggage area?" What if they were huddled, freezing in a wheel well, waiting to be deposited in a Georgia cotton field when the gear came down.

"Ja, wel, there is access, but first a person must ride down the elevator."

"Let me see it!" Shouted Sally and I simultaneously.

In the galley a metal tambour door slid up, revealing a small elevator. One level below is the plane's pantry where meals are stored until needed. Also in the pantry were two little hellers who were methodically sampling the snacks kept in bins.

"They seem to especially like the macadamia nuts," reported a sour looking stewardess who had sent the girls back up the elevator before returning herself to glare at the neglectful parents.

While Sally delivered a stern lecture, I wondered about the practicality of handcuffs, and how that would square with child-protection laws.

From M&M's **Guide to Treasure**

Confederate gold
How much? $251,000

What is it? This is all the money that the
confederate states had after the civil war to get rid
of slavery. Their president, Mr. Davis, was trying to
take the money from Richmond Virginia to
Savannah Georgia to put it on a boat to France.
That was to pay a loan from France. Some men who
deserted from the fighting ambushed the wagons
carrying the treasure.

Where is it? The wagons were ambushed in east
Georgia right in front of Chennault plantation. The
men who took the gold and silver coins and bars
couldn't carry it all and had to hide some and
dropped some of the treasure.

Proof it exists. After a big rain people still find gold
and silver coins in ditches.

Fatherhood had not been easy. You can see the challenges posed by two rapscallions who, from birth, were their own hermetically contained and complete social support system. Their parents' approval was welcome, but never essential. They weren't rebelling – not yet, that might come in a few years – they were simply indifferent to us; Sally and I were just two elements of an environment that they managed.

"What goes around, comes around." That was Sally's stock response whenever I bemoaned the picaresque ways of our daughters. She was referring to my own childhood behavior. In my day I was one of Idaho's most celebrated pranksters, but with good reason. My sissy name, Maxwell Smythe Brown IV, made me an easy target of ridicule and it was important to be seen as daring to the point of near incarceration. Obnoxiousness was a perfectly legitimate defense mechanism and I practiced it well. M&M, on the other hand, seemed genetically wired to mischievousness. They'd inherited their father's propensity for getting into trouble, and their mother's charm and beauty which usually got them out of it.

While waiting for our luggage to arrive, I corralled the two for a pre-treasure hunt briefing.

"Okay, listen up squirts. This is a new playing field. This is not our dear little Dutch island where everyone knew everyone. And it's not Switzerland where everyone is watching everyone. This is your native land where outlaws roam unfettered and small children meet fates that not even the Grimm brothers would have envisioned. Got it? We're going into the woods and tonight Daddy's going to rent an instructional video called *Deliverance* so you can see how it is out there." Sally shot me a withering look.

It didn't matter; they weren't listening. As I concluded my admonitory lecture Margaret boarded a suitcase on the luggage carousel and disappeared around the turn while her mother tried to fight free of the other luggage watchers to chase her down. I grabbed Mary's arm just as she was about to hop on a duffel bag in pursuit.

Are you getting the picture here? These were not easy children to raise.

———————

The following afternoon we bounced painfully up a dirt road in a rented SUV and stopped in front of a single-wide surrounded by heavy woods.

"Skeeter? Are you home? It's your niece, Sally."

The answer was an explosive boom as buckshot slammed into a tree six feet to our left. The twins shrieked and started to cry.

"That's it, Sal. Kin or no kin, your uncle's even nuttier than last time. We're getting out of here."

"Don' chew all move, now, y'hear. Ah don' like firin' warnin' shots 'cuz ammo's so costly these days. Next un's fer keeps."

Uncle Skeeter came out on the steps, his shotgun still pointed at us. We didn't focus on the gun – the normal reaction – because Skeeter was stark naked.

Sally jumped out of the car and slammed the door behind her. "Dammit, Skeeter. Don't play stupider than you already are. Put on some clothes and come apologize to Margaret and Mary."

That did the trick. Uncle Skeeter retreated into the trailer in search of clothing. A brindle hound came out from under the steps and followed Skeeter through the door.

———————

Let me explain. Skeeter is a casualty of war. He was Sally's mother's much younger brother, an apparent failure of family planning. Coy about his age, we guessed he was only a few years older than me. According to the family, he'd always tried to do the right thing. He'd excelled at school, been an Eagle

Scout, became a decent auto mechanic, and was among the first to sign up with the Marines to fight for our noble cause in Vietnam. When he returned to the US thirteen months later he was unrecognizable. Before his enlistment was up, he'd accumulated seven AWOL's, been arrested nine times for brawling, and had spent roughly twenty percent of his time in the base brig. He just missed a dishonorable discharge, although he might have preferred it.

How he supported himself was a mystery. Mary Taylor, Sally's mother, tried repeatedly to rescue Tom – his baptized name – with no success. Tom/Skeeter accused Mary of being a government spy sent to gather data on how the chips or chemicals implanted in him were performing. On one of her rescue visits he drove her off at gunpoint.

But, he was Family – Sally's only family – and, we were in the neighborhood . . .

None of the Taylor-Browns, huddling in the SUV, wanted to venture into Skeeter's trailer and, come to think about it, no invitation had been extended. After he reemerged, clothed, Sally talked to him for a few minutes, then returned to the car to announce that Skeeter would join us for dinner at a restaurant, the Two Wheels of Suches. The name gives it away: a biker bar – with decent food, as it turned out – that consigned four wheeled vehicles to a parking area a short walk down the road in a field.

While waiting at the restaurant for Uncle Skeeter to catch up, I got a head start on beer; the gunfire had been unsettling. Thirty minutes and 2.5 beers later, the sound of unmuffled exhaust signaled his approach and we were soon hugging, clapping one another on the back, and grinning like jack-o-lanterns.

"So," said the proud mother, "these are the twins, Mary and . . . where's Margaret?" Margaret was located talking to seven men seated at a round table in the far corner beneath a large Confederate flag. I retrieved my wandering child, with apologies to the seven for the intrusion.

"Yer a cute 'un, aintcha. I'd be careful, little girl. Some ol' boy just might take you home to be his wife." And the seven laughed while my insides churned.

Turning to me, the man in the middle said, "You tell ol' Skeeter not to be a stranger." I nodded to indicate the message would be delivered and shepherded Margaret away.

The reunion settled down. Skeeter quickly overtook me in beer consumption and listened while the twins outlined their treasure hunting plans.

"Don't forget about the gold that came up from New Orleans – the really big haul," volunteered Skeeter. His adopted hillbilly accent had been slipping away over the course of the evening.

New Orleans . . . big haul? This was exciting news to the twins: more gold. Their chances of unearthing a vast treasure had just doubled.

Margaret asked, "Is it dangerous to look for gold?" Her tone indicated that a little danger would be a welcome ingredient in their treasure hunt. "I told those men why we're here. They said I had to look out for niggers. Mom, what are niggers?"

"Later, dear." Sally was no more prepared than I was to field Margaret's question. "Uncle Skeeter, why don't you tell the girls about the gold from New Orleans?"

"Well, it seems that as Union troops closed in on New Orleans in 1862, the Confederate gold in the city was moved to the Iron Bank in Columbus, Georgia, which is maybe 150 miles from here. A General Beauregard was ordered to get the gold out of the bank in Columbus but the bank manager refused to let it go. Finally the manager was forced to cough up the gold. Beauregard took it and headed in this general direction. Beauregard later wrote, 'What became of that coin is a mystery' which I find interesting since it was him, Beauregard, who liberated it from the bank."

"What kind of gold?" asked Sally. Great. Now she was getting into it. "Bars? Coins? I don't think I've ever seen Confederate coins, Skeeter."

"And you won't. Except for four sample coins, the CSA used the original US dies to mint their coins. Beauregard was probably toting around some ingots and gold and silver coins minted in New Orleans, but with United States of America stamped on them."

How did Skeeter know all this about the gold, including Beauregard's statement? Had we stumbled onto a fellow fortune hunter? I noticed the seven men under the rebel flag were sitting quietly, watching us.

"Um, Skeeter, back to the gold in a minute, but who are those guys in the corner? They asked me to tell you 'not to be a stranger'."

His accent clicked back in. "They's Knights. I ran with 'em for a while." No one had anything to move the conversation forward, so after an awkward pause Skeeter added, "I figured they was heavily 'filtrated by Feds. I don' bear 'em no ill. We jus' go our sep'rate ways."

Confusion was written all over Sally's splendid face. I explained, "The Knights are the KKK, babe."

Her reaction was immediate. "Uncle Thomas!" she sputtered. "You *ran* with the Klan?" She was on her feet, leaning across the table. "You're a disgrace to my mother and my grandparents and everything those good people valued! You're not the only guy who went to Vietnam and got messed up!" I was afraid she was about to trot out my story as an example of someone who went to 'Nam and got only a little messed up. She didn't. "Running with racists? I'm ashamed of you! If my mother was alive she'd come down here and kick you right in your scrawny nuts."

Wow. Being the mother of two juvenile delinquents had changed her; she could serve up a white-hot scolding on no notice. The invective was all the more vivid since we'd recently seen Uncle Thomas' scrawny nuts.

Skeeter/Thomas was on the defensive. "Hey, I *used* to run with them." The accent was gone again. "When you live in the mountains you have to fit in."

Sally snorted.

"I won't defend the boys, but some of 'em are going through a rough patch and need someone to blame. And from time to time they do something worthwhile. They'll take up a collection for a family with problems. A month ago they put a scare into Jimmy Proctor who was messing around behind his wife's back. They ain't all bad.

"And," he continued, "I never use the 'N' word," as if this established his moral independence and superiority.

Two bright little minds seized on that statement, "Uncle Skeeter, what's an 'N' word?"

I wasn't ready to let him provide his own explanation. "Girls, it's related to the word you asked about before, nigger, which stirs up so many bad feelings that people now just use the first letter." Two sets of small red eyebrows remained raised, indicating that this wasn't a sufficient explanation. "The word is an insulting term to refer to the descendents of the African slaves who were brought here." That seemed adequate but, since the eyebrows remained up, I redirected the conversation onto a topic I knew they couldn't resist. "So, Skeeter, I get the impression you've studied up on the gold."

Skeeter, who'd been slipping lower in his chair behind a forest of green beer bottles, told us more than he might have revealed if sober.

"The gold could be anywhere, but I do have kind of a lead. I got my hands on the journal that General Beauregard's Aide-de-Camp kept and I followed that. It looks like Beauregard wandered around the area in a way which makes you think it's someone who's either looking for a good hiding place for the gold, or is trying to confuse anyone who's following him." He took a long tug on his beer. "I'll tell you what girls, I'll show you what I have and maybe we can figure this thing out."

I attribute that rash offer to two things: 1) Skeeter was pretty tipsy, and 2) everyone (except their parents who'd been taken in far too often) was eager to gain the approval of such pretty and guileless (ha!) young ladies.

4

The next morning we waited in the Blairsville Waffle House. The time difference with central Europe meant we were already overdue for a meal so we ordered and were addressing our breakfasts when the unmuffled exhaust approached again, more slowly than the previous evening.

Skeeter parked his truck, but was slow to get out. When he did, we could see that his right eye was bruised and it looked like his lip was split and swollen. He called from the restaurant door, "Sorry to be so late. Some stuff came up and . . ." then retreated outside and vomited on an azalea.

"I don't know, Sal. Your uncle put away eight beers last night, but this looks much worse." Sally had a supremely judgmental look on her face. I don't judge her family on the basis of this broken warrior. Show me one combat vet who wasn't at least a little bit scarred by Vietnam.

Skeeter came back in and the waitress marched over. "Skeeter. You're going to clean that up before you leave, right?" Skeeter nodded miserably and sank into the booth beside Mary who wrinkled her nose in disgust.

"Sorry about this, folks. Some shit happened last night." He glanced at the girls. "Pardon my French, ladies."

"I don't get it, Tom." One vet to another. "You'd had a few beers, but I don't understand this."

"Them boys, them Knights . . . they helped me out of a situation." The condition of his face indicated the help hadn't been sufficient. We waited for Skeeter to continue.

"That damn Deputy, Larson, was waiting for me and followed me out onto the highway and pulled me over. A DUI is a serious thing here. Big money. I was trying to talk my way out of it – and not doing very well – when Boon and the other six pulled up in their trucks. They told Larson that he didn't really want to bust me and they circled around him as they talked. Larson looked like he was going to shit himself – sorry about the French, again, girls – and when they created a little opening in the circle, he split."

I could see the twins wanted to ask about the French; their vocabulary flash cards at Ecole Int hadn't included shit as a French word. Of course they knew exactly what it meant. In our house? How could they not. Shit was just the start of a large and colorful vocabulary that they'd tutored their little Dutch buddies in.

"But you got beaten up," observed Sally.

"Yeah, well, about that. Them Knights said the least I could do was buy 'em a round – and that was true – so we went to the Boar's Nest where I can still run a tab and we hoisted a few more."

"But, you got beaten up," repeated Sally.

"I reckon I said some things the Knights disagreed with." He shrugged.

Sally had to know the whole story now. "And those things were?"

"It doesn't matter. They got their beliefs, and I got mine."

"Does race figure in here somewhere?" That's me, taking a stab.

"Maybe . . . I guess so . . . perhaps I told them I thought the whole rebel cause was a mistake and maybe a disgrace. I was pretty drunk by that time, you know. I wasn't thinking straight."

Sally beamed with pride. "Dammit, Uncle Tom (a strange title, given the discussion at hand). I knew you were made of good stuff." She walked around the table and gave him a hug. He reddened. She wrinkled her nose and her eyes watered.

"They said something else you oughta know. They said that Confederate treasure belongs to them who are loyal to the Confederate ideals."

Oho! Competition.

"That's news to you, Skeeter?" The waitress had returned and was tapping a pencil on her order pad. "Them boys been talkin' for years 'bout using that gold to finance a new rebellion. I hear 'em talkin' 'bout it almost ever' time they's in here."

"Did you hear that, girls? Seven nasty men don't want any-one else looking for that treasure. We're going to focus on the other one near Chennault."

"The little one?" asked with one whining voice.

"The safe one."

"But . . . (tears were close, their trump card) Uncle Skeeter has all this good information. We really should help him."

———

I believe your approval of me will go up when I tell you I didn't cave in to the onslaught of lamentations, threats, and appeals to family solidarity. We were going to Chennault Plantation. I did, however, compromise – you have to, every father knows this – to the extent that we would look at Skeeter's materials.

The materials were extensive. He brought a stack of maps from his truck, mostly USGS drawn to a 1:24,000 scale, as well as hiking trail maps and a few maps for tourists produced by Chambers of Commerce and municipalities.

Skeeter pushed three tables together – to the visible dismay of the waitress – and spread out the USGS maps. "This here's Columbus, Georgia where General Beauregard started off. I put in a large X and the date everywhere he stopped, according to the journal, but there's sometimes more than one possible route between the points. That's mainly a problem early in his trip because the land is flat. When you get into the foothills you have fewer good choices where you can drive a wagon. The lit-tle ink dots are my best guess of the track they followed."

Three things were obvious: 1) As Skeeter had said, Beaure-gard and his crew had wandered around aimlessly. They'd even re-crossed their path in two places. 2) The multiple possible paths made it next to impossible to narrow down the quarries, mines and other natural hiding places the treasure buriers might have used. 3) The distance traveled per day was fairly constant, allowing for terrain, except for two days when it looked like they'd gone no more than three miles, despite the existence of decent roads. The short distance covered could be accounted for by time spent hiding the treasure; but it could also be accounted for by repairs, or hunting, or resupply, or to rest the horses, and so on.

"Skeeter, this short trip in the Cavenders Creek area . . ."

"Good, Max. I've focused on that too. A short day with lots of time to salt away the treasure. And there's more. According to the journal, half of the detachment was sent by another route, but the journal doesn't specify which group Beauregard accompanied. Of course the routes aren't identified – same as other days – and I can find four paths that a wagon could have followed."

Two small red heads were pushing in. This, after all, was their event. The advantages of doddering old dad showing interest were obvious, but, still . . . Skeeter turned his attention to them.

"See this symbol here, girls. This here's an abandoned mineshaft. Over here's an active mine – or least it was when the map was drawn in 1951. I got the oldest maps I could find since they wouldn't be cluttered up with recent construction."

"What was in the mines?"

"You don't know, Margaret? Or are you Mary? We're in north Georgia. They mainly mined for gold."

The expression 'eyes big as saucers' has always seemed overblown, but it fit. Both little hoodlums stared at each other with delighted amazement. Gold mines! The odds of finding something valuable were skyrocketing!

We spent another hour with Skeeter going over his maps and listening to his theories. "Sure could use some help."

I frowned at him and addressed my family.

"Okay, gang. Saddle up. We need to get moving to get to Chennault today so we can start waving those metal detectors around first thing tomorrow."

The prospect didn't ignite much enthusiasm. The twins kept unrolling the Dahlonega topographical map that had Cavenders Creek on it until Sally and I physically herded them out the door. As we pulled out, Skeeter was pouring a pail of water on the azalea. "If you change your mind, you know where to find me," he shouted.

From M&M's *Guide to Treasure*

Boregard's Treasure

How much? Mommy's uncle thinks maybe $2,300,000 dollars.

What is it? This is the gold that was in a bank in New Orleans for the Confederate States. When it looked like the northerners might win New Orleans the goOld was moved to Columbus, Georgia. General Boregard took it even though the man at the bank tried to stop him.

Where is it? Everyone thinks the treasure is hidden somewhere in the north part of Georgia but no one knows where. General Boregard did not leave any clues and he claimed he didn't know anything.

Proof it exists. My talked to some men in a restaurant who are sure it exists and they want it to pay for another war. My asked if they wanted to have slaves again and they laughed.

5

Chennault Plantation

In 1865 Chennault Plantation was presided over by Dionysius Chennault, an elderly planter and Methodist minister. It was his misfortune that the last of the Confederate treasury was hijacked 100 yards from his front porch on the night of May 24th.

There are many theories about what happened to the treasure. The 'official' version of events is that deserters from both armies conducted the ambush and made off with the loot. Another is that the treasure was buried at the confluence of the Apalachee and Oconee rivers. And many in the area maintain that the deserter story was a red herring; the locals bushwhacked the wagons and divvied up the loot themselves. Whichever story is right, gold coins still appear in drainage ditches after a strong rain.

Why was the Methodist minister unfortunate? Because when Union soldiers arrived the next day, they were deeply upset. They tortured everyone in the household for information. Obtaining none, the entire Chennault family was taken to Washington, DC to undergo intensive interrogation. They were questioned thoroughly as to the whereabouts of the gold, but the Chennaults couldn't – or didn't – reveal anything that wasn't already known. They were released a few weeks later and returned to their home in Georgia.

"So, pretty exciting, huh, girls?" This brief narrative of the great gold heist of 1865 didn't fire the imaginations of M&M. Treasure hunts required treasure maps. Skeeter had maps. I had a cheesy brochure from the motel's lobby.

After a fitful night – jetlag was biting hard on Sally and me – the four of us drove up the first dirt road we encountered north of Chennault Plantation and, armed with our cheap metal detectors, worked across a recently ploughed field. After an hour Mary's detector chirped. Much excitement.

I produced a foldable spade and after several minutes of exertion unearthed a large bolt that must have fallen off a farm implement. The excitement subsided and we resumed the search.

After our picnic lunch, Mary – she seemed to have the touch – located another buried metal object. Excavation revealed an empty beer can (*Billy Beer*). We kept that; it was at least eight years old.

I talked up Disney World. Mary commented, "Danielle says it's really lame next to the one in France." Danielle, of course, was French. I never figured her for the sharpest crayon in the box, but she was ten years old and, consequently, enjoyed greater credibility than did a geezer who was just two pushes of his walker from the great hereafter.

By mid-afternoon the starch had gone out of the treasure hunters and we returned to the motel where the girls played in the pool and talked quietly, with occasional looks our way to make sure we weren't eavesdropping. Mom and dad were splayed in deck chairs. Mom was attired in a scanty bikini that would have gone unremarked in Europe, but was attracting attention in rural Georgia. She did look delectable and, with a deep sigh, I reflected that the future held only shared motel rooms for the Taylor-Browns. It's not that we couldn't afford a separate room for the girls. We didn't trust them on their own.

A shared room makes sleep more difficult. You have to suppress coughs, you're afraid to shift in bed for the noise you'll make, you can't turn on a light and read, and you can't dial up that sure-fire soporific, the droning TV infomercial pitching a small kitchen appliance. What you can do is replay the same dismal thoughts, with rarely any deviation from a well-worn script.

I was fourteen years older than Sally. When we'd met ten years earlier that hadn't seemed important. Her parents had checked out young, barely getting past sixty. Mine had been murdered – one of them by me – so their lifeline was unknown, but past generations of Browns have held up well, most of them getting into their mid-80s. If genetics counts for anything, Sally and I would, one distant day, walk together hand-in-hand toward the light.

But would she still be there? At the ends of the age spectrum fourteen years mean a lot. An attractive fifty-year old woman with a balding coot on Social Security? Yellow teeth – those that remain – stooped posture, faltering speech, leaky memory. A husband no longer able to keep up, who's promoting Caribbean cruises and all-you-can-eat buffets while she's plumping for unicycle tours through Nepal. I'd started working out and prided myself that I could beat up the man I was at 34 (at 34 I deserved to be beaten up). Would a trim physique, albeit in a wrinkled package, postpone the eventual rejection?

———

The next day began, just after I'd finally fallen asleep, with a perky announcement/demand, "We're hungry. We want to go eat."

Sally's response from the other side of the bed was, "Jesus Christ!" Apparently she hadn't slept either.

My response was, "In a little while, dears. Your mother and I are still sleeping." This kicked off the negotiations which ended when they took my credit cards, some cash, and the room key and headed out to the Denny's next door. "Only to Denny's," Sally shouted after them, "and then right back. Understood?"

"Sure, Mom."

I still couldn't sleep.

"Sal, are you awake?"

She recognized the tone. "Okay, let's do this. Maybe it'll help me sleep too." And we did it. No strong emotions. Just two tired animals rutting away. Is the term 'married sex' an oxymoron? And why aren't there performance problems in the morning? It's the same apparatus that lets you down fourteen hours later. Perhaps that's why they call that unreliable organ a prick.

But it worked. No sooner had we rolled apart than I was unconscious.

Unpleasant dreams. The twins were judging some kind of athletic competition and I kept falling down. I was contemplating the next event, the pole vault, certain of the dismal outcome as my pole turned to rubber and collapsed beneath me while my daughters laughed and clapped their hands (you don't need Freud to interpret that one), when . . .

"Holy shit! Max, look at the time!" It was 11:15, over three hours since we'd sent the twins off.

We threw on clothes, rushed out the door, crashed into the room-cleaning cart, and limped across the parking lot toward Denny's.

————————

"Yeah, they were in here. Cutest little muffins I ever seen. Scrambled eggs. Cleaned their plates like real good girls."

The waitress at Denny's was preparing to relive every delightful minute with the two little enchantresses when I interrupted, "Right, excellent. Do you know where they went?"

She looked stunned that this rude Yankee would cut her off in mid-reminiscence. "I guess they went back over the parking lot toward the motel. Is that where y'all are staying?"

Thanking her for the information we returned to the room. The cleaning woman had to let us in.

"Girls. . . Are you here? Mary . . . Margaret." It was a small room. What were we expecting?

Sally screamed.

Holy sweet Jesus! Had she come upon their dear small bodies?

"What? What?"

"Look, Max."

I looked and saw nothing. "I don't see anything."

"Their little suitcases are gone."

We ran to the lobby. "We have to speak with the police." The receptionist quickly dialed and handed me the phone.

"Officer, I'm calling to report two missing girls. Both age nine, red hair, last seen in the Denny's east of town."

. . .

"No sir, we don't have evidence of foul play. We think they ran away."

. . .

"24 hours? You have to be kidding!"

. . .

"Alright. Thanks for your help.

"Unbelievable! The cops won't lift a finger until a kid's been missing for at least six hours and won't start up a manhunt until 24 hours have passed."

The receptionist had been following all this. "So, those two little sweethearts are yours? They came in here with their matching suitcases about three hours ago. Cutest things. They had me call them a cab."

"And you did?" That's Sally, who's close to a meltdown. "Holy shit, man. Phone the cab company and find out where they went."

"Don't panic, babe." She was panicking. And, why not? The second disappearance in four days?

I tried to reassure her. "This is pretty normal in my family. I used to run away all the time when I was a kid. If I didn't get my way, I'd pack my little bag and walk out." I didn't tell Sally I never traveled further than next door to the house of my saintly adopted aunt, Letha Risk. Auntie Letha plied me with cookies, while, I later realized, she was discretely phoning my mother.

"Okay," announced the receptionist, hanging up the phone, "here's the deal. Martha at the cab-company dispatch said Jerry picked 'em up about three hours ago."

"Did Martha know where he took them?"

The receptionist smacked his forehead. He dialed the cab company again while confiding in a low voice, "You know, Jerry's dumber than dogshit. I think he lied about his age to get a CDL. He don't act like he's eighteen. But he's the dispatcher's kid so don't say nothin' offensive." He'd correctly guessed that offensive would surface easily in this situation. He handed me the phone.

"Martha? My name's Max Brown. Do you know where Jerry took our little girls?"

. . .

"That's a pretty long way to take children without any approval from their parents."

. . .

"I understand, Martha. We all want to earn money."

. . .

"Yes, I'm sure he meant to be helpful."

And very nearly threw the phone through the window.

"Jesus Fucking Harold Christ! Sal, that moron kid took off for Union County with the girls."

"Union County? Why would anyone in their right mind agree to take two very young girls halfway across the state?"

"His mother – who seems to understand it wasn't a bright decision – said he didn't radio back until he was on his way, reception is lousy in that direction, and then they're twisting through the mountains, so they lose contact."

Sally glared at the man behind the counter.

"Hey, lady. I'm the receptionist. I didn't know where they wanted to go. They said they wanted to surprise their uncle with a visit. I figured that'd be here in town. That's all I know. You take it up with Jerry."

6

WARNING: HIGHER ROLLOVER RISK

was placarded on the driver's sun visor. A silhouette picture of a capsizing vehicle emphasized the point.

The SUV's tires squealed as we slewed around hairpin turns; other drivers honked furiously as we overtook them in no-passing zones. *Fuck 'em.* The twins had a three-hour head start and we'd been told that Jerry wasn't one to dawdle on the highway. They'd probably been pulling up Skeeter's road at the same time we'd set out from Chennault.

"It may be Pollyannaish, Sal, but I don't think Skeeter would do anything foolish with the girls. The more time we spent with him, the saner he seemed."

Sally looked at me with concern. "Not to be too gloomy, Max, but Skeeter is not sane. He's loony-tunes. Nuts. Maybe you didn't see much of it in the Air Force, but during those two golden years I served in the Army in Kansas, we saw an endless number of guys who were messed up.

"Skeeter was always a king-sized suck-up as a kid. After he took that shrapnel in the head it just got worse. Every time he got into trouble in the Marines, it was because he was tagging along after some bad actor or had done something stupid on a dare. I call it the Zelig syndrome after the character in the movie." Conversation was suspended while we wheeled around a slow-moving Buick and ducked back into our lane as a white pickup truck bore down on us, horn blaring.

"You saw that Skeeter became like us when he was with us. When he 'ran' with the KKK he probably became like them. Remember how he was speaking when we first saw him? This is a guy who's lost track of who he is. He has no personality of his own. Or maybe he doesn't want to be who he is." That squared with what I'd seen of some combat vets, but they hadn't become Zeligs; Skeeter was different. "Maybe he wants acceptance, so he becomes like the people he's with. I don't know. Bottom line? Not stable and will go along with whoever he's with."

"And now he's with two willful nine-year old girls. He'll do anything those twerps ask him to do."

"Pretty much."

We drove in silence.

"I expect we'll find them at Skeeter's trailer, studying maps and making preparations."

"Max, baby, I don't know where you've been the last few years. This is all a wonderful game to them. They think they're Jim in *Treasure Island*, staying one step ahead of evil pursuers. They probably don't know they have such a good head start so they won't be wasting time. I'm betting they're well down the road."

This sobering assessment led to more silent travel. I tried to drive faster.

"Well, I think we should still check the trailer first. If nothing else, we might pick up some leads."

Later we learned that we'd chosen a road named Georgia's Devil. One hairpin turn after another. It took us over three hours to get to Skeeter's single-wide, where, as anticipated, there was no sign of life and a large padlock on the door. The brindle dog came out from under the trailer, sniffed us over and allowed herself to be petted before retreating.

"With a guard dog like this," Sally said, as she tried to coax the dog out for more affection, "I understand the lock."

I found a heavy piece of pipe and broke the lock off. The interior of the trailer wasn't as disgusting as we'd prepared ourselves for, but it was clearly the lair of a single man who wasn't expecting social calls. Sally and I started at opposite ends of the trailer, searching for any clue that would tell us where to look for the girls.

"I found his maps," called out Sally. "There're a lot of them."

We went through the USGS topographicals, trying to remember what we'd been looking at two days before.

"Here's something, Sal. The topo for Dahlonega isn't here – he had that two days ago – and there isn't one for Suches either.

He must have taken that. That supports the possibility that they headed for Cavenders Creek. Of course maybe half of the trails that Beauregard meandered around on are on those two maps."

Sally looked under Skeeter's bed and gingerly extracted a locked metal box. We forced it open and there, unmistakably, was the journal kept by Beauregard's Aide-de-Camp.

The journal appeared to be missing pages and the faded handwriting was difficult to read. We studied it for a minute but I was still feeling the urgency of our three-hour dash from Chennault to Skeeter's trailer. "Unless you think there's something else, let's get a move on." This was said without any idea of where we should be moving to.

We'd just turned onto the highway when three pickups with Confederate flags fluttering in the back roared by and swung into the dirt track leading to Skeeter's trailer.

"This may be a dangerous idea, Max, but I think we need to know what those assholes are up to."

I turned around and headed back up Skeeter's road. As we slowly approached the single-wide, the sounds of gunfire and a yelp brought us to a stop. Putting the SUV into 4WD low range we left the road and plowed through the underbrush until the car couldn't be seen from the road. Sally and I got out and crept toward the trailer.

"Hey, you nigger-lovin' sumbitch. I know yer in there." The seven Klansmen from the Two Wheel café were arrayed around the front and sides of the trailer. Partially protected by trees, their rifles were haphazardly pointed in the direction of the trailer. One of the Knights shot out a window and they all laughed. They seemed drunk. The brindle dog lay dead.

"C'mon' Skeeter. My ol' lady tol' me you was plannin' to go down towards Dahlonega with them Yankees and look for our gold. You tell us what you know and then we can all go git drunk together, just like the ol' buddies we are." Another window was shot out.

"Hear that, Sally?" I whispered. "Looks like the waitress is married to one of these guys." She nodded. She was looking at the dog, tears in her eyes.

"Hey, Boon. You know his truck ain't here. Skeeter wouldn't be here without his truck."

Boon reflected on this. He had to be pretty drunk or pretty stupid not to have figured this out before. "Be that as it may," he said grandly, "I don' intend to take a blast from Skeeter's squirrel gun just 'cuz he parked his truck somewhere else."

The first speaker said, "Fuck, we's just wasting time," and came out from behind his tree and walked to the door, where he inspected the broken lock. "Hey, look here. Skeeter had a lock and it looks like someone busted it off. Why would anyone do that?"

The seven went inside the trailer and I signaled to Sally to pull back. This might be our best chance to get away and back in pursuit of M&M.

As we turned onto the main road there was a dull explosion and a ball of grey smoke rose above the trees. "I'm betting that was Skeeter's propane tank. Hope it doesn't set the forest ablaze." I pushed the speed up. "Where to now?"

Sally shrugged. I think the dog was on her mind. It was on mine. I suggested, "Let's go back to that Waffle House in Blairsville. Maybe we can throw these guys off the scent while we round up Mary and Margaret."

Sally didn't respond. I looked over and saw she'd started crying softly. "The dog, babe?"

"Partly," and nothing more. Of course, why should we assume Mary and Margaret were still okay?

————

The same waitress as before was on duty, but with a significant change. She'd been hit more than once, and the heavy makeup couldn't disguise the bruises.

"Where's your cute little girls?" she asked with apprehension, and a slight slur to her speech.

"Oh, they charmed their soft-hearted uncle into taking them down to the water park near Atlanta. We're going to catch up with them. We're not much for water parks."

"Seems like a bad idea for Skeeter." Why would she say that? The answer was forthcoming. "You know, he hasn't registered that truck for a long time. He lost his driving license from his first DUI. And, if nothin' else, the noise the thing makes'll have those Atlanta nigger cops all over him."

I was really falling out of love with these people.

"In that case, we'd better catch up and get everyone into our car."

"Don'tcha want nothin'?"

"If we're going to get there before Skeeter winds up behind bars, we'd better move. Sorry. How long does it take to drive to Atlanta?" I wanted the idea firmly cemented that everyone was going to Atlanta. No one was hunting for treasure around Cavenders Creek. Atlanta.

"Two hours tops. Drive safe, y'all."

———

Back on the road, "Evasion mode, babe. I thought we'd left this behind us nine years ago. Would you take a look at the paperwork from the car rental company and see where's the nearest town we can swap this car for another one."

She rifled through the handful of papers. "I think maybe in Blue Ridge, just 20 minutes ahead." Her head jerked up, "Turn around, Max. I need to buy something at the WalMart back there."

I waited in the car, assuming Sally was making an emergency purchase of feminine hygiene products, but she was gone almost fifteen minutes before she returned.

She climbed into the car, gave me a meaningful look, and deposited a pistol – a Beretta – and two boxes of ammunition in the glove compartment.

"Fucking dog killers!"

7

A few minutes later we pulled off the road again. A plywood cutout of Smokey stood by the highway, identifying the US Forest Service station. "We need maps," I explained.

"It's 5:30. Do you expect a federal employee will still be at work?"

In fact there were several people at work. A young ranger – on his way to the exit – stopped and asked if he could help us.

"I hope so. Our nine-year old daughters have run away with their deranged uncle on a treasure hunt. We think we know where they're headed, but we need maps of the area to find them."

"Whoa. Are you serious?" Anyone could see by our drawn faces that we were very serious. "Follow me." He led us to a windowless room with metal file cabinets along two walls. Sliding open a wide shallow drawer, "Here are the USGS topos, and over here are the 1:10,000 maps the USFS produces." He started pulling the maps out, then paused. "About the uncle, did you give consent for your daughters to go treasure hunting with him?"

"Of course not," answered Sally. "We explicitly nixed the idea."

"It's none of my business, but technically he may be guilty of kidnapping."

Another ranger stuck his head in the door. "We gotta move, Jones. Some poor bastard blew his single-wide sky high and it touched off a fire. All hands to the pumps."

Jones looked conflicted. "I'm really sorry. Look, something can be organized, but right now a fire takes priority. Here's my card. Call in the morning. Take whatever maps you need and we'll settle up sometime. Better yet, just don't cheat on your income taxes this year and we'll call it even." And he was gone.

We took updated versions of the USGS topographical maps Skeeter had, plus the more detailed USFS maps of the same areas.

"Okay, Sal. We have maps, but no idea what to do with them. It's getting late so Skeeter and the squirts should be looking for a place to stay."

"Right. Skeeter may be happy sleeping in the woods, but not the princesses. I've been thinking. You gave them your credit cards this morning. If they use them, the credit card companies would know of it almost immediately." I kissed Sally on the forehead. A brilliant woman!

We went into the office with Jones' name on the door – he wasn't using it – and Sally produced her credit cards.

The 800 call to a Visa account was unproductive. After confirming that we weren't reporting a stolen card, the man at the other end informed us that the issuing bank was in Switzerland, and he didn't know fuckall.

American Express was more interested. "You say the children ran away with the card and might make unauthorized purchases? I'll cancel the card immediately sir."

"No, no, no. Do not – repeat – do *not* cancel the card. These are two nine-year-old girls. They're out there with no resources. If something happens to them I would not want to be the person who cut off their access to food and shelter. Do you understand what I'm saying?" Pretty dramatic stuff, but I was sincere.

"I'll have to talk to my supervisor."

"What now?" asked Sally.

"This colossal asshole is concerned about the girls buying an unauthorized Big Mac. The prick . . . oh, sorry, you're back."

I was curtly introduced to the supervisor.

"Mr. Brown? Please explain the situation."

I told the supervisor about the flight of the treasure hunters, going light on Skeeter's involvement. "We thought they might use the card to take a motel room tonight and we could round them up." God, that would be ideal. This guy would tell us where they were and Sally and I would have M&M back under lock and key within the hour.

"Well, I see there has been a transaction. It's a large one; that's why it's been posted." A large transaction? "The smaller transactions aren't individually confirmed with us and it could be several days before a restaurant or motel charge would show up in the system."

"A large transaction is excellent! What did they buy?"

"The vendor is J&W Best Deal Auto Sales in Ellijay, Georgia. It looks, Mr. Brown, like your nine-year-olds bought a car."

After persuading the supervisor that he didn't need to cancel the card, and that I was on record as willing to honor any charges, I was able to get off the phone.

"The little stinkers just bought Skeeter new wheels."

Ellijay is 35 miles south of the USFS station and we steamed onto the used car dealer's lot within 27 minutes. A man wearing plaid pants, white shoes, and a red sports coat was locking up. When he saw prospective customers, he hurried over.

"Good evening. Lucky you just caught me." A brief pause for breath. "Good day for you to drop by. Got new inventory coming in, so I really need to move something. Now, what can I do for you fine folks."

Sally answered. "Earlier this afternoon you sold a vehicle to two little girls – red hair – and a skinny man with a beard."

"Sorry. I can't discuss my clients. It's part of our code of ethics."

Sally and I would normally be ready to discuss the ethical code subscribed to by used car salesmen, but we had more pressing concerns.

"Alright, let me put it this way." That's me, speaking through gritted teeth. "You sold a motor vehicle to a very young child who was using an obviously stolen credit card. This would be a good time for you to start cooperating."

He deflated. "Come inside my office," and he unlocked the door to a small trailer and led us inside.

"First off, I didn't sell a car to any minor. The paperwork's all made out to a Thomas Lonegreen. You can check with Melissa up at the DMV. I called it in to her."

Behind his desk, his self-assurance started to return and he rocked back in his chair. "Yep, the three of 'em come in here about three hours ago. Cutest little girls I ever seen. I would of *give* 'em a car, they was so charming. You must be the proud parents?" Easy guess; they look a lot like Sally, but we were in no mood for chitchat.

"What car?"

"The sweetest conversion van you ever saw. Sleeps four, kitchenette, chemical toilet, water tank holds fifty gallons. I practically gave it to 'em."

"What color and make?"

"Fire engine red. I think they liked that 'cuz of their red hair. The guy, he wanted a camo paint job, but I don't have any on the lot. GM, 1988, but it looks like it came off the assembly line yesterday."

"Four-wheel drive?"

"Nah. And I don't advise it. Them vans aren't built for . . ."

I interrupted, "Would they have to buy anything more to make the van ready for use."

"Food and a propane tank. I even filled up the water for 'em."

"Did they ask you where to go for supplies?"

"Nah. The man seemed to know the area. In all likelihood, they'd go to the Ingles two stop lights down 515."

We ran out to the car – wasting no time on farewells – and headed down 515. Sally was fishing around in her wallet for recent pictures of the twins and came up with a year-old school picture. As we pulled into the parking lot it was evident there were no bright red GMC vans.

Going from cashier to cashier, "Have you seen red-haired twins that look like this?" No. "Have you seen red-haired twins that look like this?" No. We struck pay dirt at checkout aisle 7.

"Oh, those little sweethearts? So precious! Going camping with their uncle, I gathered."

"It's a little more than that, ma'am. They ran away from home to go treasure hunting with their uncle. He's a sweet man, but a little touched in the head. I think it's his childlike nature that appeals to the girls." Having said that, it sounded plausible.

"Oh dear. Should we call the police?" And have the law come after poor confused Skeeter as a kidnapper?

"We may have to at some point. Right now, it's in the family. Maybe you can tell us what they bought so we have an idea of where they might have gone."

"Oh, the usual. I don't need to get the tape to look it up. Sweet things for the girls. Some hot dogs and buns. Canned baked beans. Frying pan and a pot. Paper plates. Marshmallows. Dried firewood. You know, things you might take if you were going to spend time in the woods with children. Oh, and two tanks of propane."

"Do you remember how much they spent?"

"I think it was over two hundred dollars. Took 'em three carts to roll everything out. I can look up the exact amount, if you want."

Back in the car. "It's not getting easier, is it, Sal. There's a lot of woods in north Georgia and they're provisioned to stay out there for some time. Maybe it helps us that they're in a van that can't stray off prepared roads." There was a flutter of brightly colored cloth in the periphery of my vision. "Fuck! Get down. One of those Klan assholes is cruising the parking lot."

"Did he see us?"

We crouched quietly.

A truck door opened and slammed shut next to us.

From M&M's *Guide to Treasure*

The Waterhouse Treasure
How much? A newspaper said more than ten million dollars

What is it? The Spanish mined gold way back almost 500 year ago. They had a machine called an arrastra to grind the gold out of rocks and they melted the gold into long bars. The bars were covered with copper to disguise the gold. They had so much gold they could not get all the bars to the ocean where their ships were so they kept the gold bars in a cave. For some reason they left the area and couldn't bring all the gold with them. Or maybe they just died. So there is still a cave with lots of gold bars covered in copper.

Where is it? Most people think the cave is on Rocky Face Mountain which is near Keith, Georgia.

Proof it exists. In 1890 William Waterhouse who owned land near the cave said he found it and asked for help getting the heavy bars out of the cave. The story was in the Chattanooga newspaper. Mr. Waterhouse's family are still searching for the cave. In 1950 a lot of loose gold was found in the Coosa River near Rocky Face. How did it get there?

8

"Well. Looky here! You wuz right, Boon. It's them Yankee relatives of ol' Skeeter. What're you good folks doin' all hunched down in the seat like that?" Followed by a wheezing laugh.

I sat up, resigned; Sally didn't.

"We thought we might get a chance to see Skeeter's new van. But this here's almost as good." Sally was still hunched over. "Hey, little red-haired lady. Don't be shy. We don't bite."

"I might." Sally sat up and pushed the barrel of her pistol into the nose of the man standing by her door. That explained what she'd been doing.

"Jesus, lady! I didn't do nothin' to get a reaction like that!" The hands he'd confidently placed on the doorsill started to tremble.

"What's going on?" Boon got out of the truck, came around, and saw the pistol. "Whoa, lady. You can't just go pointin' guns at innocent folks in parking lots."

"Actually, I'm thinking of firing it."

Boon responded; he didn't have a gun barrel in his nostril. "No need for that. We wuz just lookin' for ol' Skeeter to congratulate him on his good fortune. He musta already found some of that treasure. Y'all tell him we'll catch up with him one of these days pretty soon."

"You might be delayed." Sally's announcement brought a look of increased concern to the man at the end of her gun.

"Delayed? Now don't go doin' nothin' uncalled for."

Sally pushed on the pistol and the man fell back. Then she fired two quick shots, one into each tire facing her. This act of wanton destruction, committed on the truck he loved, overrode Boon's fear.

"Hey! Them's hunerd dollar tires! Plus," as if he were about to trump all arguments, "there's a law against discharging a firearm in public areas."

"That was a million-dollar dog. Consider you just made a down payment." The two Klansmen looked at each other, trying to figure out what Sally was talking about. "And there's a law against arson."

She paused; the wheels were turning.

"You boys might consider relocating to some place without an extradition agreement with the US. Check out Antarctica. It's nice this time of year. As soon as we get the developed film back, the pictures of you simpletons blowing up Skeeter's trailer are going to every law enforcement agency in the area."

Boon was starting to shake a finger in protest, but stopped when Sally turned toward him.

It was fun to watch Sally intimidate the Knights, but we had higher priorities. "C'mon', Sal, we'd better roll." Lots of people had heard the gunfire. Even by the standards of north Georgia, shooting at trucks in crowded parking lots was probably frowned on.

Back on the highway, "Damn, you are brilliant, woman! Those assholes will be busy for days checking every drugstore and shop that develops film."

Sally smiled. "Yes, I am raaaather proud of myself." Said with a posh accent and a tilt of her head. "But I don't know if it'll slow them that much. The Klan seems to have far-reaching tentacles. 'Melissa' or someone at the DMV tipped them to Skeeter's registration application."

The sun was setting. Should we start combing the woods looking for a campfire and marshmallow roast? We decided to cover our own tracks and spent the night in a cinder-block motel on the outskirts of Dahlonega. I registered under transparently false names and paid in cash. The guy behind the counter gave me a wink and a thumbs up when Sally looked away.

Using the Aide-de-Camp's journal we'd found under Skeeter's bed, we tried to recreate General Beauregard's wagon trails on the USGS map of the area. It looked right, but I hadn't been paying careful attention when Skeeter went over this. And we hadn't had a good view of Skeeter's map; two little gremlins had pushed in front of us.

———————

Tired by the day's events and two short nights, fear crowded in. Sally was asking unanswerable questions about what might happen to the girls should the Klansmen catch up with them. How would I know? Should I share my own nightmares?

Of course not. I did what I'd done for years. I called on my most reliable defense against unpleasant realties: I intellectualized.

"Sal, I know this doesn't answer your questions, but my mind's headed off in another direction. Can these guys be as evil as they seem to be? I've never understood it. All the creatures put on the face of the earth and only one species has the capacity for evil. Lower order animals fight and kill, but for a purpose like food or reproduction. A lot of our fellow humans kill for the sheer hell of it."

This was no help to Sally. She was asking hypotheticals about the Knights' intentions and I was talking about men who kill for sport.

"Ah Jeez, theodicy again, Max?"

When I was younger I'd gotten tied up in knots over the paradox of a benign and all-powerful God who reigned over a universe chock full of evil. How could that be? By the time I met Sally the prompts and reminders that had kept me in the hunt had faded and my interest in the paradox did the same. But it does come back from time to time. There's no doubt that some men are evil. You can't explain away their behavior on the basis of misunderstood motives or misplaced loyalties or confused values. Some men are evil. Were the seven Klansmen such men?

"I'm sorry, babe. I'm intellectualizing so I don't wet myself with fear. But there is, in my defense, a practical core to this. Evil exists. How do you spot it?"

"Killing a sweet old timid dog would be one good sign," Sally answered. I didn't follow up because I knew she didn't want to believe that.

Sleep? Not much. And no sex to help us sleep. Thoughts of our two naughty, precious little girls, camping in the woods with an unstable man and pursued by seven unpleasant cretins takes the romance out of any parent's evening. And, what if I couldn't rise to the occasion? That's a hell of a note: Avoiding sex for fear of failure. I'd been doing that all too often for several months.

———

In the morning we turned in the SUV and walked to Dahlonega's other car rental agency. I was still carrying a fake passport and driver's license – both in the name of Melvin Gibsun. These were leftovers from the days when we were on the run from killers who'd taken exception to my beating them to a large treasure.

The pasty-faced counter clerk examined the documents, scowling. "I don't know, Mr. Gibsun. This is a Swiss license. I don't think you can drive in America without an American license."

Well, of course you can. At our insistence Pasty-face made a phone call, smiled apologetically, and went about renting us a black SUV – chosen to contrast with the silver SUV which we'd just surrendered. Payment led to more discussion. My credit cards were in the care of the two little thieves, and Sally's were in a name different than Gibsun, but eventually the transaction was completed and we rolled out of town toward Cavenders Creek.

And arrived immediately. The area was only three miles from the center of Dahlonega and had been swallowed up years ago by middle-income housing as the town had sprawled. There was a Cavenders Creek Road, Street, Court, Lane and maybe more. If there was still an actual creek, we couldn't identify it among the many small streams in the area.

I pulled into the Cavenders Creek Baptist Church parking lot. "Let's think this over." Said in the hope that the declaration would improve mental clarity. And then – in an embarrassing regression to an earlier identity (pompous academician) – I pontificated:

"First premise: Although Skeeter has put a lot of research into this, the twins are calling the shots, and Skeeter won't be aware of that. First corollary: If that's true, they'll go to places that fit the girl's expectations for a treasure hunt.

"Second premise: Gold is found in gold mines. Second corollary: The girls perked up at the mention of gold mines and they'll want Skeeter to take them to those.

"Third premise: Treasure, in the girls' view, is found in remote areas, not in suburban housing developments. Third corollary: They'll be bugging Skeeter to take them away from urban areas to old gold mines, especially those with tunnels – not quarry mines."

Is it possible to detect if someone's trying to *not* roll their eyes? It looked like Sally – through a determined effort – was maintaining a non-judgmental expression for the duration of my discourse.

"Got it, Professor. We should be inching down narrow mineshafts, sputtering torches in hand, bats rushing by . . ." She stopped at that point. The image was getting to her. She'd developed a touch of claustrophobia in recent years.

"Well, that's my considered appraisal. The girls are in it for the adventure. As you said, it's a game."

"Does this analysis have an action component?" We were both tired and scared and getting snippy with one another. And, in fairness, I sounded like a braying jackass.

I rose above it. "There were several signs in Dahlonega to a gold mining museum. Maybe we can get some information there."

As it turned out, we could. The museum offered maps and booklets for sale that informed the reader that the state counted no fewer than 500 gold-mining sites, 153 of which had amounted to something and many had remained active up to recent years. A few of the larger and more accessible ones had been converted into tourist attractions.

We gathered up every morsel of information the museum had and asked if there was an unoccupied room with a large table we might use. The helpful attendant opened what had been a jury room years ago. We brought in the USGS maps and Aide-de-Camp's journal from the car and went to work. By noon we'd identified seven underground mines that a) had existed in 1862, b) were not operated for tourists, c) were in rural, and fairly remote, areas, and d) were on or near Beauregard's likely routes of travel.

With feelings vacillating between a sense of progress that we were closing in on the little hoodlums, and deepening despair that we were thrashing around blindly, we came out of the museum into the glare of the midday sun.

"Damn, Max. Be careful!" I'd grabbed Sally's arm and pulled her back through the door into the museum.

A pickup truck with a Confederate flag planted in the bed slowly rolled by. The two occupants were scanning the parked cars.

"Your apology's accepted." See? We were getting snippy. "First stop is to get you some kind of head covering. Your hair's a beacon that can be seen for miles."

"I'm sorry." She looked at me for acknowledgement. I smiled, but I was still annoyed she'd assumed the worst when I'd pulled her out of view. "Do you think these guys know what they're looking for, or are they just trolling randomly?"

I shrugged. How to know? But the appearance of these turds was unnerving.

9

From a brochure supplied by the Gold Museum of Dahlonega -

> The Sixes mines were originally worked by the Cherokee and were located near the Cherokee town called Sixes. The discovery of the gold mines was the reason the Cherokee Nation was forced off their land. The Trail of Tears march began in Cherokee County, two miles from where the original Sixes Mine is located.
>
> The six mines that comprised the Sixes are the Three Hundred and One, Cherokee, Clarkston, Downing Creek Placer Mine, Macou Project, and the Putnam Mine.
>
> The Cherokee Mine is located on what is now Army Corps of Engineers property. Public access is difficult, and there is no easy approach. The mine can be reached by boat from Allatoona Lake up Sixes Creek, or by foot into the Corps property across from Bridgewood and is marked by red blazes on the trees.

It was no overstatement that 'access is difficult.' The red blazes on the trees were indistinct, or gone. It looked like the power company had felled most of the trees near the road, probably annoyed at the occasional inconvenience caused by a tree toppling onto a power line. But, as we worked through the tangle of shrubs and climbed over fallen tree trunks, we were encouraged that we were getting closer to the mine. Occasional signs warned that the full weight of the federal government would descend upon any who proceeded further. We doubted Skeeter would be deterred by these warnings; we were sure that the twins would be spurred forward. We plunged on, uncertain of where we were or what we were looking for.

You've probably heard of kudzu; if not:

> *Kudzu* '*ko͝odzoō*' *noun. A rapidly growing eastern Asian climbing plant, used as a fodder crop and for erosion control. It has become an ineradicable pest in the southeastern U.S.*

The trees were covered with the stuff, often climbing to the highest branches. Some trees had given up the ghost, smothered by the rapacious vine, the trees themselves leafless and missing limbs. The kudzu created thick veils between trees; it obscured fences and the Corps of Engineers' warning signs; and it made progress slow and painful.

"Do you really think the twins made it through this stuff?" A reasonable question from Sally. We weren't doing well.

"Skeeter might have known of a better way in. There is the water access. He might have found a boat he could borrow."

"Or be instructed to steal," said his niece.

We plunged forward.

"I found something," shouted Sally. It was an historical marker rewarding anyone foolhardy enough to come this far with the information that they stood where the entry to the mine had once been; the whole kit and caboodle had caved in in 1861, a year before Beauregard's trip with the gold. The information available in the Gold Museum hadn't included that nugget.

We were briefly encouraged when we found the remains of a campfire, but it was surrounded by empty beer bottles and a few ripped open condom packages.

"This was tough to get to, Max. Let's make the effort worthwhile and look around a few more minutes. Where's this Sixes Creek that they might have floated up on?"

I pulled out the USGS map and decided the creek would be 200 yards to our west. The sun was past the mid-point in the sky so it was clear which way we should go. After five minutes battling with the kudzu we arrived at a small creek; the water level looked low and red mud banks were exposed. We were excited to find footprints in the mud, some of them small, and indents that might have been made by a canoe that had been hauled up on the bank.

"Paydirt, babe. Look over here." There were the remains of an extinguished campfire, the partially burned wrapper of a marshmallow bag by the ashes, and three sticks lying on a rock, each coated with white gooey marshmallow despite the best efforts of three armies of ants to carry off the trove. "I'm no Kit Carson, but it looks like they were here yesterday, looked around, had their picnic, and retired to the comforts of the van."

Sally surveyed the scene. "I can't believe we missed them. But this vindicates your theory. I feel really good. We know how they're thinking. We're going to catch up with them, and I'm rehearsing the chewing-out of the century. Yessiree Bob. One queen-sized ass-chomp."

She kept this up for much of our long slow thrash back to the road. This was the first time we'd been optimistic enough to allow thoughts about how mad we were at the girls. Of course we knew, as did the kids, that when we were all reunited, mom and dad would be so tearfully relieved that there'd be no retribution. All that aside, I had to admit I felt pretty positive about our prospects.

We came out on the road at an unfamiliar point. Our first sortie took us the wrong direction and after walking half a mile, we reversed course. We were hot, tired, and worried that we were losing valuable time when, finally, we saw our car. The passenger window had been smashed in; the hood was open; our personal effects were strewn around in the grass; and, etched into the paint on the door –

WHOSE DELAYED NOW?

From M&M's **Guide to Treasure**

Cherokee treasure tunnel
How much? No one knows. A lot. All the gold and silver the Cherokee Indians had.

What is it? After gold was found in Georgia the government kicked the Cherokee Indians off their land and gave it to the white men. The Cherokees had lots of gold and silver and they wanted to hide it before they had to leave so they dug a deep tunnel in an area they thought the white men would not want to use for farming. They also robbed some gold from a government wagon to put in the tunnel with their own treasure.

Where is it? Someone wrote you can get to it on the Etowah River. Someone else said it's near Settendown Creek.

Proof it exists. The Indians carved secret clues into rocks to help them find their way back to the gold but they were never able to return.

10

While I stuffed our clothes back into the suitcases, Sally inventoried the losses in the car. She summed up her assessment, "We're screwed." Missing from the car were her purse with our remaining credit cards, the pistol and ammo, the Aide-de-Camp's journal, and our maps. The car's battery was also gone. "Please tell me," she asked, "that you put the list of the seven potential sites in your pocket when we left the Museum."

I had, and I was also carrying the USGS topographical map for the immediate area – the map with the red dots and x's that would have alerted the Klansmen to our plans.

"Thank you, Lord, for very small favors," she muttered.

In my wallet I had some cash and an ATM card issued by Credit Suisse. Would it work in the US?

We made a call to the car rental office from a house a short distance up the road. The apprehensive woman required a lot of convincing, but finally permitted Sally inside to use the phone. A tow truck arrived 45 minutes later. The driver installed a new battery in the SUV and followed us back to the agency's office in Dahlonega.

"Tentacles," muttered Sally. "First order of business for me is to buy another gun." I guessed she was trying to concentrate on revenge rather than the increasing peril our daughters were in.

"The only way I can piece this together is this, Sal: Their contact at the DMV – the one who told them about Skeeter's application for a van – helped them find us."

"But it was a rental." Sally reasoned.

"Right, but all they needed was the license plate number from our encounter with them in the Ingles parking lot. Their contact in the DMV told them which rental company owned that car. They found we'd turned it in and that we'd walked away, dragging our luggage. Simple for them to go to the only other rental agency in town and they got Pasty-Face, the dimwit behind the counter, to help them."

"How? We used different names. Oh, you're thinking the red hair."

I was. The Klansmen probably hadn't known our real names – they didn't need to – since my beautiful redhead was invariably noticed and remembered by any man with a pulse.

"First order of business for me is to squeeze Pasty-Face." Now I was muttering angrily.

That wasn't possible. To our initial disappointment, Pasty-Face was no longer on duty. He'd been replaced behind the counter by the first African American we'd seen for two days: Shawn Ferguson, according to the name plate on the counter. This was an improvement; Shawn wouldn't be cooperating with the Klan.

"Where's the guy who was here this morning?"

"Um, he had an accident and had to go home." Small credit to Pasty-Face. Perhaps he'd not given us up easily. I studied the clerk. How much did he need to know?

"Mr. Ferguson, we know the guy who was behind the counter this morning gave out information to some Klan guys. They were the a-holes who broke the window of your company's SUV and stole the battery."

"And they stole some valuable property from the car," added Sally. "We called the police and someone's going to meet us here to fill out the report."

Ferguson's head jerked up. "You asked the police to come here?" At that moment, a squad car rolled up and a young muscular cop with a buzz cut came into the office.

"So, who had the little problem out west of town?"

Sally answered. "That would be us, officer. While we were exploring in the woods, someone – we think it was two Klansmen from up around Blairsville and Suches – broke into our car. I've made a list of the things that were taken."

"Klansmen? Why do you say that, ma'am? They're more often interested in helping maintain order." Sally was about to protest; she can be a little slow sometimes when it comes to understanding how rotten people can be. I muttered 'tentacles' under my breath to her, and addressed the cop.

"Just a hypothesis, officer. I think our first priority is filing this report, getting a replacement car, and then we'll be back on the road."

Officer Buzzcut smiled. He and I understood one another. Why cause a fuss when it'll only lead to complications.

We completed the report, and the cop left, but not before checking his watch and speaking over his shoulder to the clerk. "Surprised to see you here so late in the day, Ferguson."

"The boss hit me with an emergency request to fill in at the counter, sir."

"Hmm," from the cop; he looked at his watch again and left.

"Did I just miss something?" asked Sally.

"It's a sundown town, isn't it, Mr. Ferguson."

"Sundown town?" asked Sally.

I'd read about them when studying sociology. "They're all over the country. African Americans are prohibited from being inside the city limits after sunset."

Ferguson nodded, and added, "It's not out in the open like it used to be when I was a kid. Then they had the sign and blew a whistle in the late afternoon to signal that the Black folks had to leave. A few women who cared for the children of white folks were allowed to stay longer, but they were taken out in a bus that picked them up."

"What sign?" Sally was into it.

"A lot of towns had them. They were usually some variation on, 'Nigger, don't let the sun set on your black ass in this town.' They put them out on the highway. It wasn't to tell us anything we didn't know. It was to proclaim their racism to anyone passing through."

"You can't be serious! This is America. This is 1993. Certainly it doesn't happen anymore?"

Ferguson remained expressionless. He'd seen this white indignation before. Naïve liberals exposed to the unpleasant realities of his life. "Things have steadily improved. Like I said, it's not out in the open anymore and there are a lot of newcomers who know nothing about it. But still, change can be slow, especially with some people." He looked out the window at the cop car pulling away.

"How late does your boss expect you to stay?" I asked.

"Lock up at 7:00. Sun sets at 6:36 tonight. I was thinking I might just sleep in the back office, but I'm not sure how that would work now that the cop knows I'm here."

"Don't worry. We'll get you out of town. Won't we, Max?" That hadn't been my intention. We had two babies out there in the woods traveling with an unstable man who was, himself, the target of seven bad guys and their many associates. But . . . Ferguson was in a jam because of us, so, it would be the right thing to do.

"Of course. We can use the time getting ready. We need another car, we need to get on the phone to the credit card companies, we need to get some cash, and we need to figure out where we're going."

"And I need a gun," Sally reminded me.

Ferguson, now an ally, processed the repair charges and new rental from the record of the credit card we'd used before.

Then I called to cancel the card since Sally's was in the hands of the KKK.

"So, stolen when, Mr. Brown?" asked 'Rex' in an Indo-Texan drawl.

"Just minutes ago. Right after we did our business for the car rental. We've filed a police report. I'm afraid I don't have the report number." We'd neglected to ask Officer Buzzcut for that.

"I apologize for the inconvenience, sir. Can you confirm a charge made about an hour ago at the Mountain Construction Supply Company in Dawsonville?"

This would have to be the Klansmen using Sally's card. Did I just purchase another car for someone? Only the big charges were posted immediately.

"Refresh my memory, please. I'm not sure we made any large purchases this afternoon that would have come through so quickly."

"Not a large amount, Mr. Brown. Some purchases are of controlled materials and the law requires immediate notification. It says here that Mrs. Taylor-Brown purchased $87 worth of dynamite."

My mouth went dry. "I'll have to check with the lady when I see her, Rex." *Jesus! What were those bastards planning to do with dynamite?*

When I hung up – my palms damp – it had been agreed that the credit card the Klansmen had stolen would be cancelled, but the one the girls had was still effective. The final four digits on the cards were different.

"Dynamite, Sal. The assholes are buying dynamite."

She turned to Ferguson. "Where can I buy a gun?"

Ferguson directed us to a bank two blocks distant to try the ATM. We discovered that we could withdraw cash from our Swiss account, but no more than $100 per day. Added to what was in my wallet, we were strapped.

From the bank we followed Ferguson's directions to a pawnshop. If we wanted to hang onto any money for food, Sally's gun budget was $180.

History has a way of repeating itself. The only affordable handgun at the pawnshop was a Smith & Wesson Masterpiece, the gun that had figured in our first engagements with the Indian thugs ten years earlier. After a box of .38 ammunition had been included, we calculated we had just enough spare change to add an order of fries to our evening meal.

When we got back to the rental agency Ferguson had gassed up the replacement SUV and was closing down the office, although it was still well before 7:00.

"I want to be out the door with no delays," he explained.

While waiting we learned that he'd joined the company because they'd advertised that they prized diversity. He hadn't expected he'd be given the role of Black ambassador to racists.

I'd been thinking about what the Klansmen might do next. "About that, getting out the door with no delays? I think these a-holes spotted our car here in town and followed us. They knew we'd have to come back to this office and it's possible they're watching to see where we go next."

"If you don't mind my asking, why are these men after you?"

"It's not so much us, it's Sally's uncle. They think he's on the verge of digging up the Confederate gold of legend."

"And why would they think you'll lead them to the uncle?"

"He's traveling with our nine-year old daughters."

"Jesus Christ! They stole a pistol and now they're buying explosives?"

Sally gripped the counter edge. I didn't feel very good either.

Ferguson's response was immediate, "We've got to get you clear of this place. Here's what we have to do. We'll leave early. That might catch these idiots at the McDonald's. I'll drive. You two stay out of sight."

"I appreciate that, but I would expect them to follow any car that comes out of here at this hour."

"True. Okay, I think I might have something for that." He went into the back office and got on the phone.

While Ferguson was setting up our escape, I located our next mine on the map and traced the road to it. "We can get there in about 45 minutes, Sal. The roads look twisty and slow, but I think more important than speed is not having anyone following us."

11

At 6:45 – a compromise between official closing time and sundown – Ferguson drove our third SUV of the day slowly out of the rental agency's lot and headed south. Sally and I were lying in the back where we'd put the rear seats down and were concealed by a moving pad that smelled like it had been used to transport fish.

"You were right, Mr. Brown. Here they come, stars and bars a-flapping behind them. Don't become alarmed by the driving."

"Why should we?" asked Sally through the odoriferous wool.

"I intend to lead these idiots someplace they normally wouldn't go. That'll work better if they're more focused on the chase and not paying attention to where they are."

Ferguson had a lot on the ball.

After ten minutes of sedate driving, with an unusual number of turns, Ferguson warned, "Hang on." And he floored it.

We squealed around corners, Ferguson's foot moving constantly between the accelerator and the brake pedal. I wondered if he'd noticed that placarded warning on the visor.

"You can look out, now," as our speed slowed.

It was almost completely dark. The streetlights were few and the houses, crowded together on narrow lots, looked modest. Cars parked on both sides of the street reduced it to one lane. We coasted to a stop and Ferguson said quietly, "I hope I got the directions right."

The pickup truck screeched to a stop behind us. "Hey nigger, we know you got them two treasure hunters in there."

"Jesus Christ," muttered Ferguson. "These are the two dumbest crackers in Georgia. They haven't figured out where they are? A failure of Darwinism?"

I had a feeling that was a prepared line, but I still liked it.

Sally asked, "The cavalry is on the way?"

"They'd better be. Can you see a house number? I don't know my way around yet."

"1098." My eyes were still undimmed despite the advanced years my daughters were fond of commenting on. 20-20. I should take up flying again.

Ferguson smacked the steering wheel. "Ah, shit. Two blocks too soon." He leaned his head out the window. "Hey assholes. Let's see if you can keep up with this driving." And we shot forward, the pickup truck's tires squealing behind us.

Two blocks later we stopped again.

"Got you now, nigger. And it ain't gonna be pretty . . ." The voice trailed off as the distinct sounds of pump action shotguns and the click of ammunition being chambered registered on the Klansman. On both sides of the street gun barrels were visible in car windows. Faces were not.

A muffled voice said, "Motor off. Keys on the street." We heard the rattle of keys hitting the pavement.

Ferguson muttered, "Welcome to Pea Ridge, pea brains. Known to you as Nigger Town."

Sally was excited and climbed over me to get out, her newly acquired pistol in hand. Was this a good idea?

She strutted up to the pickup truck. "So, dog killers. New tires, I see. Maybe you assholes didn't know you shouldn't be in this part of town after the sun sets." She'd moved to the driver's door. "I believe you boys have some things that you followed us down here just to return. Am I right?" And she pushed the Smith & Wesson's barrel into the cheek of Boon, the wide-eyed driver.

"Don't do nuthin'. I'll get 'em," said the passenger and he reached into the jump seat of the truck and retrieved a shopping bag.

"Thanks for the delivery," said Sally as she took the bag. "Max, would you check and see if this is complete?"

It seemed to be. Gun, two boxes of ammo, Sally's purse, three credit cards and the Aide-de-Camp's journal.

"The battery's in the back, if you want it."

Ferguson did, and he retrieved it. A company man.

"The maps?" asked Sally.

"They was in the bed too. If they ain't there now they must of blowed away."

"What should we do with these imbeciles everybody?" Sally looked around at the invisible army crouching in the surrounding cars.

"Nothing," said Ferguson, the voice of reason. "They took some stuff. We got it back. Everybody's happy."

"Strange. I just don't feel the happiness," muttered Sally. *What's she up to now?* "I still feel deep sadness."

Hold on, Sal. This is where we say goodbye to these pinheads and go looking for M&M.

"Something is missing from my life."

"Not that ol' dog agin?" whined Boon.

"That's it! The dog! Thanks, now I know how to ease some of my pain."

"C'mon', lady. That dog couldn't hunt worth a damn. We done Skeeter a favor."

"Second installment on your debt," announced Sally, and she walked around the truck, firing a shot into each tire.

The noise was alarming to everyone. Gunshots attract attention.

Ferguson smacked the steering wheel for the second time. "Ah shit, no! We gotta move. Now!"

I took Sally firmly by the arm – she resisted, she wasn't finished yet? – and pulled her into the SUV. I could see our posse slipping out of the far sides of the cars and melting away.

Ferguson was ready and we sped forward, followed more slowly by the sound of the pickup, flopping along on disintegrating tires.

"Nice going, Annie Oakley. I'm sure that was a lot of fun, but it didn't help our cause."

"But I slowed them down, Max. Wasn't that important?"

"By pushing the town closer to a race war?" Okay. I was exaggerating. But I really was pissed. I'll grant we were beyond diplomacy; still, this seemed like a provocation that would escalate tensions between the Klan and the Black population that lived – apprehensively – near the town.

Ferguson was even more upset and trying to speak calmly, but you could hear that he was seething. "See, ma'am, they'll have to retaliate. Bullets will come flying through living room windows. Some kid walking home from school will be taken for a ride and terrorized. There'll be some kind of response."

Sally wasn't giving up. "But I was the one who shot their tires. Logically they should be coming after me."

"Sure. Logic works real good with racists." Ferguson was talking to himself by this time. "I don't know who's the bigger menace, the helpers or the haters."

"I'm very sorry, Mr. Ferguson. Sally had no idea how this all works. We've been isolated from American racism for so long our instincts have dulled. But, it's occurred to me – and probably you – that your career in Dahlonega is at an end. We need to get you somewhere."

Apparently that had not occurred to Ferguson. He smacked the steering wheel again.

"You're right. I'm in the crosshairs." He sighed, let his shoulders slump, and put on the brief act of someone who'd been shafted yet again – but, why should things change? "I'll pick up my car at the office, clean out my apartment, and crash with an ex-girl friend in Atlanta."

"Where's your apartment? I have a bad feeling that the clock is ticking."

He lived on our route back into the town. We picked up empty boxes at a liquor store and Sally and I waited in the car, pistols in our laps, while Ferguson went up to pack his clothes and the few things he most wanted to protect. I was growing apprehensive. We knew it isn't easy to pack up, but he didn't start hauling things downstairs until an hour had elapsed. Sally and I helped carry out boxes of books, suitcases, and trash bags stuffed with bedding.

"Is that it, Mr. Ferguson?" It had to be. The SUV was full.

"The apartment came furnished. This is most of what I own and all I really need."

I took over the driving into town, Ferguson giving directions. "Just a few more blocks, my office is right up ahead where the . . . turn, turn, turn!" he shouted. I pulled right into a one-way street – opposite to the direction of traffic, but no one would notice.

A rolling two-part explosion rocked the night, accompanied by a brilliant flash of light.

We crept around the block until we had a clear view of the rental agency across an empty parking lot. A red Mustang was burning out of control in front of the shattered windows of the car rental agency. Sally opened the door and vomited.

12

"I'll replace the car, Mr. Ferguson. I have some money . . . Mr. Ferguson?"

He was stunned. "Sally . . . Sally."

"Yes," answered a gagging Sally. No response from Ferguson, who stared at the burning car and rubbed his temples.

"Just a wild guess, babe, but I think he named his car Sally. You know, Mustang Sally in the song?"

Ferguson's mind was somewhere else. Time for a verbal slap across the chops. "Come on Ferguson. We've got a situation going here. You can grieve for your car later. How do we get out of this disaster of a town?"

Ferguson was still looking back at the blazing car as we pulled away. "Down 400 to Atlanta. There's a sign up there at the corner. Just follow the signs to 400." His voice was faint. After a few minutes and several turns he rejoined the sentient. "Take this left. Then 400 is just a couple hundred yards down by that filling station."

I turned right. "You must have misheard me, Mr. Brown. We need to go the other way." I pulled into a side street and turned off the lights and ignition.

"See that white pickup at the filling station?" Head nod. "See the flagstaff in the truck bed?" Head nod. "What do you want to bet that a rebel flag is attached to that flagstaff?" For the second time that night, Max's superior vision had averted disaster. I planned to work that into the story when I told it to M&M. Then I was immediately sorry I'd thought about them.

As we watched, a second pickup truck joined the first one at the gas station. The men got out and gestured in various directions.

"I'm fucked. They're patrolling the roads to Atlanta."

"What about other towns?" I asked.

"They're pretty much the same as here. Cumming, Ball Ground, Alpharetta – I heard they were all sundown towns up to a few years ago. Probably some people of that era still around.

A person of my hue will be noticed, reported and outnumbered."

"I saw a sign to Dawsonville. How about that?" Trying to be helpful.

"The Grand Dragon lives there. Does that answer the question?"

Sally had recovered enough to join the conversation. "Which direction are they least likely to think you'd go?"

"North."

"North it is," I said, and we wove back through the town.

"Declined? Try this one." All three of Sally's recently recovered credit cards had been blocked. I paid for our burgers with the small amount of cash left. We thought that small purchases didn't post quickly. Apparently the banks are on the lookout for invalid cards, but little else.

"Our situation hasn't improved a great deal," I announced. In fact, by some measures we'd taken a step backwards. We had a car loaded to the gills with someone else's life's possessions; we had a passenger who wanted to go the opposite direction we needed to go; and we'd earned the enmity of a number of people who were short on subtlety and long on violence.

"Look, I'm sorry to impose on you two . . ."

"Oh no, Shawn. It was your willingness to help us that got you into this fix." Plus Sally's theatrics; she'd been uncharacteristically quiet since. "We won't abandon you now." But it was tempting.

"Having said that, we need to make a decision. Sally and I need to look for our girls." Shawn sat up; I think he'd forgotten about the missing twins in the recent dramatic events. "The options are two: Either we have to set off together, the three of us, after the girls. Or we need to get you to sanctuary somewhere so that Sally and I can resume the search."

That concentrated Shawn Ferguson's mind. "Well, my limited experience with these so-called Knights is that they have short attention spans. They'll remember this day until they die, but they'll get bored sitting around waiting for something to happen. I'm thinking that in another couple of hours we can pick up 400 a little further south and be in Atlanta in 45 minutes."

"I'm trying to think like them." That's Sally. "I wouldn't be surprised if they didn't start patrolling these roads. Movement seems to be their thing. Those guys had a lot of time back there in Pea Ridge to memorize our license plate. We can't swap cars again and if they see a black SUV they'll be able to confirm it's us from the plates."

"Is your car unlocked Mr. Brown?"

I clicked the remote and the parking lights flashed. Shawn went out and started rummaging around in one of his boxes. Then he disappeared. Five minutes later he returned.

"You got a new license plate." We looked alarmed. "Don't worry. I just swapped it with another car. Those folks won't realize anything's wrong until they register their car next year. Who checks their license plate?" He smiled. We smiled back uncertainly. "Who says you don't learn anything useful in high school?"

———

Ferguson made another trip to the car and brought back his Little Black Book. He smiled at us confidently as he thumbed through the entries. "A little of that old Fergy magic and I'll be set."

There was no doubt in his mind that he was a ladies' man. Which is why he received his ex-girlfriend's rebuff with ill humor. After several minutes on the pay phone, his free arm waving as he argued, he slammed the receiver into its cradle and stomped back to our table.

"What is *wrong* with people? We had something, and now I'm in a little bit of a jam, and she won't give me the time of day?!"

"I take it," asked Sally, "that you're without a place to crash tonight?" She was enjoying Shawn's fall from grace.

Before the conversation turned snarky, I interjected, "Then we're in this together. Here's the deal, Shawn. We've drawn up a list of the places we think our girls will get their uncle to take them. The nearest is about 30 minutes away. If they did go there, they'll be parked in a red GMC conversion van within easy walking distance of this mine. Wherever they went, they got there earlier today, did their exploring, and now are picnicking and getting ready for bed."

Ferguson asked for the map and studied it for a few minutes.

"Okay, it doesn't show up on your government map, but there's a KOA campground here." He indicated a spot on the road less than a mile from a mine.

"How do you know that?" Sally asked.

"Part of the job. Everyone – and I mean everyone – who rents a car asks for directions to some place before they leave the office. After a few weeks you're repeating them in your sleep. The KOA isn't a biggy but I did have a couple requests."

Perhaps Mr. F was going to pay his freight.

We crowded into the SUV – Shawn's possessions didn't leave much room for passengers – and headed west toward the KOA campground. As we left town and were picking up speed a pickup with a Confederate flag flapping in the bed roared by, then suddenly pulled to the side of the road and doused the lights.

"Fuck, they saw us." I was driving. "You two get down."

I put on one of Ferguson's baseball caps and drove at a steady speed. The pickup pulled out behind us, headlights out, and followed closely on our tail for a short distance before swinging wide and taking off up the road.

"That's one for you, Shawn. The license plate did the trick."

Arriving at the KOA, we slowly circled through the parking pads, each one occupied by a rolling palace, a cozy teardrop trailer, or something in between. Turning into the last lane we saw a red GMC van parked at the far bend. Sally started to cry and laugh with relief.

The van was dark. Our naughty little angels must have been exhausted by the day's exploring, so we knocked lightly on the side to rouse Skeeter. No answer so we knocked more insistently. Was he drunk and deaf to us? Others weren't and the elderly couple sitting under an awning by their Winnebago shushed us.

I tried the door. Locked. I tried the passenger's door . . . driver's door . . . tailgate. All with the same result. They weren't there. Nine o'clock at night and our babies were not there. The laughter went out of Sally's sobs of relief and they became sobs of despair.

13

The elderly couple shushed us more insistently. "There are children sleeping here," the woman said waspishly.

"Two little red-haired girls?" I asked, grasping at hope.

"Our grandsons," answered the man.

We were defeated. I expected Ferguson to try to stoke false optimism, but he was wise to the situation and kept his mouth shut.

"We did see the little redheads," the woman offered. "Are you related to them?" and she looked at Sally.

"Their parents. We can't find them."

"The two of 'em and the skinny guy went off with someone in a pickup truck about two hours ago."

Nightmare. The Klan had them. Not wanting to know, "Can you describe the truck and the men driving it?"

"Black 250. Stickers all over the window and tailgate. There was only one man driving the truck. Great big bear of a guy."

"A Confederate flag?"

"I wouldn't think so. There were the usual bunch of bleeding-heart stickers about the whales and peace and love and stuff like that. And a few USMC stickers mixed in. A jarhead hippy, wasn't he, Ruth?"

"I don't understand" That's Sally, coming out of her black hole. "This guy's a peacenik? Where'd he come from?"

I laid it out for the Winnebagoers. "Our daughters ran off with their uncle on a treasure hunt. Dangerously, some Klansmen are after them, probably because they think our daughters and their uncle might know where an actual treasure is. We're trying to catch up with our children, but we keep bumping into these guys and that's slowing us down."

The man reflected on this. "Hmm. I guess that explains all the interest." Our expressions signaled he should continue. "Your kids and the uncle were out of here on foot early this morning. One of your daughters told our grandsons that they planned to go to a mine. They packed a little lunch and headed off. About noon a pickup like you were describing – flag and all – pulled in and tried the van doors. We told the guy there was no one in there and he looked like he was about to scratch something in the van's paint but he saw we were watching. He came back a few hours later – was it maybe four o'clock, Ruth?" Ruth nodded. "And the fella' just parked and played music on his radio."

Ruth picked up the story. "Loud music. Kenny asked him to turn it down and he did for a few minutes and then we could see he was sneaking the volume back up so Kenny went up to the campground attendant and complained. Well, that attendant's the nicest fella' you'll ever want to meet. He came right down and asked that redneck to turn off his radio. There was some discussion we couldn't hear and then the attendant said the guy had to leave since he wasn't renting a space. More discussion but when the attendant said he was going to call the police the pickup driver left, radio on full blast."

"So, who did our children go with?"

"Not five minutes later they came straggling up the back way, looking pretty parched and tired. Me and Kenny talked it over and agreed something didn't seem right so we told the skinny guy, the uncle, about that redneck that'd been looking for him. Uncle Scooter – I think was his name – he took off like a shot for the attendant's booth. I reckon he phoned the jarhead hippy," they seemed to enjoy this name, "because not forty-five minutes later that guy showed up and they all left together."

I looked at Sally who seemed afraid to get her hopes up again. "Hear that babe? They're with some old Marine Corps buddy of Skeeter's."

She asked, "Anything more happen, or did you hear anything about where they were going?"

"No, it was a big reunion between Scooter and the hippy. Some talk about having a beer. So they left, but there was more that happened. A different pickup with a rebel flag rolled in not thirty minutes later with two rednecks. They started asking around. We didn't say anything but I think the people in the Airstream down there must of told them something because the rednecks shot out of here. Almost hit a kid on a trike, didn't they, Ken."

Ken nodded agreement. Then he inclined his head toward Shawn, "Who's he?"

The tone was not neutral, so I answered, "My son by my first marriage. You may know his work. Among other things he invented the Frisbee and now goes around looking for charities to give his fortune to." Shawn went along with a shy nod.

"Don't that beat all, Ruth? And he's giving his money to good causes?" The wonder in the man's voice made it clear he was baffled by the existence of a Black man spending his money on anything other than drugs, cars, and gold chains.

Shawn was unfazed. "Since I've been introduced, may I ask if you remember anything about the hippy's truck? License from Georgia? Which county? Dings and dents? Any of the stickers from a local organization? I really want to find my little sisters." I think he was relishing the turmoil he was creating in the old couple's minds of a Black man who was a) successful, b) charitable, and c) M&M's brother. His questions were the right ones, but I was afraid he might get so involved in the act that we'd lose focus and leave a memorable trail. The Knights were likely to keep coming back to the campgrounds as long as Skeeter's van was there.

Ruth had noticed something. "According to one of the stickers, the truck was bought at J&W Best Auto. I only noticed it because it's the same sticker as on Scooter's van."

"Dad?" Shawn was having a great time with that role, "Do you think we should take uncle Skeeter's van? I have a spare key."

"You do?"

I needed time to think this through and discuss it with Sally, but she looked like she was still out of it. The van was a homing beacon. Skeeter had decided not to continue traveling in it since it was known to Boon and Co. and easy to spot. If Skeeter came back and took the van, we would have lost our best lead. But if we took it, Skeeter would make inquiries and we could leave instructions on how he should contact us.

The Klansmen would also have their eye on the van. Another reason we should move the thing: to confuse our adversaries.

Decision made: "Sure, boy," I could enjoy this role too, although it brought sour looks from both Sally and Shawn. "Get the key."

The Winnebagoers looked uncertain. Were they witnessing a heist? After all, a Black man was involved.

"Ruth, Ken, if Skeeter comes back, tell him to ask the attendant for information on where to find his van. Don't tell the Klansmen that unless you want to witness them beating the information out of the attendant." The old couple paled and shook their heads rapidly.

Shawn rooted around in one of his boxes and went to the driver's door of the van. A minute later the van started. "Sally, would you follow us in the SUV." She seemed to be pulling herself together. Perhaps the demands of driving would keep her mind off her daughters.

I got in the van with Shawn. "Where'd you find a key?"

He grinned and produced a large screwdriver. "Don't get the wrong idea, Pops; I've only been the victim of this kind of 'key.' First time I've tried it myself, but it's as easy as claimed."

We stopped at the attendant's booth – he *was* a nice fella' – and asked him to watch for Skeeter and the girls. "If Skeeter comes back, tell him his niece, Sally, took his van and he should go to the central Atlanta police station where we'll meet him. I'll call you every few hours to see if he's come by." The attendant looked questioningly at Shawn, then handed me a card with the campground's phone number on it. "And please don't talk about this with anyone else. Those rednecks with the rebel flags are dangerous. Our daughters are out there and at risk." I fixed him with a serious stare; he nodded reassuringly. He seemed okay.

We got back into the van, me driving. "Where you taking me now, Daddio?" The joke was wearing thin.

We needed to leave the van somewhere that would send the opposition off in the wrong direction. "Run through your memory banks, Shawn. Where's a trailhead near here? One with a parking lot."

"The granddaddy of them all, the AT, crosses the road not fifteen miles from here. I think there's good parking there."

AT turned out to stand for Appalachian Trail which would be perfect. The presence of the van at the trail would signal that Skeeter and the girls had headed up the AT in search of treasure. The Klansmen were welcome to hike all the way to Maine in search of their prey. The closeness of the trail also got the van off the road quickly.

I drove slowly. Sally's not a good driver and we were all exhausted. Still, we pulled into the small parking lot at Woody Gap twenty minutes later. We found a spot that was visible from the road – let's make it easy for these bozos – and parked with the driver's door and deformed lock against a mountain laurel bush. A sock – Skeeter's, by its size and aroma – draped over the steering column concealed the damage to the ignition switch.

"Don't you think we should look for clues, Max? They might have left something that would tell us what places they intend to explore." Sally was right. With one of Shawn's flashlights, we went through the van. The twins had taken their suitcases with them when they left with the hippy jarhead but there were wadded up papers and a carefully maintained **Guide to Treasure** that they'd apparently been compiling for some time. The **Guide** included a section on treasure in the area – twelve possible sites – including a recent entry based on Skeeter's description of the Confederate gold taken by General Beauregard.

Pocketing these items we climbed out the passenger's side, locking the door behind us.

We did this with deep regret. It was late and the bunks in the van beckoned, but it was easy to spot from the road, even at night. We did the best we could in the SUV.

Morning brought stiffness, gummy eyes, irritability, and a craving for caffeinated beverages.

"Where to now, Pops?" asked with no evidence of good humor.

"Can it, Shawn. We need to go to Ellijay, get some cash and breakfast, and then ambush our used car salesman."

We made a welcome discovery. I could withdraw $100 on my Credit Suisse ATM card and Sally could get an equal amount on her recently recovered card. But still concerned about finances – the SUV gobbled down $32 of gas – we breakfasted at a McDonalds directly across the highway from J&W Best Deal Auto Sales. Perhaps owed to our circumstances the food tasted magnificent.

We ate in silence, sparing me any further annoying references to Shawn's paternity. What was difficult to tune out were the stares directed at our racially mixed trio. The family in the next booth got up and moved across the room. Does a person ever get used to this? Their two children asked for an explanation; perhaps that's cause for hope.

A call to the KOA attendant. No sign of Skeeter or his pursuers yet, but the day was just beginning.

Taking turns watching the car lot and cleaning up in the bathroom, we were about as prepared for the day as we were going to be when our used car salesman pulled into the lot and opened for business.

We'd decided intimidation was the best tactic and the three of us crashed into his office.

"Hey," he shouted, unsure of our intentions. Then, recovering, "Are you ready to buy something? If you are, you're in luck 'cuz I've got some . . ."

"No, Mr. Harris," his name plate was on his desk this morning, "we're here to offer you a way out of a difficult situation." Harris' left eye began to twitch, but he regained his composure and wagged his finger to signal he wasn't going to be cowed.

Before he could say anything I resumed. "It seems, Harris, that you aided and abetted a kidnapping. If you're really lucky, the kidnappers won't have crossed any state lines, although I gather Georgia views this crime rather dimly too."

"If you're talking about that van I sold two days ago, there was nothing wrong with that."

"Really?" Sally jumped in. "A credit card presented by a small child. The only logical explanation was that she was doing so under duress. You didn't trouble your mind with that possibility, did you? Your only thought was the sale, not the well-being of two children who were purchasing a vehicle under the most suspicious circumstances."

"And you overcharged them in the bargain!" Shawn wanted a speaking role. He needed better lines.

"Who's the ni . . ." began Harris, who was just bright enough to stop there.

"You're not a fight fan are you, Harris," I observed. He shrugged and turned his palms up to signify there was no reason he should be a fight fan. "Still, I'm surprised you don't recognize Kid Ferguson, WBC champion in his weight class. No opponent's made it past the third round in Kid Fergy's last seven bouts." Shawn seemed to like this and cracked his neck from side to side. "He's joined us in case we need someone with his particular skills."

"Are you threatening me?" Harris wasn't a complete fool. It's hard to bullshit someone who does it for a living.

"Threatening you? Those are our daughters out there and we're not interested in legal technicalities. We're here to get information." Shawn smacked his fist into the palm of his hand. He was overdoing it. "You can start by supplying us with the names and addresses of everyone who's purchased a black Ford F-250 from you."

"That's privileged information. I can't have my customers being harassed."

Shawn leaned across the desk. "It's us or the FBI. When they figure out how deeply you're involved in this kidnapping they'll march your saggy old white ass off to prison where you'll spend ten to fifteen in close confinement with a very large brother – probably nicknamed Ramrod." He delivered that line pretty well.

The twitch had returned to the corner of Harris' left eye. "How far back do you want me to go?"

Harris had sold nine black F-250's during the preceding three years; apparently not a popular color. Two of the sales were at auctions to other dealers, leaving seven possibilities. As he laboriously wrote down the name and address of each buyer, he gave every indication that this betrayal of the Used Car Salesman's Code of Ethics was draining the life force from him.

Of the seven sales, one was to a woman and one was to a buyer who lived in Tennessee; a third black 250 was returned when a mechanical defect disabled the truck within a mile of the lot. Harris didn't elaborate on the nature of the defect. That left four candidates.

"Let's go down these. I hope you have a good memory, Mr. Harris." Shawn nodded grimly and tried to crack his neck again. "Describe each buyer."

"Well, Tom, here, the first one, I've known Tom forever. He trades every two or three years and I cut him a deal."

Sally pointed out, "That's not a description. Age, color of hair, height, weight. That's what makes a description."

"Okay, Tom's a slight fella'; he attaches blocks to the pedals to make them easier to reach. Balding, grey hair – what's left of it. Is that what you want?" We nodded yes.

"This second fella' is hard to forget. Great big guy, Rocco Snyder. Address is over near Dawsonville. Never seen him before that day, or since." Sally's expression brightened and I jumped in.

"Nothing so far, Harris. Keep going, but write down all the addresses."

Harris described two more men who by age and build seemed unlikely candidates. I tried to show unusual interest in the last one, hoping I wasn't dooming him to an unpleasant encounter with the Klan.

"We'll take that list Harris. Good you saw the wisdom of cooperating. If you're indicted, we'll come forward and testify that you did help, for what it's worth. In the meantime, you might want to keep your big mouth shut. I understand the Klan and the militias around here are so heavily infiltrated by Feds that you never know who you're talking to or who they'll turn around and blab to next."

Harris appeared to take this advice seriously.

From M&M's *Guide to Treasure*

Lost treasure of the Red Bank Cherokee
How much? $2,600,000.

What is it? When the Cherokees were forced to
leave they hid their gold and silver. The Red Bank
group of Cherokees didn't trust the others so they
hid their own in pots that they buried.

Where is it? It is buried along the banks of
Bannister Creek and Bruton Creek. The Red Bank
Cherokees carved clues in rocks all over the area to
help them find the buried pots. One large stone had
the key to all the buried pots. But, and this makes us
nuts, someone moved that key stone with a road
grader and now the directions don't work.

Proof it exists. Three boys found the big stone by
Bannister Creek in 1932 and dug under it. They
found a pot with gold and jewelry worth $15,540 but
the mean farmer who owned the land took it away
from them.

14

"I'm Moondance, Rocky's lady." The three of us stood at the door of Rocco Snyder's yurt, taking in the scene. Moondance was a Walt Disney Indian Maiden, from her long braids, to her fringed buckskin dress and turquoise jewelry, down to her moccasins. The only discordant note was Moondance's obvious Nordic ancestry. She towered over us and had bright yellow hair; her light blue eyes gazed dreamily through our little group. The stale aroma of smoked cannabis drifted out of the yurt.

We introduced ourselves and described our mission.

"So you're the proud parents!" It's amazing so many people use that adjective to describe our status. Proud? No, we were the alternately annoyed or panic-stricken parents. "The four of them left early this morning with their maps and everything."

We must have looked concerned, so Moondance hastened to reassure us, "Oh no, Rocky doesn't want any of the gold. We live off the earth's bounty." The garden that surrounded their yurt did look bountiful.

Sally spoke up, woman-to-woman. "It's the children. That's who we're looking for. We never wanted to find gold and it's just a game for the twins." She described the confrontations with the Knights.

It seemed to be dawning on Moondance that the treasure hunters might, at that moment, be in peril. Her eyes came into focus but her only comment was, "Oh dear."

I noted, hopefully, "From the descriptions of your husband, we gather that he can take care of himself."

"Oh, yes," another dreamy pause, "he can. He's committed himself to inner tranquility and non-violence." We must have looked unconvinced. "He's really serious about it. Last year some bikers forced him off the road because of a sticker on his truck and beat him so bad he had to spend a week in the hospital."

"That's terrible," Sally and I said simultaneously.

"Oh no," Moondance assured us. "Rocky never raised a hand to strike back. It was a test and he passed. The last aggres-

sive act he ever committed was in Vietnam on 27 April 1973."
This was said with unmistakable pride.

————————

Moondance had no idea where the treasure hunters had gone so
our best option seemed to be wait for them to return. Sally
wanted to check the next mine on our list, but there were three
mines that were equidistant from the Snyder's yurt. And any
searching would put us out on the highway in a known vehicle;
the false license plate would provide less protection during the
day when the occupants could be seen.

I asked Shawn if we could take him somewhere; he seemed
surprised by the offer. He was still recovering from the rejection
of the night before and hadn't developed another plan.

I was trying to feel good about our prospects. The Knights
had to have been thrown off the scent by the red van on the AT
and they weren't looking for Rocky's truck. Then again, maybe
they were if the Airstream occupants had given them a good
description. And, when I inventoried our assets, we didn't present a formidable force:

- A large ex-Marine committed to non-violence.
- Copycat Skeeter, who might, by this time, have also taken a
  vow of non-violence and was escorting the twins to an ash-
  ram.
- Shawn, who'd seemed willing enough thus far, but this
  wasn't his fight and at some point he'd remember that.
- Sally, our shooter, who'd only used her talent to dig us into a
  deeper hole.
- And me, who brought decent eyesight to the fray, but little
  else.

On the other side? A large number of ill-tempered thugs nursing
a grievance. The optimism evaporated.

————————

With evident pride Moondance served up a wholesome lunch of bland vegetables. Shawn accepted the offer of Rocky's home brewed beer and retired for a nap on the futon. Then we waited. Another call to the KOA attendant. The KKK had been back; Skeeter had not.

At 5:00 Moondance walked a short distance up the gravel road that led out to the highway. She was pacing so I joined her. "Anything wrong?"

"Rocky's late. He's always here before 5:00 for our meditation." She looked genuinely concerned.

"A few minutes can't make any difference," I offered.

"Rocky's never late for meditation. Fourteen years and this is the first time he's been late."

I ran back to the yurt and woke Sally who'd dozed off in a hammock. "Something's wrong, babe. Moondance says Rocky's never come back later then 5:00 and we're well past that now."

Not a good awakening. Sally sat up groggily, slumped when she heard the news, and the hammock pitched her backward onto the ground. I was barely able to catch her arm to break the fall. "Oh Max, what do we do now?" She looked on the point of tears. Put an adversary in front of her and she'd disable the person. This was different.

"Let's not jump to any conclusions. I'll ask Moondance to call the highway patrol and hospitals."

Moondance was receptive to that. One of their few concessions to modernity was a telephone. After ten minutes she came out.

"No accidents. No one who fits the descriptions of our four showed up at an emergency room around here."

Shawn emerged from the yurt. He'd overheard enough to have figured out what was going on. I unfolded the USGS map and located Woody Gap, where we'd left the van, and the three mines that we'd believed would be the twins' next targets. "What's the most efficient route around these four locations, Shawn?"

He studied the map for a minute then said, "First Woody Gap; then west to Horner mine. A few miles south of that is Ivey Cut mine; and then it's a pretty good haul down to Whim Hill mine."

"C'mon, Sally. Let's roll." She and Shawn headed for the car. "No offense, Shawn. I think we'd all be better off if you sit this one out."

"Why? Because I'm too *visible*?"

Well, yes, but I was also uneasy about repeatedly exposing him to perils of our making.

"Exactly."

He looked accusingly at Sally's red hair.

"Sorry, Shawn. I agree with Max. And I'm going to wear a head scarf and glasses."

Shawn looked petulant. He *was* acting like one of my children.

"We can leave a pistol with you."

"No guns!" shouted Moondance from up the road where she'd resumed her vigil. Okay, that's consistent. I shrugged at Shawn, and Sally and I got in the SUV.

Fifteen minutes later we approached Woody Gap. I slowed and tried to scan ahead. Skeeter's van was where we'd left it. There was a second parking area across the road and we pulled in, moving as far toward the rear as possible.

The other vehicles were a mix of Subarus with roof racks for mountain bikes and kayaks, and pickup trucks – none with rebel battle flags.

As we were closing the doors, we saw the same USFS ranger we'd met in Blairsville, Jones, running away from Skeeter's red van shouting. "Get back! Get back! Run!" The few people who were loading their cars after a day of hiking were tired and slow to respond. "There's a bomb!" shouted Jones.

That galvanized attention and there was an immediate rush across the highway toward the lot we'd parked in. I grabbed Sally's arm and pulled her behind our SUV. The conversion van was over 50 yards away.

The fleeing mob ran past our car and took refuge behind parked vehicles or in the forest. A few were peering from behind trees; most were hidden. Jones was the last to arrive; he'd been shepherding the stragglers across the road. I intercepted him. "Is it the red van?" He appeared to recognize us and nodded yes.

"That van belongs to the guy who's running around with our daughters. What kind of a bomb is it?"

"Dynamite. One stick. But enough to blow that thing sky high and maybe set off explosions in some of the gas tanks in cars nearby. It'll be a mess."

"Could you see the fuse?"

"No, the fuse end was pointed away from me."

"Any sparks?"

Head shake.

"What made you look under the van?"

"The idiot who parked it put it almost on top of a mountain laurel. I was trying to see if there were any more damaged plants underneath."

"We may have lucked out Ranger Jones. If that thing doesn't blow pretty soon it's likely the fuse went out." That's me, the idiot plant-killer, talking.

"I'm still not letting anyone near it. We're warned that the fuse can continue to burn slowly inside, especially in conditions of high humidity."

"Understood, and Sally and I have no interest in getting closer than nece . . ."

Sally had paled. "Did you check to see if there's anyone inside?"

"After I saw the damage to the mountain laurel, I looked in the car's window but I didn't see anyone. Not anyone sitting up in a seat anyway. There could be someone lying out of sight on the floor, I suppose, but it would have to be someone pretty small."

Sally bolted out of our protected area and ran across the parking lot toward the red van. I was so stunned it took a second to react before I followed her.

From M & M's *Guide to Treasure*

Confederate pay train
How much? It was a railroad car full of sacks of money to pay the Confederate soldiers.

What is it? A Union train filled with soldiers and horses was being chased by a Confederate train. The Confederate train also had lots of soldiers and weapons. One car was filled with money. Some Confederate soldiers tried to blow up the Union train but they messed up. They blew up their own train by mistake and the money flew everywhere. They must have been pretty stupid.

Where is it? It's in southeast Tennessee south of a town Chatata.

Proof it exists. In 1970 a boy found a saber that was part of the shipment of weapons in the Confederate train. An expert said that the heavy coins had all sunk down in the mud.

15

I didn't know Sally could run that fast. I was still several steps behind when she slammed into the side of the van and started tugging wildly on the door handles. The division of responsibilities left me in charge of bomb disposal. Dropping to the ground as I neared the van, I slid to a stop inches short of the running board. The stick of dynamite was visible in its brown paraffin paper wrapper, just at the limit of my reach. As Jones had said, the fuse was not visible.

I reached for the dynamite and only succeeded in scooting it a little further under the van. *Fuck!* A stick, I needed a stick to fish it out. *Not a lot of time to search. We're in the forest; there must be sticks scattered everywhere.* As it turns out, no. They get picked up by campers for use as kindling. I went around to the other side where Sally was tugging on the driver's door. I ripped a branch off the unlucky mountain laurel and went back to the passenger's side. The stick worked. Slowly – too slowly? – I coaxed the dynamite toward me. I really wanted to push it the other way. *Another inch.* Got it. I pulled the dynamite out, holding it with two fingers at arm's length – as if that would protect me from the blast – and examined the fuse. It looked dormant.

Sally was beside me. "Remove the fuse, Max." I started to rip it out. "No, very slowly. Don't . . ."

The excellent Ranger Jones joined the small party of heroes, produced a knife and cut the fuse. He took the explosive from me, also holding it with two fingers, picked up dust from the ground and sprinkled it on the dynamite. Paraffin paper turns out to be an excellent medium for capturing fingerprints. "Look at that," exulted Jones. "Now we're getting somewhere. What else can we find?"

Ranger/detective Jones retrieved a half-burned cigarette from under the van. "Well," he concluded, "their plan is obvious. See the hole where the fuse was punched through the cigarette? They were using the cigarette to light the fuse which would give them time to drive away." He picked up the end of the fuse he'd cut off. "They need to switch to a more combustible brand of smokes. The cigarette went out before it could ignite the fuse."

I confess to a moment of disappointment. There was never any real danger. And Sally had satisfied herself that the twins weren't in the van.

Jones pulled a plastic dog-poop bag from a dispenser by the trail and gingerly put the dynamite into the bag. "I so want to crush these assholes," he muttered. Then he looked at us. "Okay folks. It's getting serious. No more mincing around. We have to bring in the cavalry."

We told Jones everything that had happened, starting at our dinner with Skeeter in Blairsville, emphasizing repeatedly that Skeeter was a confused innocent who meant harm to no one.

I concluded, "We think it's pretty clear that the Knights who hold court at the Two Wheels in Suches are involved in this. That's one place for the Feds to start. Another would be that waitress at the Blairsville Waffle House. She's married to one of them and it looked like she'd been roughed up. Maybe she'll talk."

"Not if she's smart," opined Sally.

Jones, who'd been writing furiously in a small pad while we talked, was silent for a minute; the toe of his shoe traced lines in the dust. "Okay. Some good leads for the FBI to get started on. We work more often with the BATF – you know, dealing with moonshiners and such – but I have a direct line to the FBI guy responsible for this district. We've worked with him on some militia activities in the national forest. These guys? Boon is suspected of militia involvement. He's the bad actor in the group and the others either put up with him or listen to him be-cause he's seen combat." Another shining legacy of our war in Vietnam. "I'm guessing that's why they want Skeeter to stay with the group – you know, a combat vet.

"The gravity of your uncle Skeeter's offenses don't stack up to much compared to some of this other shit that's going on. These jerks seem to like to blow things up. From your descrip-tion of the two-part explosion of that guy's car in Dahlonega, I'd guess that was dynamite setting off the gas tank. More explosive power in a full tank of gasoline than in nitroglycerin. Same would have probably happened here. Benefit of the doubt? This was intended as a warning, but these pinheads don't understand how this stuff works. Anyone nearby would have become a casualty in some degree." He seemed, increasingly, to be talking to himself so I cut in.

"Right. Looking to the future? Our twins?"

"Of course. Give me any pictures you have. I'll get in touch first with the FBI. I have a radio so I can probably contact them before you can. They may have all kinds of jurisdictional issues to dither over, but no one trusts the cops around here. The Feds have to dive in and even the dimmest among them will figure out a hate crime was involved in blowing up Ferguson's ride. Besides, no one hangs back in a child kidnapping."

"Technically, not kidnapped," corrected Sally. "Missing? Yes. In danger? Maybe. Not actually kidnapped." That, at least, was our hope.

"The Knights purchased dynamite from the Mountain Construction Supply Company in Dawsonville with a credit card they stole from Sally. Might be another bit of evidence you can hang on them."

A shout interrupted our conversation. "Hey, over there. Is the coast clear?" That came from one among the masses huddled on the far side of the road.

"Damn," said Jones. "Eyewitnesses," and he trotted back to the group that had taken refuge. He quickly learned that none of them had seen anyone around the red van. We concluded the perps had placed the dynamite earlier in the day.

"Sally and I have to split. There's not much daylight left and we want to get to these three mines." I pointed them out to Jones on the USGS map.

He shook his head. "I can tell you not to bother with this first one. The entrance collapsed years ago. Heavy equipment would be required to get into that. The second is a problem. It's on private land. The owner clings to the dream of opening it to the public and retiring on the ticket sales. But the mine couldn't be less stable. Every good rain, water floods down through it.

The timbers must be shot. And the adit is so narrow in places I doubt your Marine flowerchild could get very far. The owner's been warned the courts consider the mine an attractive nuisance and he's liable when someone gets hurt. But he just tacks a few one-by-fours across the entrance and figures he's done his duty to protect the public from its own bottomless stupidity. I expect to read about the tragedy any day now." Sally didn't need to hear this. Nor did I.

"Your third mine here is small potatoes. The adit extends no more than ten feet into the hillside."

"Adit? Not a shaft?"

"Sorry – maybe not important. A shaft is vertical. An adit is horizontal – the kind you see in old Western movies. I think the miners also call a horizontal tunnel a drift. Adit, drift; same thing. There're lots of that kind around here." Ranger Jones looked like he was ready to share more on mining terminology, but we were pressed for time.

"We'd better move. Give us your phone number and, by the way, we don't know your first name, Ranger Jones."

"Fred." He looked down; was there more? "There're two Freds in the station and the other guys identify me by my initials. If you call, ask for F.U." We tried not to react. Burdened with an easily ridiculed name myself, my sympathies always lie with anyone similarly cursed. "I know. It's my personal cross. Thanks for not snickering."

We left F. U. Jones sadly contemplating the mountain laurel by the van. A good guy, but he needed to address his floraphilia. He also needed to get in touch with the FBI and Sally shouted a reminder back to him as we pulled out.

————

It took us almost half an hour to get to the mine and the light in the sky was fading. While I drove, Sally ransacked Shawn's effects, looking for flashlights. She found two – one only a small penlight – but not before unearthing a trove of titty magazines.

She repacked the magazines carefully to avoid embarrassing Shawn.

We bounced off the main road up a dirt track for a few hundred yards before the path was blocked by Rocky's black F-250, clearly identified by the stickers plastered across the tailgate and back window.

"Bingo. They're here."

Sally's set expression indicated she was keeping her hopes in check.

We half-walked, half-ran up the path. My mind, and I'm sure Sally's, alternated between positive and bleak thoughts. Here was Rocky's truck. Where were our people? Cave in? Trapped? Rocky had become wedged in a narrow passage, Winnie-the-Pooh like, and no one could get out? Or were they digging excitedly for gold?

The sky was almost dark by the time we saw the mine entrance. The one-by-fours Jones had mentioned were strewn around on the ground. The breaks in the wood were white and free of dirt. The boards had been broken off recently.

Kudos to Shawn for keeping fresh batteries in his flashlights. We entered the mine, stooped over, expecting a colony of bats to part our hair at any second. There was the expected refuse from long past parties: empty beer cans and bottles, remnants of a fire, some wrappers. It didn't seem a congenial place for a cookout, but the ambience must have been a selling point – for high school kids, anyway. We picked our way through the litter and the adit opened up after twenty feet. I guessed that it would continue to accordion as the miners had expanded the dig outward, looking for that elusive vein of gold. There was the occasional wood beam. Jones had been right about their condition; the beams didn't look like they could support their own weight.

Sally started calling the girls' names. No response. Her louder shouts produced a gentle rain of dust from the ceiling of the tunnel. She called more softly.

The going became difficult. Large rocks on the floor of the mine were difficult to get over. I wondered if Sally's claustrophobia would kick in. Thinking it might do so, of course, summoned it.

"I'm so ashamed, Max. I'm panicking." She bent forward, hands on knees, eyes closed, "I have to focus on the babies. They're somewhere down in there. I have to keep going."

The tunnel flattened out for five feet and I examined the floor for prints. There appeared to be small footprints. "Look, Sal. That has to be them."

This took her mind off her claustrophobia and she lunged forward, shouting testily over her shoulder "Well, come on!" I hadn't been lagging.

We lost track of the distance covered – slight twists and turns, our backs complaining from the stooped posture – when Sally cried out, "Noooo!"

I looked around her. From floor to within a few inches of the ceiling, a mass of dirt, boulders and smaller rocks blocked the passage. There was a small opening at the top. "They're trapped. Oh dear Lord. Our precious little babies." She started scrabbling at the rocks in the wall of debris.

I felt sick. A father who can't perform the most basic function: protect his children from harm. *Are they under or behind the pile of rubble?*

"Wait, Sal . . . stop." Sally turned and looked at me, dumbfounded. "Don't move anything else." I played the penlight on the rubble, then borrowed Sally's larger flashlight. "See. Small footprints in the dust going up the wall of rocks and dirt. There . . . a child's handprint. They didn't get past this point," triumph ringing in my voice. "They're not even in the mine."

The implications of that discovery were quick to set in. If not here, where were they? We hurried back up through the mine. Sally took a painful looking fall but didn't make a sound. Back on the dirt road down to the cars, we traded theories.

"Maybe they circled around the mountain, looking for another entrance." Remotely possible; Skeeter and Rocky might have information that would lead them to expand the search.

"Maybe they came out and found that Rocky's truck wouldn't start. They had to hitchhike." We both liked that one.

The theory we didn't say out loud: maybe they've been collected by Klansmen.

As we neared the cars I asked Sally to wait while I went ahead. With the better flashlight I looked under both vehicles. No dynamite.

"Let's check the status of Rocky's truck." With Shawn's ersatz 'key' I turned the ignition – *I'll cover the repair bill, Rocky.* The truck started. That eliminated one comforting theory; they weren't hitchhiking.

While I was checking the truck, Sally was looking around the immediate area. "Bad news, Max. There are tire tracks all over the place. You can see the tracks going back into the bushes. Someone turned around here."

It was undeniable. The unspoken theory, kidnapped by the Klan, had just jumped into first place.

From M&M's *Guide to Treasure*

Spanish gold bars of Paint Rock Valley
How much? It took 20 mules to carry all the gold
bars. So, a lot.

What is it? 300 years ago the Spanish had gold
mines in Mexico. The gold was taken back to Spain
three times every year but the officers at the mine
hid away a little bit all the time until they had a lot.
They killed all the Indian slaves at the mine and
started toward the Atlantic Ocean with their gold.
When they got to Alabama they were wiped out by
Yuchi Indians who took the gold and hid it in a
cave. The Yuchi only used the gold for jewelry and
had to leave most of it behind when they were sent
to Oklahoma.

Where is it? Somewhere near Paint Rock Valley.

Proof it exists. In 1920 an old Indian showed up and
hired two boys to help him. He blindfolded the boys as
they went to the cave. The boys helped load heavy
bars onto the Indian's mules. Years later they
realized that the bars were gold.

16

"Let's not panic," I said, my voice quavering. *Have to focus. There must be something we can do. Steady deep breaths. The helplessness.*

Close it down. Don't think. Do something, anything.

"I know it looks like the girls were taken, but there are other, slim chances that Rocky and Skeeter went somewhere with them on foot." There wasn't enough light to see Sally's reaction. Was she comforted by this 'slim chance' bullshit? I wasn't. *Don't think. Action.*

"I'm guessing these tracks were here when we arrived but we were so hell-bent on getting up to the mine we didn't look around. Let's see if we can find anything."

We started back up the road to the mine, carefully playing the flashlights on and around the tracks. Nothing. Then we returned to the vehicles and worked out in expanding circles. I found an empty beer can, possibly left there recently. I tried to hold it by the tab so as not to disturb any fingerprints. While I was conducting this delicate retrieval I could hear Sally pushing through the brush. "Find anything? I've only come up with a beer can." I was trying to sound calm. We had nothing to go on and no idea what clues we might be looking for.

Sally screamed.

"Oh Jesus, no. They killed Rocky!" Her flashlight illuminated a very large man, bound to a tree by duct tape, his head hanging forward, a drying trickle of blood coming down his chin through his beard and onto his massive chest.

Overcoming my initial revulsion, I approached Rocky, "Are you conscious?" He didn't look alive. I put two fingers on his carotid artery. There was a pulse, but it didn't feel strong.

"He isn't dead. Let's get him out of here."

Here was something we could do. It didn't bring us closer to our daughters but it was activity, and it was a good act. Maybe we'd earn merit? I started to strip away the duct tape when Sally stopped me.

"Look, writing." She pointed her flashlight at the tape covering Rocky's stomach. "

BEAR MEAT
HiPPY FAGGET

"They have a way with words, don't they." The writing appeared to be in blood.

"Wait, Max. You can't just cut him loose."

Why not? We can't leave him here either.

Sally explained, "He'll fall to the ground and we won't be able to lift him into the car."

She was right. Rocky looked like he weighed over 300 pounds, more dead weight than Sally and I could hoist into our SUV.

"Hang on, babe. Physics to the rescue." I ran to Rocky's truck, started it with Shawn's all-purpose key, and backed up until the open tailgate was just a foot from the unconscious Rocky.

"This seems undignified, but if we can get the top half of him to fall into the truck bed as we release him from the tree, maybe we can lift his legs and shove him in."

Shawn had a thin roll-up mattress in his bedding. We placed that and two of Shawn's pillows in the truck bed in front of Rocky. Sally unwound the tape as I tried to brace Rocky so he didn't collapse into the truck with too much force. I was thinking I should spend more time with the free weights at the gym.

"Here he comes," Sally warned as she stripped off two more rounds of tape. Then we saw why Rocky was in rough shape. Blood started to ooze from a wound in his stomach.

"Ah, Jeez. Get some tape around that. A compression bandage or something. Those savages shot him in the gut. He'll bleed out."

Sally wrapped the tape back around Rocky's mid-section. I held him upright so he wouldn't fall into the truck bed before we'd re-closed the area over the wound. My arms were starting to shake from the exertion when Sally announced, "That's about as good as I can get it. I don't see any blood coming out around the edges of the tape. Ease him down."

I tried to lower Rocky's top half slowly into the truck, but my muscles were used up and he fell out of my grasp. The thin mattress and two pillows cushioned the fall – a little.

Sally tore off the remaining tape around his legs and the two of us picked up his ankles and inched him forward, the mattress sliding into the truck bed.

We closed the tailgate. '𝕷𝖔𝖛𝖊 𝖔𝖓𝖊 𝖆𝖓𝖔𝖙𝖍𝖊𝖗,' urged one sticker. '𝖁𝖎𝖔𝖑𝖊𝖓𝖈𝖊 𝖎𝖘 𝖓𝖊𝖛𝖊𝖗 𝖙𝖍𝖊 𝖆𝖓𝖘𝖜𝖊𝖗,' declared another. Bullshit to that. I wanted to put a bullet into the belly of everyone who'd had any part in this.

―――――

Sally rode in the truck bed with Rocky to keep an eye on him and to try to prevent him rolling around as I drove along the winding rode toward town. A large white H on a blue sign directed us to a hospital.

―――――

"We found him duct-taped to a tree. It looked like he's taken a bullet to the gut. We tried to wrap that up to stem blood loss." It took five burly orderlies to extract Rocky from the back of the truck and put him on a gurney. I felt better about my own struggles to ease him into the truck bed. "I'm sorry we can't tell you much more than that."

Sally looked at me incredulously. Why wasn't I telling them the men who'd shot Rocky were KKK who'd also kidnapped our daughters? Because, Sally, sometimes I get it right. We needed to get on the road – although we had no idea where to go – and we didn't know who we were talking to.

Vindicating my caution, a minute later a police car squealed to a stop behind us. "Who's been shot?" We turned and the buzzcut cop who'd threatened Ferguson got out.

I put a warning hand on Sally's arm. "A big guy, Officer. We found him duct-taped to a tree. We were just able to get him into this truck and bring him here. He's in rough shape. Maybe lost a lot of blood."

Buzzcut went over to the gurney and shook his head. "I figgered it'd just be a matter of time. Have to say, he brought it on hisself. Hell, I tried to warn him to go easy on the leftie shit."

He shrugged with resignation and, moving away from the gurney, he studied us. "Didn't I see you somewhere before?" Rocky was rolled away.

"Yes sir. We were at the car rental the other afternoon when you came and took that report from us."

"You folks seem to attract trouble. First you get broken into. And now you bring in a shot up body."

"We do seem to be bad luck. Mentioning that break in, don't we need to get some kind of police report number from you for insurance purposes?"

That banal side excursion seemed to work. "Didn't I give you that? Well, you need to come down to the station with me and make a complete statement about this shooting – if that's what it turns out to be – and I can scare up the info you need."

"That would be great." I was trying hard not to paste this asshole in the mouth. "If you can spare a minute, I'd like to check on the man we brought here. I can't help but feel a little involved."

The policeman shrugged so I pulled Sally through the sliding doors into the ER. She arched an eyebrow, "You have a plan, Ace?"

"Not yet, but I'm afraid that the guys who did this to Rocky won't want him to regain consciousness and start talking. It doesn't seem like the asshole cop knows what went down, but eventually he will."

I looked around the ER for any sign of sanity. A physician, older, balding, and stooped, came in and started to cut away the duct tape. I moved to the other side of Rocky's gurney to get a better look at the doctor's nametag.

"Doctor Levine? An urgent word with you sir." The doctor looked annoyed, and with good reason.

"This is really not the time . . ." he started.

"Are you Jewish?"

"That's offensive. Get out of the ER before I ask that policeman outside to remove you."

"That's part of the problem, Doctor. He's a Klan sympathizer and the guys who shot Rocco Snyder – the guy on the table in front of you – are also Klan."

Levine stepped back, glanced nervously through the glass doors at the policeman, and led me into a small office.

"Klan?" Dr. Levine looked unwell.

"Yes sir. They followed us down from Blairsville and Suches. It looks almost certain they've kidnapped our daughters. We don't know why. They're trying to find some gold. Maybe they think the girls can help them. Or maybe a ransom note will arrive."

"How can I know you're serious. That's a pretty fantastic yarn."

"Look at that guy on the table out there. Does that look serious to you?"

He shook his head in distress.

"Here's what you need to do." I liked the way I was taking charge. "I approached you because you're Jewish, a group high on the Klan's hate list. Make sure anyone who's assigned to watch over Rocco Snyder has good reasons to despise the Klan. Jews, Blacks, Hispanics, maybe Catholics. No good old local boys."

"Yes, of course. We have a foreign medical graduate from Jamaica. Probably doesn't know much about the Klan yet, but not a likely recruit."

"Okay. But you'll need more. Snyder can never be alone. If the local cops put someone outside his door, that's not necessarily a good sign." Levine nodded.

"Next thing is to call the FBI. They've been informed that our daughters are missing. Now it looks like they've been kidnapped. Tell them that this attempted murder was done by the same people who kidnapped the Taylor-Brown children."

I almost lost it as I said those words. *The Taylor-Brown children are my children.* "Rocco there probably witnessed the kidnapping. The Feds may be able to get something out of him about where the kidnappers were heading. Which leads me to my last request. I want you to try to get that information too. Those are my babies, Doctor. If Rocco knows anything that might help us, we need it. I trust the FBI to do their job, but we're talking manpower here. I saved those two children once before. I can do it again."

Who was I trying to convince with that? The assertion stopped me cold and I started to sob, leaning forward on the small physician.

Pulling back, "Sorry. Too little sleep during the pursuit. If you're a father, you'll understand." *Fuck. Now he was tearing up.* I guess that signaled a willingness to cooperate. "Okay. Sorry I had to pull you away from your doctoring duties. Go save Rocky's life and call the FBI."

He handed me a card with his direct phone number on it and I rejoined Sally. "What now?" she asked. "Do we go to the station with this Neanderthal or make a break for it?"

"Fewer complications if we go to the station if it can be wrapped up quickly. Question is, how much do we tell them? Notably, what were we doing up a dirt road at night pulling bodies off of trees?"

———————

We didn't have to address that question. Officer Buzzcut came into the ER waiting area. "I just got a call. You can either go down to the station now and give your statement to whoever's on duty, or, if you'd rather give it to me (why him, in particular?) I come back on at four in the afternoon."

"Okay, you go fight crime, officer." Was that too wise-ass? "We'll take care of the statement one way or another." The cop hesitated, then left. He was speaking into his microphone with official urgency as he pulled out.

"C'mon, Sal. We need to recover our car, get Moondance down here with her man, and try to pick up a trail."

The shortest route to Rocky and Moondance's yurt took us past the mine. This was good. We could collect our own car and give Rocky's truck to Moondance. If Moondance knew how to drive – she looked like someone who might have elected to pass on 20th century life skills – she could go down to the hospital by herself and we could go . . . where?

There were only two potential sources of information to help us find the girls: 1) Rocky would regain consciousness and give us a detailed route of travel for the Knights. Unlikely. In fact, I hoped that the twins had been nowhere around when Rocky had been beaten, trussed up and shot. 2) The Knights did want M&M as guides to the gold – and Skeeter too – and they would go to the same mines that Sally and I had identified. It didn't take a lot of imagination to picture the twins accepting the Klansmen as Long John Silver sorts of associates: basically untrustworthy, but potentially useful. Skeeter, of course, would hitch his star to anything or anyone.

Sally and I discussed this as we drove back out to the mine. We also tried to figure out why a barely live man was left tied to a tree. Alive he's a liability. Did something go wrong? Or did these dimwits make a mistake? It was hard to believe they'd tie someone to a tree and shoot him – non-fatally.

In the dark we couldn't see the references that had guided us earlier to the faint dirt track that went up the hill to the mine. We were slow to realize we'd overshot the turn-off and were creeping back along the highway, scanning for the entrance, when Sally hissed, "Douse the headlights and pull over."

On the hillside up to our right, lights were moving around and we could hear a voice shouting,

"That fat hippy sumbitch got loose," then indistinct responses.

"We need to hide this truck and see if we can overhear anything useful." That's me, saying the obvious.

There was a long curving gravel driveway across the highway from the dirt track that ran up to the mine. I pulled into the driveway far enough around the curve that the truck wouldn't be visible from the road. The stickers would identify it to anyone who saw it.

Sally distributed the guns – I was given the Smith and Wesson Masterpiece – and we started up the track to the mine, hugging the tree line so we could duck into cover quickly. More lights playing – flashlights – and the conversation became more distinct. Sally could make it out; I couldn't; the price of too much time on Air Force flight lines with howling jet engines.

"They're talking about our SUV. They can't decide whether it's ours. I think there are three of them."

We moved steadily closer and now I could make out what was being said. "How'd that big ape get loose? After Boon here stupidly put a slug in his gut I figgered he'd be dead by now."

"Can't we leave that alone? I didn't plan on droppin' my rifle."

"It wouldn't of gone off if you didn't have to have a fancy hair-trigger Mannlicher. You oughta buy American guns."

This led to an uninformative argument over the merits of different rifles.

"Someone who fought for America oughta buy American guns, that's all I got to say."

Then a voice we hadn't heard before, "I didn't count on none of this. I was okay with Skeeter and them kids showing us their stuff. But I never figured we'd go throwin' dynamite around or shootin' anyone."

"I don't deny it, Len. Some of that was different from what we planned." Boon talking? "And I don't deny we got us a problem here. That fat hippy might could put the finger on us. I figgered he'd take the warning as a warning. But a bullet? He might just go to the police. What that makes me think, though, is the first place he'll go is back to his Scandinavian squaw. She'll pro'ly use some herbs and magic chanting to fix him up."

"I'd sure like her to fix me up. Wooeee. What a body! Wasted on that fat peacenik."

Then words we didn't want to hear, "Ya know? I'm pretty sure this here's the car them two Yankee gold hunters was driving. They mighta switched tags."

Then, words we were happier to hear. "If their car is here, they musta gone up to the mine. Maybe we can give 'em a surprise."

Voices and flashlights receded up the track toward the mine entrance.

Sally and I went quickly up the hill to see if we could recover our car. The Knights had obligingly parked their truck in the turn-around area near the tree where Rocky had been taped up, leaving the dirt road to the highway open. I removed the cores from their tire stems and threw them into the forest. After determining how we needed to maneuver to turn around, we got into our own SUV, backed into the turn-around, and bounced rapidly down the track. There was a shout, then the report of a rifle. The shot frightened me, but got Sally's blood up.

"Fuck. These guys don't care who they shoot at!" I think she would have preferred to stay and duke it out with the Knights. Given her skill with a gun, the odds were tilted against them.

"No, babe. I think they do care about shooting at us." Reaching the highway, we pulled up the drive where we'd left Rocky's truck. I was careful not to touch the brake pedal and send a beacon of red light through the trees to our adversaries.

"Okay, Sal, you choose. One of us should warn Moondance and get her and Shawn out of that yurt. Even these morons seem to realize they have to silence Rocky, so they'll start looking for him. And I think the best place for Shawn might also be the hospital. Too many people around for the KKK to do anything there. Maybe that Dr. Levine will even check him in to keep him out of sight." Sally took this all in.

"What about the twins?"

"Well, I may have outsmarted myself. If I'd left the Knights' truck in driveable condition they could have led us to the girls. Still, I think one of us should stay here in case they do get moving."

"I don't like it . . . splitting up. We're a split-up family already."

True. The emotional burden of dividing further was too great. "You're right. It won't take long to drop Rocky's truck off with Moondance and then we can come back. These guys aren't going anywhere soon."

————

It wasn't that easy. Moondance fell into a stupor at the news of Rocky's condition and Shawn didn't want to be left behind again.

"C'mon, Shawn. Listen to reason. The bad guys are headed this way as soon as they get air in their tires. Moondance here is in la-la land and someone has to drive her to the hospital. And that's where I would like you to be to keep an eye on things while staying out of sight."

"Look, man. I am not actually your son. No ordering me around, okay? If all you need is a chauffeur and baby-sitter for Moondance, why can't Sally do that?"

That was too much for a panicked mother. "Because, you petulant jerk, you're not the mother. I am!"

Shawn had no response. I could see he wanted to defend his already dented manhood against this attack, but he was learning what countless men before him had learned: Don't cross Sally Taylor when she thinks she's right. And, in all fairness, she usually is.

I handed Shawn the screwdriver that operated the ruined ignition lock in Rocky's truck, and, with this parting advice – "I wouldn't waste a lot of time" – Sally and I set off to see if we could catch up with the goobers.

Parking across the road and out of sight, we again crept up to within listening distance of the stranded Klansmen.

"That red haired cunt sure has it in for your tires, don't she, Boon? This the third time, ain't it? Ever' time she passes by, you end up buying new rubber or pumping air."

"I'd sure like to have her here now. I'd pump her pussy full of something, and it wouldn't be air." They laughed. Sally sunk her nails into my arm. *Was I bleeding?* "She might like that, Boon. Get some real white-American man-juice in her. It don't look like she gets it from that old noodle-dick husband." *Were my declining abilities that apparent?*

This witty exchange was interrupted by the squawk of a radio. One of the revelers answered. "White one, white three here." The message was indistinct but apparently involved an ETA. Should we stay there in the hope of eavesdropping on information about M&M? Or should we be poised for pursuit in our car? Indecision meant we stayed where we were. Five minutes later another truck swung into the dirt road and crawled up the hill.

"Chew bring some new valve stems?" The answer was yes. A small compressor was hooked up to a truck's battery terminals and after ten minutes all four tires had been re-inflated. As he packed up to go, the rescue truck driver said, "Ya' oughta know, Snyder was checked into the hospital down in Dahlonega. I heard he's in a bad way."

"Pro'ly not bad enough," muttered Boon. "I knew I shoulda finished the job." He kicked at a tire. "How's our little tour-guide princesses doin'?"

Sally and I stopped breathing. A lot hung on the answer.

"Out like lights. Lookin' forward to a big day tomorrow." That sounded better than expected.

"Look, Boon. I know you said they might come in handy. But they's a big problem. Now with the fat hippy shot and you blowin' up stuff, we can't just turn 'em loose and we can't kill 'em neither. They ain't enough friendly judges in the state of Georgia to keep us from fryin'. Besides, I ain't up for killin' no little children. Maybe you got used to it in Vietnam, but these is American children. I gotta level with you straight out: I just can't count'nance it."

I didn't dare look at Sally. Was she about to open fire?

"Don't you worry, Billy. I been thinkin' 'bout this. Due to circumstances, we're fugitives. I didn't want it, but sometimes shit happens. Now we got to adapt to a new situation."

"You thinkin' about ransomin' them two for our freedom?"

"Hell, Len. We got our freedom. We can live in the forest forever. No one'll find us and sure no one'll turn us in. No, I'm thinkin' bigger. We don't need to live in the woods. That gut-shot to fatso was an accident and we're all witnesses to that. Blowin' up that nigger's car? Who saw that? No one."

"I'm still worried 'bout them two little girls. They've heard talkin'. They might of seen somethin'."

"I understand yer concerns, Len. You see, one of the side advantages, you might say, of lookin' 'round in mines is that tragic accidents can happen. A person might get trapped and not be found for years. In fact, we might even be heroes tryin' to get those two poor little tykes dug out."

Billy answered, "Well, I think we need to talk more 'bout this before anyone does somethin' rash."

I did look at Sally. She was frozen.

From M & M's *Guide to Treasure*

General Morgan's stolen treasure

How much? At least a million dollars

What is it? General Morgan was a Southern general who was verys good at winning battles but he started stealing money and letting his soldiers get out of control. The other generals did not like Morgan and the head general told him not to go somewhere but he did anyway. He went into small towns and took all the money. His men were terrible to the people. Pretty soon Morgan was defeated and he buried his treasure before escaping. He was killed in a battle before he could get back and dig up his treasure.

Where is it? Maybe some is buried outside a town called Cynthiana

Proof it exists. Everyone knew Morgan was taking money and had a lot. The Confederate government demanded he share some of it. Other generals wanted Morgan punished and made to pay back the money.

17

"Let's go, babe." I took Sally's arm. "We need to follow the truck that just arrived. They came from wherever they're holding M&M and they're getting ready to leave." Sally came out of it and headed down the road ahead of me.

We ran along the rutted track as fast as conditions allowed, our flashlights off. I tripped and took a fall. It was timely. I was on the ground and Sally leaning over me when the headlights of a pickup swung over the top of us. Staying low, we dove off the track into the brush. The first truck bounced past.

Damn, damn, damn, damn. That's the one we need to follow.

We were back on our feet when the second pickup pulled out of the turnaround onto the track and headed downhill. Pinned in the trees again, we were crouched in a runner's starting position, waiting to bolt down the track. Then both pickups were on the highway and we were racing down the hill, each of us taking another fall. We crossed the highway, still with 100 yards to go to our SUV, and saw the taillights of the pickups receding up the road. I was first into the car and almost tore off before limping Sally could get in and close the door.

I pulled out onto the highway and floored it. Nothing but darkness ahead. On the short straight stretches between the sharp curves in the road I pushed the speed up to 90. Several intersections flashed past; they could have turned off at any of them. I accelerated to 100 mph and we nearly left the road at the next bend in the twisting highway.

"Easy, Max, we can't find the kids if we're dead."

After a few more minutes and two more brushes with death we acknowledged that we'd lost our best opportunity to find our children.

Defeated, we pulled in at a one-pump gas station and general store, surprised that it was still open as it was almost midnight. "Do you have a pay phone?"

The acned high-school kid behind the counter nodded at a well-used phone on the wall by the bathroom.

I dialed 911.

"Please connect me with the FBI."

. . .

"Yes, it is an emergency."

. . .

"No. I don't want to speak to the Dahlonega Police Department."

. . .

"Well, then, can you give me the number for the FBI?"

. . .

I hung up and dialed 404-679-9000. It was busy. Was the kid behind the counter trying to listen in? After a minute, I tried the call again and got through.

"My name is Max Brown. You should have reports from Dr. Levine in Dahlonega and Fred Jones of the USFS about the kidnapping of our two children." The kid at the counter was trying to look busy rearranging the cardboard display boxes. He should be looking bored if he wasn't listening, or concerned if he was.

. . .

"That's correct. That's us. We just had a chance to overhear the kidnappers. We have three first names, Boon, Len and Billy."

. . .

"Yes, I understand they're common names."

. . .

"No. We tried to follow them and we lost them. They were headed north on state 52."

. . .

"Yes, I'm sorry too."

. . .

"Yes, I'm sure the Bureau is."

. . .

"I'm sorry. That's out of the question."

. . .

"Alright, then. 'Bye."

"What's out of the question, Max?"

"She wanted us to come to Atlanta to make statements." I looked over at the guy behind the counter, who kept his head down. "Any suggestions on a motel around here?"

He hesitated. Why? At length he answered, "There's a place two miles up the road. On the right. Probably have to go to the owner's shack out back to get a key at this hour."

We thanked him and left. Sally said she didn't think she could sleep, with the girls taken. I was watching through the store's window; the guy was watching our car. "Sal, what do you want to bet that no sooner do we pull out of here than that kid's on the phone?"

"He did seem strange. Someone's talking about kidnapping and he's rearranging dispensers on his counter?"

"It's clear where we won't be checking in, but maybe we can get out of sight there and if someone does come looking for us, we can tail them."

———

Five minutes later we drove past the Mountain Meadows Inn and found a place from where we could watch the motel's parking area without being seen ourselves. Sally wanted the first shift; she said she was too keyed up to sleep. I dropped off immediately, my last waking thoughts being to chastise myself for indulging in shuteye while my babies were in danger.

"Max, wake up. Something's happening" According to the dashboard clock two hours had passed. A minivan was parked in front of the motel. A man got out and headed around to the back of the building, presumably to rouse the owner.

Sally and I took the pistols out of the glove compartment. She checked them both before giving me the .38.

"So? Take them down or follow them?"

I wasn't sure. "Let's see how this develops. Following them might be better and then we can call in the Feds." It seemed unlikely Sally would wait for help to arrive if she knew where her children were.

A few minutes passed. No activity. Then the driver returned to the car. He opened the back door and carefully lifted a small child out while his wife did the same on the other side. They carried the sleeping children into a room and returned for suitcases. And that was it.

We were both wide awake. "The assholes have had two hours to get here, if they wanted us. I vote we move on."

"Where to?"

"The next group of mines is north of here. We could go up to the Blairsville Ranger Station, sleep in their parking lot, and then coordinate with Jones about how to cover the remaining mines."

Sally shrugged; she had no better idea so we headed north on 52 again.

I thought Blairsville would be closer but we didn't get there until three o'clock. Sally was already asleep and I was fighting to stay awake as I drove. I parked at the far end of the USFS parking lot and after a few minutes of thrashing around in the reclining seat was asleep.

———

An insistent tapping on the window brought us both bolt upright. The tapper was Fred Jones. "Rise and shine. You have company." The dashboard clock announced it was 8:15.

A black Suburban parked in front of the ranger station signaled the arrival of the FBI. Agents Malkowitz and Bernstein were waiting for us in Jones' small office. A Mutt and Jeff combination: Malkowitz was tall, bespectacled and bookish in appearance and manner. Bernstein was short, wide and muscular; her mouth set in a permanent clench of disapproval.

While Jones brought coffee and a half-empty box of stale doughnuts, we briefed the agents on everything up to that point, including our unsuccessful stake-out of the motel. Bernstein was quick to respond.

"I know how hard it is for parents to stand back, but you really need to."

That pissed Sally off. "We came within a whisker of tailing them back to our girls last night. What have you got to show?"

"Not a whole lot; we're new to the case. But it's been our experience that parental involvement usually leads to the parents themselves becoming hostages or casualties and that makes the job just that much harder."

Bernstein was right. In normal circumstances, that is. But Sally and I were different. We'd been through this before and our instincts had been pretty good; we just hadn't been able to close the deal up to that point.

"Now," she continued, "we understand you have some ideas about where the girls might lead their kidnappers."

I brought the maps in and showed them Beauregard's route and the candidate mines we'd identified. Of the four we'd not gone to, Jones said all were adit, or drift, mines.

Malkowitz spoke for the first time. He was the senior agent. "These are interesting theories, and we've noted these mines. First stop is going to be the Two Wheel Café. You've identified suspects. We start with them."

We were given the agents' cards with phone numbers that would alert them via pager . . . and they were gone.

I looked at F.U. Jones. He was silent. "More coffee?" he finally asked.

"What gives, Fred? You're not telling us something."

"Well, yeah. I'm a little disappointed. These agents are new to the region. The guy I've always dealt with in is on vacation."

"So?"

"So the folks up here won't tell 'em anything. A waitress may have been topping up Boon's coffee this morning but she'll tell those agents she never heard of such a person, and 'wouldn't it be a good idea to clean up the crime all those coloreds are committing in Atlanta'." He put on an exaggerated mountain accent.

"There's no better place – aside from Russia – to hide from the Feds than north Georgia and western North Carolina."

"You're telling us it's back on Max and me."

"Not entirely. There's mostly decent people up here. No one would approve of kidnapping little girls under any circumstances. They just tend to forget what's at stake when they see those federal badges."

I was wondering if Jones was going to be an asset, or if he suffered from the same federal taint. "And you? How do you operate?"

"It's not easy. I'm from Oklahoma so I'll never be one of the locals. Nor will my children, in all likelihood. The Forest Service has so many running problems over land encroachment, poaching of trees, hunters building blinds in the national forest, out of season hunting – you name it – that there'll always be friction.

"How do we operate? Community meetings. We join local organizations. Go to church. It takes a few years, but I think we come to be seen as a bunch of working stiffs just trying to do our jobs."

In other circumstances this soliloquy would have been interesting. What I wanted to know was whether Jones could get information that Malkowitz and Bernstein couldn't.

"What if you asked these same questions?"

Jones thought about this. "I'd need legitimacy. Like I said, I'm seen as someone doing my job. But that hasn't involved hunting down Klansmen."

"Would legitimacy come from doing distressed parents a favor?"

"It might. Could I recommend, though, that first you take advantage of the showers in the locker rooms and get cleaned up?"

We'd forgotten how we looked – or smelled. I brought in our suitcases and Sally and I went back to the ranger station's locker rooms. Twenty minutes later we were back in Jones' office.

Sally chewed on her lower lip. "I've been thinking about what Fred said. It might go over better if it was just me, the desperate mother." She looked at Jones and me for approval.

She was right, of course, but she didn't know who to talk to. Jones suggested, "Maybe I could make the intros and then make myself scarce while you to talk to the person."

This sounded good and Jones and Sally left in our SUV – the fewer official federal cues the better – to make the circuit. While they were gone I resumed study of the Aide-de-Camp's journal and the maps. What would Skeeter have spotted that might suggest itself as a likely hiding place for gold?

There was one over-riding assumption that fueled Skeeter's and the Klansmen's interest: The disingenuous General Beauregard ('It's a mystery what happened to that coin.') never got back to retrieve the treasure. Given the General's other behavior, it's possible he may have been so stupid he forgot where he'd cached it. In support of that assumption, if he or his immediate descendents had suddenly adopted a lavish lifestyle, the many amateur sleuths who were interested in the treasure would have noticed it.

The expanded criteria were:

- a tunnel mine, not open pit, that's what the girls would think of as a mine,

- that had been in operation in 1862,

- that lay somewhere along one of Beauregard's many possible routes where the day's travel distance had been short, and

- was not easy to return to.

Would Skeeter have used the same criteria? It probably didn't matter what Skeeter thought; the twins would be calling the shots. Think like them.

From M&M's *Guide to Treasure*

The Miller's Treasure
How much? Maybe one million dollars

What is it? There was a miller who always wanted
to be paid in gold. His name was Mr. Sharps. He did
not trust the bank so he put his money in a sack and
every week he went into the forest and buried the
gold he had just made. His nephew worked for him
and the nephew wanted the gold. The nephew
followed Mr. Sharps into the forest to see where the
gold was being buried but he always chickened out
and ran away. One day in 1899 Mr. Sharps fell into
the mill pond and drowned. No one knew where the
gold was buried.

Where is it? Near Florence, Alabama. Probably
northeast of the town.

Proof it exists. The nephew looked for it for many
years.

18

Sally and Ranger Jones returned after two hours.

"What'd you learn?"

"Not much. Fred made the introductions, but the trail is cold – or well covered. That waitress at the Waffle House called in sick today. The manager gave us her telephone number but when I called it one of her children answered and said his mother was unable to come to the phone. The kid said that daddy wasn't there and hadn't been seen for over a day."

Fred picked up the report, "We went down to that restaurant in Suches to see if we could get the names of the seven guys who meet there. Total amnesia. And it didn't help that we came in on the heels of Malkowitz and Bernstein. People's attitudes had hardened when they saw those badges. Even your wife's tears didn't move them."

"Those were real tears, Max. We're running into a wall and I'm losing it." I tried to hold her but she pushed me away. A first. I was stunned and hurt.

Fred had a theory which he shared, perhaps to break the tension. "I've always suspected news travels fast in these mountains. From what you said you overheard in the woods, it sounds like the twins weren't hauled off kicking and screaming." That was our conclusion as well. "The guys who have them have probably put out the story that the little girls are willing participants in this venture. Maybe some folks have even seen them and concluded they don't look like captives. If the good folk of Union County go with that reasoning it becomes more of an internal family matter. Uncle Skeeter and the girls on one side, mom and dad on the other. Mountain people stay out of family squabbles."

Sally and I had come to a parallel conclusion: Grumpy Old Dad wouldn't let the girls go treasure hunting – *real* treasure hunting – so they were obliged to head off on their own, linking up with like-minded fortune seekers wherever they found them. What M&M didn't know was that at least one of their newfound allies intended to bury them alive when their usefulness had been exhausted.

"Back to plan A. We go where we think they'll go. I was working on the Aide-de-Camp's journal and maps while you two were gone. Fred, take a look at these possibilities and tell us what you think."

"So, you've added two more mines. This one, on Pisgah Mountain, is on national forest land and the Service seems to have made a determined effort to keep the public out. It's difficult to get to and you'd need dynamite to clear the entrance." Sally and I looked alarmed, reminded that our daughters' escorts were packing explosives. Fred noticed our expressions and hurried on. "Another thing about Pisgah. We rangers try to get out of going up there because it's not only miserable to move around in that area, but there're more copperheads than you can shake a stick at." This information didn't help; Sally gasped. Fred should think before speaking. "Still, I think the mine didn't collapse so it can't be ruled out. The other one, down on Three Sisters . . . I don't know. Let me make a call." Jones consulted his Rolodex and dialed.

"Doreen? Fred."

. . .

"Yes," with resignation, "F.U."

. . .

"Yeah, long time. No, his broken heart is healing. The resilience of youth."

. . .

"Look, your husband worked with that logging outfit that had a concession on Three Sisters. There was a big mine there that played out a long time ago. Did he ever mention it?"

This was followed by a lengthy response, Jones throwing in the occasional 'really' or 'I see' as the story unfolded.

Finally, "Thanks so much, Doreen. Say hello to Angie and tell her, 'No hard feelings'."

I wanted to know about the mine. Sally asked, "Broken heart?"

"My son was sweet on Doreen's daughter but she didn't feel the same about him." Sally looked distressed. "They're six."

"And the mine?" I asked with barely concealed exasperation.

"Very interesting story," answered Jones. He rubbed the back of his neck. Apparently he was organizing the mass of information Doreen had provided. Or maybe editing out the alarming bits, given how we'd reacted to his description of the dangers awaiting our children on Pisgah.

"That mine closed down for the first time around 1870. They were only getting two to three ounces of gold per ton of rock that they pulled out and sent to the stamper, and that wasn't enough to cover costs. When the US let the price of gold float in the mid-1970s people got interested in the mine again and there was some small-scale poking around in there, but no serious effort. When the gold price went over $700 an ounce in 1981, things heated up. The road was improved and they started taking out several tons of rock an hour. They were getting four to five ounces of gold out of every ton, which wasn't fantastic, but Doreen guesses they were breaking even. Then gold prices went back down to $300 so they just kept on a small crew, and finally sold the concession to a retiree from Florida. The mine is in the national forest, but the concession and lease are grandfathered and transferable. The old man who bought it and his grandkids mostly just farted around in the mine, playing at mining."

"All very interesting, Fred, but can you fast-forward to the part that might have some bearing on whether Skeeter would find this a promising mine to explore?"

"Sorry, Max. Coming to that. Three things: First, the old adit that was in use in 1862 was not followed up. When they reopened in 1976 they found that the vein took a slight right turn just a short distance in, so the tunnel Beauregard might have used was boarded up. Second, I said the new owner just played at mining with his grandkids but this ended badly. The little girl went down a side tunnel and may have battered away at an old timber. The roof collapsed."

Sally paled. I felt sick. She looked at me beseechingly. I put an arm around her; there was no rejection this time.

"Third," Yes. Let's get to point number three and move away from the image of a little girl crushed under rocks. "Doreen said Skeeter called her a month ago and got all the same information."

That statement did focus our minds.

"Max, that place has to be on Skeeter's hit list. We need to check that mine."

"Well," drawled Jones, "there's a complication." We waited.

"You see, the shaft where the cave-in occurred was judged too unsafe by the Bureau of Mines for any work."

"So?" asked Sally.

"The little girl is still in there."

This statement was followed by a long silence. Jones finally added, "Her grandfather closed off the entrance. He doesn't want anyone messing around in what he thinks of as a mausoleum."

Sally finally spoke, "It seems we can take this one off the list then?"

"Not necessarily. I'm not sure you two want to hear this, but Doreen's words were, 'It'd take dynamite to open that thing up.' My fear is that's just what these morons will do and that'll just shake things up in the mine."

We were absorbing this new intelligence when Fred's phone rang. He answered and handed it to Sally. She listened, nodded, said, "Thank you," and hung up.

"That was a waitress at the Two Wheels restaurant. She told me not to worry about the girls. They were with good people, men who had daughters of their own, and who had principles."

The three of us looked at each other. The woman had meant well and we wanted to believe her, but it confirmed the growing conviction that we'd run into a wall of silence.

19

Jones' office was becoming a busy place. No sooner had Sally reported on her phone conversation than Bernstein and Malkowitz stormed in; Bernstein was shaking her finger at Sally before the agent was through the door. "Look here, lady; we asked you to stand down and that's what you have to do. At some point your crashing around becomes obstruction of justice."

It would be difficult to devise a worse way to talk to Sally Taylor-Brown – or a worse time to do it. She was out of her chair, across the room, and toe-to-toe with the FBI agent. She was – I'm not exaggerating, I'm not making this up – Sally was growling. A low feral growl from deep within her. Days without adequate sleep, the terror of missing children, the inability to make progress – this is not a foundation for diplomatic behavior. Another few seconds and the men in the office would be treated to a catfight: Bernstein's FBI training pitted against Sally's Army hand-to-hand combat skills.

I tried to step between the two women and was rewarded with "Let me handle this, Max. I've had it with this tin-horned, two-bit deputy dawg. She's fucking up the case and looking to blame it on someone else." As Sally delivered this she put her hand on my chest and pushed me away forcefully.

Sally growled again and Bernstein inched backward. But not far. Maybe she was trying to summon up her own growl. I was trying to figure out how to avert a brawl. At the very least, we couldn't afford to expend our resources fighting amongst ourselves. At the worst, Sally's adversaries wound up in the hospital. Or, Bernstein might be as good.

Help came from an unexpected direction. Malkowitz, who had seemed dreamily unengaged to this point, commanded, "That's enough, Bernstein. You're dealing with a victim. One more word and you're on the next plane back to Miami." Bernstein hesitated for a second, then wheeled and left the room.

From this we learned two things: 1) Bernstein does respond to authority; if it weren't for her name she might have made a good Nazi. 2) This pair was from the Miami office and they were floundering as they tried to function in an alien environment.

We heard a car door slam and from Jones' window we could see that Bernstein had taken refuge in the Suburban, pouting. I checked Sally; she was pouting too.

I suggested that I check in with Dr. Levine at the Dahlonega hospital. A break from the recent drama was needed. This turned out to be a longer break than anticipated. I was on hold for at least five minutes before Levine came on the line.

"Max Brown here, Doctor. Anything to report?"

"Nothing yet, Mr. Brown. Snyder is still unconscious, but his vital signs are looking better. The bullet tore through a lot of fat but we got it out. Meanwhile he's receiving plenty of attention. His wife or girl friend, the tall blonde woman in Indian garb, hasn't left his side. Sometimes we need her to get out of the way, but she's immovable. The Dahlonega police did send someone over to sit in the hall but he seems more interested in chatting up the nurses than finishing off Snyder. Your friend Ferguson is salted away in the isolation ward. I'm told he started clamoring for release soon after he saw his breakfast. Have you made progress?"

I told Levine about our near miss the night before and that the Feds had arrived. He acknowledged this with a protracted "hmmmm."

"One caution, Dr. Levine. If you got a good look at that buzzcut cop who was there last night, we think he's a Klan sympathizer. If he picks up the guard duty you might have to step up your security for Rocco."

"Not a problem. Three beefy guys from my temple are going to rotate the duty. The first one should be here any minute."

"Snyder is beefy too. It didn't spare him, Doctor."

"That's been considered, Mr. Brown. I'm told that these men will have an Uzi at their disposal. You probably aren't familiar with the Uzi," he continued, pride in his voice, "but it's a machine gun invented in Israel for the IDF, and . . ."

Jewish pride is rooted in a gun? How about music, art, literature, science, medicine? "Doctor, I'm far too familiar with the Uzi." I wasn't, but this behavior shouldn't be encouraged. "Let's hope there's no need for it." He murmured assent. "And keep the gun a secret from Snyder and his woman. They're anti."

I gave Levine the pager number of the two agents and promised to call back in the afternoon.

"Now," I said, turning to Malkowitz, Jones, and the still fuming Sally, "let's get back to work finding Margaret and Mary."

Sally told Malkowitz about her unsuccessful attempts to obtain information and the phone call from the waitress at the Two Wheel. Then she glared out the window at Bernstein, who glared back. After ten mostly wonderful years with Sally I knew the signs: she was at the breaking point.

Jones had assumed the role of moderator and took the floor. "My reading on this is that we're not going to get any assistance from the public. They're deeply anti-Fed and the story they've been told is that the kidnappers are simply helping two little kids on a lark. Harmless stuff.

"What we have is what we've always had: a list – now with two additions – of mines where these kidnappers and their three willing associates might look for Beauregard's gold."

We went over the maps again with Malkowitz. "Well," the agent offered, "more manpower would be useful. I'll put in the request. You heard that the Atlanta office is short-handed. Normally this would be their case but two guys were caught at Hartsfield airport yesterday trying to board different flights with guns. Over half of our Atlanta personnel is working on that. Bernstein and I got hauled out of bed after midnight. The Bureau trotted out one of their own planes to get us up here from Miami. There's just a lot going on."

He sounded tired, and while the explanations helped us understand why no larger effort was underway, it was clear that our most reliable and effective federal help was going to come from Ranger Jones, sworn defender of the mountain laurel.

"Thanks for the explanation, Agent Malkowitz. From that we gather it won't be possible to cover all of these mines simultaneously. Jones seems to think the Pisgah mine is not high on their list. The Three Sisters mine sounds intriguing and Skeeter knows about it. But it appears that blasting might be required to get into it. I assume anyone within a few miles would hear the noise. Shall we start with the four around here we identified earlier?"

That brought nods of agreement and we headed out to the cars. I was studying our map as we walked. Bernstein was quick to react to our appearance; as we passed in front of the Suburban she opened the car door and shouted, "Malkowitz, you can't be serious. Get these people out of the way. They're emotionally involved and have no skills or training."

Without changing expression Sally drew the Beretta from her jacket pocket, aimed it with both hands, and shot the little wire antenna off the top of the Suburban. "I have skills, Agent Bernstein. Do you need another demonstration?"

Let's pause here for a description of the reactions to this dramatic event.

- As the sound of the shot ricocheted through the trees, Bernstein dropped to a knee, pulled out her own pistol and trained it on Sally.
- Malkowitz pulled his own gun and pointed it first at Sally, then at Bernstein, then he put it away.
- I almost wet myself (but didn't). I stepped between Sally and the deranged federal agent. I can do the right thing sometimes; I just need an opportunity.
- And Ranger Jones laughed, but not a natural laugh.

Sally, who'd kicked this off, put the Beretta back on safety, pocketed it, and resumed walking toward our car. "C'mon, Max. We have mines to explore."

It would be pleasant to report that that was the end of it, but of course it wasn't. Bernstein was howling incoherently. Malkowitz had moved to the Suburban where he was examining the damage to the antenna, and Fred was now giggling – nervously.

The dynamic changed again, fifteen seconds later, when a Union County sheriff's car slid to a stop in the parking lot's loose gravel. The Deputy Sheriff, a paunchy caricature from Central Casting, sized up the situation: There was a deranged woman with a gun, shouting. And there were three unarmed men and one woman in peril. He threw his car door open and kneeled behind it, his own pistol out. "Put down the gun, lady, and no one's gotta get hurt."

Bernstein didn't know how to respond to that. She turned toward the Deputy's car, her pistol only slightly lowered. The Deputy must have read this as a threatening act because he fired at Bernstein over the windowsill of his car door. Apparently marksmanship is no more important to sheriffing than it was for me in the Air Force. His bullet hit the rear fender of the Suburban, ten feet from Bernstein, but only a few feet from Agent Malkowitz whose attention, to that point, had been directed to the damaged antenna. Malkowitz came to life.

"We're federal agents, dammit! Everybody put away their guns. Jesus Fucking Henry Christ!"

Sally stopped walking. She could see that events had spiraled out of control. *That often happens, Sally, when you shoot at government cars that have government agents in them. She really, really should not be allowed to play with guns when she's in a volatile state.*

Malkowitz grabbed Bernstein's gun – a courageous act in my book – and addressed the car door behind which the Deputy Sheriff crouched. "Sheriff. We're FBI Agents called in on a kidnapping. It's safe to come out."

The Deputy's head inched above the door sill. Holstering his pistol – but not taking his hand off it – he stood, hitched up his britches, and strode over with a self-assured waddle intended to convey that he was accustomed to being in charge in situations like this.

"Alright, everybody. I heard a shot and I seen this woman here waving a gun around. If you're really FBI let's see some identification." Malkowitz flipped his wallet open; Bernstein followed suit reluctantly after a questioning look from Malkowitz. The sheriff examined the badges and laminated IDs intently. Then he looked at Sally and me. Sally had donned an expression of angelic innocence and the sheriff smiled apologetically. I don't think my presence registered.

"F.U., you're the only familiar face here. What's goin' on?"

"Just a demonstration, Sheriff. Nothing special, but you missed some great marksmanship. Since you're here, though, I been meaning to ask you, is your boy planning to play again this year? They sure need him at fullback."

And that did it. The wily Ranger Jones had the Deputy Sheriff talking about his son's recovery from arthroscopic surgery, the physical therapy regimen, and the value of knee braces. The word 'kidnapping' had not registered on him. Until, of course, Bernstein opened her mouth.

"We gotta move. First, though, something's gotta be done about Calamity Jane here."

Malkowitz looked to the heavens in despair, and the sheriff came back to matters at hand.

"You two got some kind of jurisdictional issues you'd like to take up with us? Thought you Feds was supposed to report in and we could coordinate efforts. Or are you two honeymooning up here in the north Georgia mountains?"

That suggestion brought a look of disgust to Bernstein's face. With a partner like her I was starting to understand why Malkowitz's mind often seemed to have strayed off into another dimension.

"We were on our way there," answered Malkowitz. "Trying to figure out what we're dealing with before we sat down with you people. Your trip out here has saved us time."

The Deputy didn't appear convinced that a chat in a parking lot was 'coordination,' but he let it go. "So, y'all are lookin' for those little redheads I keep hearin' about?"

"What are you hearing, Sheriff?" Sally and I asked with one voice.

"I heard they run away from home and now they're out lookin' for some old treasure with their uncle Skeeter Lonegreen and a couple of his friends."

"Did you also hear that these 'friends' are planning to kill the little girls?" asked Sally through taut lips.

"Yer imagination's gettin' the better of you there. Them boys wouldn't hurt a flea. I'll grant they're a little rough around the edges. But look, if it'd help you sleep better, we'll put out a bulletin that those youngsters need to come home and face the music." He smiled. The helpful public servant, rescuing cats from trees and herding willful young 'uns back to the nest.

"I overheard them," insisted Sally. "Boon said he planned to bury them in a mine."

"I don't know what you thought you heard, Ma'am. They could've said all sorts of things. They kid around a lot and they talk big." I didn't know what to say to this. We'd heard our children threatened with death, and it was being dismissed as idle boasting?

"Since you know who these men are," interjected Malkowitz quickly – perhaps fearing Sally would open fire again, "why don't you take us to talk with them. Then we can clear this up and I can get back to my family in Miami."

The Deputy looked unsettled by the request. He should have expected it. "Well," and he paused, "that may not be so easy. Danny and Bill, they both got full time construction jobs over near Clayton right now. That also means they're probably not able to participate in nothin', 'cept on weekends. The others? Real hard to know where they might be." He swept his hand over the surrounding skyline. "If they're out there digging for pirate treasure, there's a lot of mountains to cover."

"There is indeed," acknowledged Malkowitz, "but you don't want to be on the wrong side of this thing, Sheriff."

"Is that a threat?"

"Of course not. It's a statement of fact. The allegation is kidnapping of very young children. Any failure to secure their safety – or take it seriously – is sure to be seen poorly by the public and the courts."

Sally wore a blank expression. I think she was silently repeating a mantra.

Fred thought the message needed reinforcing. "This thing is getting pretty big, Karl. A man's been shot down near Dawsonville and Boon and his pals look to have had a hand in it. They bought some dynamite and now a couple of things have been blown up. I found a stick of it that was planted in a parking lot and I'll bet their fingerprints are all over it. This isn't just running an unregistered day camp for little kids."

"That's quite a list, F.U. I'll spread the word around." He pulled up the back of his sagging britches again, got in his car, and left.

Sally and Fred looked satisfied. I wasn't. I'd liked the scenario the Deputy had painted: The 'boys' were just messing around in the forest with some kids, and 'here the little urchins are, folks, safe and sound.' That happy ending assumed that Boon and company believed they could sell Rocky's shooting as an accident, which it seemed to have been. No hard feelings. We all go our separate ways.

No chance of that now. Fred had made it clear the 'boys' were fugitives wanted for serious crimes.

"That may have sobered him up," from Fred.

"You did good, Fred," I assured him. I thought he'd made matters worse – maybe thrown away an opportunity to solve this and get our little mischief-makers back.

20

Sally and I started walking toward our car again. We weren't interested in coordinating with these bozos. Just consider . . .

- Bernstein was a nut-job: a full-frontal, free-range offender, willing and able to piss off anyone she encountered. And quick to pull out her gun.
- Malkowitz was tuned out much of the time. Because he didn't want to tune in to Bernstein?
- F.U. was one of the good guys, but he seemed more interested in protecting flora than fauna. I carried the vivid image in my head of F.U. dolefully contemplating a broken mountain laurel when he should have been raising the alarm about our missing children.

We didn't get far across the lot. "Hey! Stop right there!" That's Bernstein, of course. "Where are you two going? We got some things to sort out."

Sally spun around. I stepped in front of her and spoke first. "Of course. As soon as we've found our daughters I'll write a handsome check for the antenna. Now we need to get moving. We'll go to the Three Sisters Mine first to see if anything is going on there. You have the list of the other places. As soon as we've scouted the Three Sisters, we'll call your pager number."

"Good luck with that," spat Bernstein. "I doubt the signal will get through without an antenna." The pager signal went through that little rooftop antenna? The world needed a better way to communicate.

"Try a coat hanger." That's Sally, committed to making any situation involving Bernstein worse.

Fred spoke up before the exchange between the women could heat up. "I'll pass by the McIntosh mine. It's hard to find if you don't know your way around there."

"Okay," I added in a tone that signified this would be the last word, "you folks know what's left on the list. We'll try to get back here by five this afternoon and we can compare notes."

Take-Charge Max, that's me. My first wife frequently accused me of being a control freak. Not so. It's just that sometimes the situation cries out for a little leadership.

This feeling of potency and self-importance stayed with me as we pulled out and I started scolding Sally for her trigger-happy ways. She wasn't having it.

"I'd do exactly the same thing again."

"But . . . but . . ." I was prepared for contrition, not intransigence.

"Look. That bitch wanted us out of the picture. Are we out of the picture? No. We're rolling down the highway and you've handed out the assignments. You used to teach us in that management class to judge the effectiveness of actions by results. The results are good." She sat back, smiling.

How could she remember something I said in a class more than a decade ago? That's the danger of arguing with a younger person. You've started to doubt your own memory and you defer to the younger person when they assert – with absolute conviction – that you once boasted of sodomizing barnyard animals, or something along those lines.

"I expect repercussions." I said loftily; the tone signaled there was nothing more to be said on the issue. It seemed to work.

We used our ATM cards in Ellijay and headed east – Sally navigating – toward the Three Sisters Mine which sat on the southwestern face of a mountain of the same name. When we got to the access road the way was blocked by an old metal gate, secured with a rusted lock.

"It doesn't look like anyone's been through here recently."

I agreed.

"Maybe there's another entrance, or maybe – wait, look there, Max – tire tracks through the grass down at that break in the fence."

Someone had driven off the highway and onto the property through a ten-foot gap in the galvanized fence. How long ago? These tall weeds would recover and stand up at some point. Ranger Fred would know how recently they'd been driven over.

Shifting the SUV into 4WD low range, we followed the same path through the fence. The tracks were faint, but joined the access road that led up the side of the mountain. After half a mile the road forked. Our maps provided no guidance. We took the road to the left because that fit best with our political inclinations. Another few hundred yards the road ended in front of an old, but very large, log house. A Toyota sedan was parked at the side. I turned off the ignition and we scanned the building for a sign of life. It was lurking inside a screened door.

"Go away. Scram or I'll call the cops."

I might have complied, but the accent wasn't local. This could be someone who'd take our story seriously.

We got out of the car and I shouted back, "We're looking for our daughters. They've been taken by some men. Have you seen anyone?"

"Daughters run off with their boyfriends all the time. Try Las Vegas. Now get out of here."

Fearless Sally marched angrily toward the front door. "Our daughters are nine years old. They've been kidnapped. How about a little civility and a little help?"

The screen door swung open and a wrinkled man in green Bermuda shorts and a fluorescent pink tank-top stood just inside. We'd found the Floridian grandfather.

We explained our situation and why we wanted to check on his mine.

"I go up every day or so and put fresh flowers at the entrance. I was up there yesterday and no one had broken in."

"Can you see the road from here so you'd know if someone is driving up?"

"I can't see it for all the trees but I can hear any traffic if I'm not watching the TV." The sound of a fake courtroom show –

the defendant had borrowed a friend's car and damaged it – indicated he'd been watching when we arrived.

"Traffic?" Sally asked.

"Kids. They go up to the mine to party or show their girl-friends what their rig will do. Usually harmless. Most respect the locked gate but maybe they think the place is deserted. I don't know." This said with a tone of 'I don't care either.' As an after-thought, "Can I offer you something to drink?"

We accepted. Sally and I had planned on staking out this mine for a few hours to see if anyone showed up. Florida Grandpa's living room was as good a place as any from which to monitor comings and goings.

I asked if I could use his phone. The utility lines were visible coming up through the trees. We hadn't planned on calling Levine this early, but we didn't know when we'd have another opportunity.

After the customary wait on hold . . . "Dr. Levine? Max Brown. Anything?" I assumed anyone who'd kept me waiting this long must be very busy or very important. As a courtesy I spoke economically.

"Snyder came around and gave his statement to the Dahlonega police. I wasn't there but Moondance said Mr. Snyder wished ill to no one and hoped that goodwill would enter every heart so that this kind of thing would become distant history. It doesn't sound like he named names."

"Damn!"

"Someone is coming up from the state prosecutors' office in Atlanta tomorrow. Maybe Snyder'll be more forthcoming with them. Any progress on your side?"

"We're at the Three Sisters mine just north of town. One of several possible mines we need to keep under surveillance."

"Keep your head down," advised the doctor.

"And Ferguson?"

"Secure and bitching up a storm to get out. He claims you're his father."

"Tell him to knock it off or you'll lace him up in a canvas camisole and ship him off to the loony bin. Put that book by Kesey in his room, *One Flew Over the Cuckoo's Nest*."

Levine laughed and we rang off.

"Honey, do we have company?" A thin nasal voice came from the back patio, followed by a bikini-clad blonde who tottered through the door on sandals with four-inch heels. Florida Grandpa emerged from the kitchen with a tray carrying four sweating glasses of iced tea and signaled for us to sit.

Introductions were made. They were Bob and Brenda; Brenda was obviously not Bob's first wife. No longer standing in front of the bright sunlight, her bikini revealed more leathery tanned flesh than I needed to see. She was in her early fifties; Bob in his seventies. A woman whose looks were too far gone to trade up, and now she was stuck with an old man, slightly stooped, brown teeth, a meadow of grey hairs sprouting from his bony shoulders, and an unsuccessful comb-over.

Would Sally see the parallel? I avoided looking at her.

"So, congratulations on finding your way in," said Brenda. "Bob keeps the gate locked since we don't leave very often." This was announced with a frown. "To what do we owe the pleasure of your visit?"

Sally answered with a thumbnail account of our mission. She ended, "We think that at some point these goobers will show up at your mine with our girls. We understand the entrance can only be opened with dynamite, but they have that."

Bob looked stricken. "Dynamite?" Sally nodded. "Not Roberta's mine!" he said defiantly.

Roberta? Had the dead girl been named after her grandfather?

He left and returned carrying two rifles, both with scopes. "Here, honey, you take the Remington. You're more comfortable with it." I wasn't sure this was a step in the right direction. Brenda was holding her gun uncertainly, the barrel pointed at my mid-section.

"Are those loaded?" asked Sally.

"They're no use empty," confirmed Bob.

"Okay," continued Sally calmly, "then she's pointing a loaded weapon at my husband." Brenda almost dropped the gun. I winced, watching the trigger guard to see if her fingers slipped inside it. Finally she laid the rifle on the couch beside her and I resumed breathing. Sally, with a disarming smile (that's the weak pun that came to mind in the moment – the mind does funny things), clicked the safety on for both weapons.

"The way we'd like this to play out is to separate our girls from the kidnappers before any shooting starts. For example, maybe the girls will be told to wait outside while the Klansmen explore the mine." I didn't seriously see that happening for two reasons: First, the girls would resist any attempt to exclude them as the treasure hunt reached its climax. Secondly, the Knights would want them in the mine if they intended to kill them. But the separation scenario was representative of the wishful element that ran through our planning.

"Could they have come already?" Brenda asked.

"Anything's possible. They have a half day's head start on us."

"Well, I thought I heard someone going up there last night."

"I didn't hear anything," countered Grandpa Bob.

"That's because you were watching *Jeopardy* at full volume and shouting the answers at Alex Trebek. I had to leave the room – if you noticed. And your answers were mostly wrong." Bob ignored this.

"Perhaps Sally and I could go up and check."

"We'll all go up," announced Bob. "It's time for fresh flowers." Brenda rolled her eyes. Apparently she didn't share her husband's dedication to the memorial where Roberta had been entombed.

A few minutes later Bob returned, bedecked in camo down to his socks and combat boots. He held a small bouquet of lilies in his hand. Brenda was making no concessions to the conditions ahead. She planned to make the trip in her bikini.

"Should we all ride in our SUV?" I offered. When we stepped outside I was reminded that it was still crammed full of Shawn Ferguson's personal effects. I emptied the back seat, putting the boxes and trash bags on the ground. After a little discussion over seating arrangements we clambered in and got underway.

The road up to the mine entrance was badly rutted. Bob's Toyota wouldn't be able to make the climb so he must have had to walk part of the way in order to pay daily homage to the little girl. Very touching. I tried to focus my mind on something else.

Bob directed me behind some trees to park. "The shade'll keep the car cool. We have to walk the rest of the way. It's close."

Brenda announced she'd stay in the car. She rolled the windows up, despite the heat of the day. "Too many stories lately about a crazy bear that's killing animals around here," she explained. She had her rifle.

Bob shouldered his own rifle with a sling, looking like an ancient WWI veteran decked out for the Memorial Day parade, and led the way up the path through the trees. After a few minutes of steep climbing we came out onto a flat gravel-covered area thirty yards across and surrounded by a tangle of blackberry bushes. As aggressive as kudzu, the blackberries take over any land that's been disturbed and they'd had more than a century to establish dominion over the fringe of cleared land that ringed the mine entrance.

The entrance itself was in front of us, filled with large rocks and rubble, and clearly impassable. Signs, hand-painted in red warned 'Danger' and 'Keep Out;' these were nailed to the timbers that framed the entrance. At the foot of the rubble a collection of wilted and brown flowers provided testimony of Bob's steadfast devotion. To the right, the remains of a campfire and a few empty beer bottles were evidence of the visitors the night before. Not KKK; just high school kids.

We were taking this all in when Sally announced, "Company's coming." From below we could hear the sound of a straining engine. A rising cloud of dust confirmed that a vehicle was approaching up the road.

21

"This way – into the trees." That's me, Take-Charge Max. Ten yards into the dense brush and threatening blackberry thorns, we could just make out the path. If we stayed low no one would spot us.

"What about Brenda?" Sally asked.

Bob wasn't concerned. "She'll be okay. The car's hidden in the trees unless someone knows about that spot and goes looking. I don't believe the stories about the aggressive bear." Does he think a bear's driving the approaching car? "Besides, she's got her gun." Misplaced faith, if ever I'd encountered it. Maybe Bob was thinking about trading up. Alone on the mountainside they must get on one another's nerves. They got on mine.

Minutes passed. The sound of the climbing vehicle came closer. We remained crouched in the trees, hidden from anyone coming up the path, but visible to mosquitoes.

The engine noise stopped, followed by the squeak of a parking brake being set. "I recognize that from somewhere," whispered Sally. Highly likely. Then silence. Whoever was coming up the path wasn't talking. It wasn't like the twins to keep their yaps shut. Had they been muzzled?

Sally and Bob trained their guns on the path. I kept my pistol handy but knew there was no point in trying to hit something at the thirty-yard distance that separated the path from our hiding place. We could hear the crunch of footsteps advancing.

"Mr. Brown? Are you up here?" Shawn Ferguson stepped out onto the gravel, wearing a pale blue hospital nightie – the one with the undignified opening down the back. Bob squeezed the trigger on his gun.

This act of titanic stupidity justifies a brief detour:

We seem to be agreed about keeping guns out of the hands of the insane. How about the stupid? Can we require gun owners to pass an IQ test? It's easier to get a gun permit than a driver's license in the US. A car can kill, granted, but that's not its primary function. A gun has very limited applications. The most obvious one is to put an end to a life, in this case, Shawn's.

Fortunately Bob didn't know, or had forgotten, to switch the safety off. He tugged on the trigger again before Sally wrested the gun from him. "You incredible, senile old moron!" She can really lay it on. "You're trying to kill one of ours!" Then she threw the rifle into the woods. Unfortunately it didn't go far. It hit a tree, bounced to the ground, and a querulous Bob went to retrieve it.

"Better safe than sorry," he grumbled. Sally and I ran toward Shawn.

"This looks like an emergency trip, Shawn. What's up?"

"Bad shit, folks. I climbed out a window to get here after an orderly told me what went down."

"Is Rocky okay?"

"Maybe. But he won't be for long. The orderly said that that doctor was bragging about the gun those big goons from the Jewish temple had."

"The Uzi. Right."

"Did you know it was invented in Israel?"

"Yes, but please get on with it."

"Sure. Sorry. Turns out that an Uzi is a fully automatic machine gun. That makes it fully illegal in the US. That buzzcut cop had come on watch. He confiscated the gun and called his buddies over to take the big Jews to the town lock-up for possession of a banned firearm. The orderly said Dr. Levine went with them. He didn't know if Levine was going to be locked up too."

"Holy shit!"

"In triplicate, man. The only thing standing between the Klan and Rocky is Moondance. I thought of standing with her, but then thought of coming for reinforcements. Levine has been checking in with me through the day and he told me you were up at this mine."

We bolted for the path, bewildered Bob bringing up the rear. Our departure was delayed by Brenda who, as we rounded the turn into the parking area, was sighting down the barrel of her rifle at us. Is stupidity contagious or are the equally stupid drawn to each other? No apologies from Brenda; she'd seen a strangely attired Black man. Perhaps she thought Shawn was a runaway slave.

Silencing Brenda's explanations and protests, we got underway and bounced back down the road to Bob and Brenda's, our vehicles leaving a trail of swirling dust.

———————

I dialed the pager number for our Federal friends and followed the instructions. When Malkowitz and Bernstein saw the page – if they'd fixed their antenna – they'd call back to Bob's phone.

"Shawn, two FBI agents arrived this morning to work on the case. We're having trouble communicating with them," I couldn't help it; I glanced in Sally's direction, "and it would be good if we could get them to join us at the hospital."

Sally and Shawn both scowled, for different reasons. Sally found a corner of the ceiling to glare at. Shawn had something to say.

"Yeah, well, no love lost on those turkeys. The minute the FBI sees you're working with a Black man, they'll tap the phones and put a microphone under my bed." Intended as a fierce display of scorn, his statement was undermined by the blue hospital gown which he was trying to hold together in back with one hand while gesturing indignantly with the other.

Sally's scowl changed from annoyance to incomprehension.

"The FBI were pretty aggressive in their attempts to discredit civil rights leaders, babe. Notably Martin Luther King. It's claimed that there've been changes at the Bureau, but you can see the distrust hasn't gone away."

Shawn nodded vigorous agreement and gripped the ridiculous gown with both hands. Sally chose this inopportune moment to offer career counseling. "You should join the FBI, Shawn. Reform it from within, you know?" *We are not actually this guy's parents, Sal.*

Shawn and I wore matching expressions of exasperation. Again, for different reasons. Before she could resume, "Can we talk about this later, Sal? Rocky's in deep doodoo." She shrugged; she was still pissed that I held her accountable for the Feds being incommunicado.

Take-Charge Max issued further orders. "Alright, Bob. We're going down to the hospital. You're in charge of the phones. Try to get this right." He didn't look embarrassed or offended. "When the FBI calls, you tell them that security for Rocco Snyder has collapsed and they need to get someone to the Dahlonega Hospital ASAP. Snyder's life is in danger." I made him repeat the message.

A call to Fred's office number; a different ranger answered. F.U. was not in the ranger station. I left the same message. As I hung up it occurred to me that the ranger's sympathies might lie with the other team; a good thing I hadn't disclosed our location.

When we came out of the house Shawn was pulling on clothes he'd dug out of the car. Brenda had left her rifle in the SUV and he appropriated it.

"A Black man with a rifle in north Georgia's in a world of trouble. A Black man with a concealed handgun? Worse; guaranteed prison time." He shoved the rifle under the truck's seat and without further discussion was speeding back down the road.

You had to admire the man. Not one to dither or stand around waiting for instructions. Maybe he would make a good agent. Certainly better than Bernstein.

I did dither. Should we go over Bob's instructions again? Sally thought not, "Time's awastin', Studly." My concurrence was not needed; immediately she was at the wheel of our SUV, grinding the starter.

———

Despite Sally's erratic driving, we caught up with Shawn as we approached the hospital. In the parking lot two police cars sat next to a pickup with a flagstaff in the back. Shawn continued past the hospital; we followed, parking a block away.

"This is so not good," muttered Shawn.

Sally nodded, "But we still have to get into the hospital. I'll wrap something around my hair." We looked at Shawn, wondering how he'd disguise himself.

"Officer Buzzcut's the one who might recognize me. I'll just shuffle and keep my head down. We all look the same to white folks, remember?"

After Sally had secured her unruly hair with a scarf, we walked cautiously toward the hospital. I had the .38 and Sally the 9 mm Beretta. Shawn left the rifle under the seat of Rocky's truck. As we got closer we could see that a mobile metal detector had been placed at the main doorway and another was being installed at the entrance to Emergency Admitting. Then, a small stroke of fortune: the balding head of Dr. Levine glided by as he guided his car toward the staff parking garage. We picked up the pace and were only a few yards behind by the time he'd parked. Ocean liners are berthed more assertively.

"Dr. Levine?" He jumped and looked around. "It's Max Brown. Wait up."

"Oh, Mr. Brown." He threw his hands in the air. "You have no idea what an old fool I've been." To the contrary, I had a very good idea. "That loose talk about that machine gun and now Sol and David are in jail and I've been charged as some sort of accessory."

"How's Snyder?"

"I don't know. He was okay when I left, but sedated, so you can't talk to him if that's what you were thinking.

"They kept me down at the police station for almost an hour. I told them there were urgent cases I needed to attend to, although that's not completely true. I'm sure another physician was called in when I was escorted out."

"Well, here's the problem, Doctor. Metal detectors have been put up at the two primary entrances. Sally and I are carrying guns, and we'd like to keep them. Is there some other way in?"

"Of course. An emergency exit at the far end of this parking garage. It has an alarm, but I can override that. Let me go in and I'll open it."

He headed toward the entrance to Emergency Admitting while we three musketeers slunk toward the door he'd indicated.

Almost before we got there, it swung open, and Levine peered out. "It's not good. That policeman you warned me about is standing guard outside Snyder's room."

Levine led us up the emergency stairs and cracked the door that gave way onto the hallway. "Funny. The policeman's not there now."

"That's definitely not good," I hissed, squeezed past him, and sprinted down the hall. An empty folding chair signaled Rocky's room. Visible through the small window in the door, Moondance was standing behind Buzzcut whom she had in a strangle hold. The muscular cop's arms flailed ineffectually.

Sally and I pushed in, Shawn close behind. Moondance was weeping as she cut off the cop's air and blood supply. The arm flapping was growing weaker; Buzzcut could only make a few unintelligible sounds. Moondance was droning an apology.

"Rocky baby, oh Rocky baby. I've failed you. I just couldn't watch him kill you." Moondance's remorse at her violent action didn't translate into a weakening of her grip. She'd soon be guilty of killing a policeman.

Sally to the rescue; she's good in these situations. She pulled Buzzcut's handcuffs from his belt, clicked one cuff onto his left wrist, and motioned for Moondance and Shawn to drag the semi-conscious cop to the corner where she wrapped the cuffs behind a vertical water pipe and clicked the other cuff onto his right wrist. Shawn and I pried Moondance's arms from around Buzzcut's neck while Sally fished some filthy looking bandages from the trash and stuffed them into the cop's mouth. Released, the policeman slid heavily to the floor. He was out of it, but he'd recover soon and figure out how to raise an alarm. I removed his pistol from its holster, considered putting a slug into his gut, then dropped the gun into the toilet. Only a statement. The dousing would have no effect on the gun.

Was help on the way? There was a phone in Rocky's room. After initial fumbling, I got an outside line and called Grandpa Bob. He reported that no one had come up the road to the mine and the FBI hadn't responded to our page. Sally's show-off shooting was biting us. I'd told her there'd be 'repercussions.' Perhaps I should clarify that 'repercussions' means 'unwanted consequences.'

We noticed Levine, watching from the door with an expression that vacillated between admiration and horror. "Doctor. Can Rocky be moved? His chances to live long enough to make a full recovery don't seem to be great here."

Levine thought about this longer than we had time for. Of course; ingrained in every physician is an abhorrence of providing care outside a clinical setting. Buzzcut stirred; that helped Levine decide. "I guess we could move him, but he would need support wherever he went. He lost blood and the concussion was severe. He can't sit up, if you're thinking of taking him in a car."

"An ambulance, then," said Sally. "How do we get him into an ambulance without anyone noticing?"

Levine was faster with this response. "Down the maintenance elevator. No one's using it at this time of day. From there we can wheel him through that same door you came in. But we need a driver. I don't know who to trust and I don't want anyone else to get into trouble over this."

Shawn stepped forward, beaming. "Well, I guess I could do it . . ." vastly understating his enthusiasm to get behind the wheel of an ambulance.

Levine sized up Shawn and went looking for an EMS uniform: light blue shirt, dark blue pants.

The brief silence was interrupted by a low moan. "I just went into the bathroom for a second," explained the distraught Moondance. "When I came out this policeman was smothering Rocky with a pillow. I snapped." She resumed lamenting her lack of resolve. This was getting old. She'd saved Rocky's life, for Christ's sake.

Levine was back almost immediately with clothes for Shawn who went into the bathroom and changed.

"How do we do this, Doctor? This is your show."

Levine was now engaged. He picked up the room phone and dialed three digits. "Morris? Harvey here. Look, I want to move a patient down to a trauma center in Atlanta. Would you have one of your boys leave a transfer vehicle at the parking garage emergency exit door?"

. . .

"Trust me, Morris. Those are things you don't want to know."

. . .

"I understand your concerns. Think about cats and curiosity."

Levine hung up. "Morris' last name is Rubin, if you were concerned." He secured the unconscious patient to the bed with two straps and left, returning a minute later with blue scrubs for Sally, Moondance, and me. Moondance's disguise as an orderly was pointless. It was too small for her and didn't cover the faux-Indian apparel, jewelry and hair braid. Levine took one look at her and said, "Moondance? Please take the emergency stairs and wait for us at the door to the parking garage. It's alarmed so don't open it."

He pulled the sheet over Rocky's face and the four of us rolled the bed out into the hall and toward the elevators. At the first corner we were met by a young policeman who peered past us and spotted the empty folding chair in the hall.

"Wasn't someone on duty at that room?"

"Pee break," answered Levine immediately. The cop looked inquiringly at the bed with the large, covered body.

"We can't win them all, can we officer," said Levine sadly. "No lower moment in a doctor's life than to take them down to the morgue." The young cop stepped back and crossed himself. Good, a Catholic.

Moondance was waiting by the emergency exit. Levine keyed in the override code and we bumped Rocky's rolling bed down the three steps to the parking garage. As requested, there was an ambulance. Shawn's first order of business was to check if the keys were in it. He wasn't going to be denied this.

The transfer from the bed to the ambulance's lock-down gurney was difficult. Five people of varying strength and confidence barely accomplished the transfer without dropping the giant on the cement. Then Shawn and I conferred on how to get out of town – initially head south as if going to Atlanta – and avoid using the siren. "A transfer ambulance doesn't need a siren, okay Shawn?" Moondance got into the back of the ambulance with her man. Levine seemed undecided.

"Damn. In for a dime; in for a dollar. I'd better ride along to monitor Snyder," and he climbed into the ambulance. Sally and I threw our scrubs in after him, closed the doors, and walked toward the parking garage exit furthest from the hospital.

As we circled around the block to recover our two vehicles we heard the wail of a siren, heading toward the south. Okay, Shawn can have a little fun this time, but he really needed to stay on script.

22

"You people have a lot of nerve. This is *not* a hospital. It's all very irregular and fishy." Not a warm reception from Brenda.

"Very fishy," added Bob, unable to come up with denunciations of his own.

Levine knew how to handle these situations. After establishing that he was a physician – Bob had to recognize that he would need a physician's services one of these days – Levine tapped into a childhood yearning: everyone wants to play doctor.

Brenda was given explicit instructions on when and how to administer the medication Rocky required. Bob was instructed on how to swap out the two IV bottles that swayed above Rocky's gurney. Both were told which danger signs would require a return to the hospital, or, more likely, Levine's return to their house. A bedpan lay conspicuously under the gurney. No assignment was made for that. I hoped Moondance saw it as one of her duties.

Levine spent a few more minutes with Rocky, declared that the trip had done him no harm, and left, explaining, "Morris will want his precious ambulance back. If I don't hear from you first, I'll drop by tomorrow evening to change the dressings on the wound and check on the patient."

We could hear the siren as the ambulance reached the highway. No one's immune. I'd probably turn the thing on myself.

Another call to the pager number and a call to Fred's office. He wasn't in.

There were still a few hours of daylight left so Sally and I headed to the Whim Hill mine. The road took us back through Dahlonega and Sally concealed her hair again. According to our map, the mine was just a few hundred yards off the road to Auraria. The town received its name when gold was discovered in the area.

After three slow passes along the highway, we settled on an overgrown trail as the most likely access to the mine. We parked the car on a dirt road nearby and started up the path. As we pushed our way through clinging branches and over fallen logs our optimism wavered: were we on the right track, or were we wasting time? It was five o'clock and the two FBI agents should be checking in; we hoped they had more progress to report than we did.

Sally needed good news. "This has to have been recently traveled, Max. Look at these broken twigs." She was turning into a tracker. But should we be speaking so loudly?

The question was answered by a shout from above, "I hear you down there. I've just about had it. Show yourselves."

Sally pulled out the Beretta and held it behind her. I had misgivings; her recent use of a gun had produced setbacks. And these voices were different from the Klansmen. No backcountry twang.

"We're looking for our daughters," I called out. "Is this the Whim Hill mine?"

"Who's asking?"

"The parents of two missing children," snarled Sally. I worried about that gun. We took the last few steps up the steep path and immediately saw the mine entrance. A man and a boy, perhaps father and son, were glaring at us. Behind them was the wreckage of the door to the mine.

"They've been here, Max. We're too late again." Sally was oblivious to the disapproving looks of the two who blocked our path. She started toward the mine entrance, replacing the pistol with a flashlight in her hand.

"Not so fast, missy."

Sally finally acknowledged the presence of the two.

Would she pull the pistol out again? I spoke, "Let me explain why we're here. Some thugs kidnapped our daughters, thinking the girls could lead them to gold. This is one of the places they might have come to. Our daughters are very young

– nine – and may not fully understand what's happening to them."

"Wow, a lot going on today, huh, Dad." The boy was excited to be part of a story.

"What else is going on?" I asked warily.

"Well," said the boy, eager to be the one to break the news, "there was that attempted murder of a policeman in Dahlonega. Cops are looking everywhere for the woman who tried to kill him. Then a body is missing from the hospital. It was a dead man who disappeared on the way to the morgue. And then something's happening at the Atlanta airport, but no one knows what." His face radiated excitement. Pity he hadn't been at the Hindenberg tragedy. He would have loved it.

"Where's all this news coming from?" asked Sally.

"We got a Bearcat scanner," explained the father. "This stuff has been coming in on the police frequencies all afternoon."

"There was also something about lost girls," the boy remembered. "A law enforcement officer up north reported the parents were looking for them and they had red hair. I only heard that once. Are those yours?"

"They are and they were kidnapped. Something local law enforcement is reluctant to accept. The FBI have been brought in." The boy's eyes grew.

Sally started into the mine again. "Please don't go in there," asked the father. "It's unstable, it's a pain in the ass, and today some jerks tore up two hundred dollars worth of lumber and lots of hard labor to get a peek inside."

"Is there any chance they're still in there?"

"No. We heard them from over at the house about two hours ago. We could hear the demolition going on. By the time we realized what was happening, they'd done all the damage they'd intended and were long gone down the trail."

"I wanted to go after them," claimed the boy.

"Good you didn't. That man that disappeared from the hospital was shot by those thugs."

Sally wasn't satisfied. "I really need to have a look. We overheard these assholes say they intended to trap our children in a mine."

"Alright," said the father, with a theatrical sigh. "Follow me, and whatever you do, don't put any pressure on a beam."

We entered the mine. The boy was ordered to stay outside; he kicked at the broken boards to register his displeasure.

The floor of the adit was wet and drops of water fell steadily, splashing into large puddles. "That's the big danger," explained the father. "Water's been rotting the timbers and washing out dirt that might stabilize the mine. I thought it would be sexy to have a gold mine when I bought this place. Huge mistake. It's a lawsuit waiting to take me down the drain. And now I'm looking at more expenses and lost weekends closing it up again."

"They were here." Sally shone her flashlight on small footprints in the muddy floor.

"Those prints are heading back toward the entrance," said the father. "Can we get out of here now?" I was on board.

————————

Back in the car, "I guess I'm a little relieved," announced Sally. "We know they're alive and okay. We also know we're on the right track." Positive news – except for the simple fact that we were always a step behind. Had it not been for the Rocky rescue this afternoon we would have intercepted the treasure hunters at the Whim Hill mine.

As we approached Dahlonega I saw a pay phone outside a convenience store and pulled in.

"Fred, glad to catch you. Update?"

"You're not going to like it, Max." What was new there? "I did get to the McIntosh mine. Nothing happening. It's a possibility they might show up there tomorrow or the next day, but it's hard to find. On the other hand, those boys have been deer hunting all over these mountains. They probably know the land better than I do.

"Second item: I'm what's left of your federal help for now."

What?

"Something really huge is going on down around Hartsfield. Malkowitz and his fiery girlfriend were pulled off the kidnapping case – 'unsubstantiated' was the word – to rally to the cause in Atlanta. I'm guessing more guns found by security at the airport. Apparently the Mayor's going nuts and all three of the local channels are promising a huge breaking story this evening.

"Are you ready for the biggie?"

Biggie? "Sure, it can't be worse."

"Depends on your perspective. You, Sally, and Moondance are fugitives from justice. That Black kid too. Moondance is accused of attempted murder of a law enforcement officer and you three of forcibly restraining him and preventing him from exercising his duties."

We should have seen this coming. I described the events at the hospital to Fred.

"Your word against his. He's a cop. He's a local. The word has it that you're a wealthy jetsetter who prefers Europe over the good old USA and who can't control his children."

"There was a credible witness."

"I hope so. You might be helped by this thing at Hartsfield. An attempted cop-killing story is usually guaranteed the headline, but it may get pushed off the front page."

"Where do we go from here, Fred?"

"Do you still have faith in your list?" I hadn't told him about our visit to Whim Hill mine. That news had also been pushed off the front page.

"So far, yes. We missed them by two hours at Whim Hill."

"Alright. I think you, Sally, and that other guy have to stay out of sight. I'll do the Ivey Cut and Horner mines tomorrow. You keep your eye on Three Sisters. Based on what Doreen told me, it's logical they'll check that out sooner or later."

Some pleasantries, expressions of concern for each other's welfare, and we rang off.

23

"Do you think there's any chance they know we're at Bob and Brenda's?"

"I doubt it, babe, unless Levine blabs, and I can't believe he would. He has every reason to hate these guys and I don't think the cops have enough to put the squeeze on him. His pal Morris Rubin might be another story. But you mentioning that makes me think we should wave off the good doctor tomorrow if Rocky seems to be doing okay. Levine might be followed."

We snuck back through Dahlonega. Light was failing. We risked a stop at a drugstore to buy bandages and gauze. Sally stayed in the SUV while I went in. Sometimes being nondescript can be an advantage.

Arriving back at Bob and Brenda's we were told that Rocky was awake but groggy and Moondance was begging for his forgiveness. Some situations are too silly to even try to comprehend.

Everyone was waiting for the big story out of Hartsfield airport. Thanks to their elevation on the mountainside, Bob and Brenda received a snowy signal from the Atlanta stations via a repeater tower. As anticipated, the lead story was about a spate of attempts to sneak guns onto planes. The coverage alternated between shots of an earnest looking reporter leaning into the camera, with shots of legions of protectors, some in military uniforms, some police, some in blue jackets and baseball caps. We looked without success for Malkowitz and Bernstein.

The next camera shot was unmistakably the exterior of the Dahlonega hospital. Easy guess what that story was going to be about – a story that would further undermine Brenda's grudging participation. "Well, enough of this." I switched off the television. "That picture's giving me eyestrain. Let's discuss what needs to be done." Brenda looked startled. "First, Brenda, where should we put Rocky for the night. A man that large can't be kept on a narrow gurney forever."

She'd already thought about this. Rocky would go into the room kept ready for the visits of grandchildren. Moondance announced she would sleep on the floor next to Rocky's bed. Sally and I would receive the guest bedroom. Shawn was consigned to the couch.

The six of us were able to get Rocky into bed. He was alert enough to assist a little and to signal when we were bending him the wrong way.

Sally pulled me aside, "Max, we have to level with these people."

"I know. They've been good about keeping their questions to themselves."

With Rocky and Moondance put up for the night, Sally, Shawn and I sat down opposite our hosts. As usual, Sally was our presenter. She's always more credible.

"Bob, Brenda, we need to bring you up to date and this has been our first chance." As she said this she glanced down the hall toward the room from which we could hear Moondance chanting in a low voice. "As you've guessed, there is something irregular about a doctor bringing a wounded man to a stranger's house." Brenda and Bob exchanged 'I told you so' looks.

"Rocky was shot by the same Klansmen that have our daughters. When we went to the hospital we interrupted one of them trying to kill Rocky – the guy happens to be a policeman – and Moondance prevented the murder. Dr. Levine helped sneak Rocky out the back way. What we've heard is that the would-be killer, the cop, claims Moondance tried to kill him and that Max, Shawn and I are accomplices."

"You're wanted?" exclaimed Brenda. She looked shocked; Bob was delighted and clapped his hands together.

"We are," I answered. "There are witnesses, and eventually the cop's story will fall apart. Meanwhile it's his word against ours and we might be locked up when we need to be looking for our daughters."

This was a wonderful development for Bob who asked about every detail. He wanted a demonstration of Moondance's chokehold; he liked the part about me depositing the cop's pistol in the john; and he approved of Levine's quick response to the policeman in the hall. This had been going on for half an hour when I noticed that Sally had dropped off to sleep beside me and Shawn's eyelids were drooping.

————————

In the morning our enjoyment of Brenda's breakfast was interrupted by the sound of a vehicle going up the road. Sally and I grabbed the two rifles and ran out to our car, Bob protesting his exclusion. Shawn was asleep, despite the activity around him.

Dust hung over the road at the fork up to the mine. As we approached the parking area we slowed. A glint of reflected sunlight off a windshield came through the trees. It turned out to be the car of a Union County sheriff. How did he know to come here? We were outside of Union County. Whose team was he playing for?

"Turn the car around, Max."

"Why?"

"The girls won't be with this guy and he can hear us just as easily as we heard him."

She was right. We went back down the road to the highway, kicking up as much dust as we could to mark our trail. We didn't need a sheriff dropping in at the house. Pulling up a side road just down the highway, we watched a boiling cloud of dust signal the sheriff's car coming back down the dirt access road. The sheriff stopped at the entry to the highway and got out. He examined the road surface, inclined his head in the direction we'd taken, and headed up the highway, siren wailing.

"This is *so* not good, Sal."

"How did he know where to look?"

"Obviously they don't know we're at the house, or he would have gone there." I checked the time; maybe we could still talk to Fred.

We returned to the house where we found Brenda excitedly talking on the phone. She was not, we hoped, spreading the story of the adventure that had arrived on her doorstep. Liberating the phone, I dialed the ranger station.

"Fred, so glad you're still in your office." I reported Deputy Sheriff Karl's visit to the Three Sisters mine.

"I made a decision last night, Max. I hope it won't upset you. With the Feds pawing through luggage at the airport, I felt we needed more eyes on the mines. Karl isn't the quickest bunny in the forest, but I think his heart's in the right place. He said he'd check all the mines on your list that are down there."

"He blasted out of here with his siren going, Fred. That seems like someone who's hoping to make a bust. Probably us."

"Could be he wants to justify the time he's putting into this by clapping the cuffs on someone. Sorry I'm not more help. Mother nature's on a tear in the national forests and that's had me tied up. We have reports of an aggressive bear down in your area and three hikers have been struck by copperheads up on Pisgah in the last week."

"A bear? In this area?" I'd grown up in Idaho where a brown bear could be a problem and a grizzly was a guaranteed disaster. The black bears of the southeast were portrayed as close to house pets by comparison.

"You know the old saying about one bad apple. Over five thousand black bears up here and then this one kills some dogs, a calf, and chases a farmer on his tractor. At least we hope it's just the one bear."

"Well, we're armed to the teeth, and you saw what Sally can do with a gun."

"Right. But the woods are not as friendly as they've been and it looks like that's where you're going to have to stay for a while. Karl's aware that you're wanted in Dahlonega so you need to keep out of his sight. He's willing to give me the benefit of the doubt about the little girls, but he's a cop and he's been told your group tried to off one of his own."

"Merde! Our movements are really restricted by the APB. Maybe we should just go up to the Three Sisters mine and keep it under surveillance. We discovered this morning that it's difficult to follow anyone up the road to the mine without being detected."

"I'm tied up doing USFS stuff today – plus bears and copperheads – but I'll try to get down to meet up with you tomorrow."

We agreed to talk again in the late afternoon.

The call to Fred concluded, Sally and I finished our breakfast and tried to think of assignments that would keep everyone productively occupied and out of mischief. Moondance emerged, looking troubled. Not another bout of guilt about saving a life, I hoped.

"Rocky's got a fever."

Brenda produced a thermometer. Rocky's temperature was over 102 degrees and he winced when any pressure was put near the site of the bullet wound.

The usual interminable delay to get through to Dr. Levine.

"Not surprising, Mr. Brown. In our hasty departure yesterday we didn't pick up the meds he's going to need. We were lucky to find extra IV bags in the ambulance. Unfortunately, I have the distinct sensation I'm being watched. If I come up there we might all wind up in jail by the end of the day. I'll call in a prescription. Put that woman – Brenda? – on the phone, would you?"

Brenda made notes as she listened. Hanging up she announced with satisfaction that she was being dispatched to pick up antibiotics at a pharmacy in town. Serum to Nome. Bob volunteered to accompany her.

"Bob, you're needed here. Could you get Rocky's truck out of sight in case the Klansmen come up this road by mistake? Then, the big one, if they show up here you have to redirect them on up the hill to the mine. They can't be allowed into the house. We'll leave a pistol with you if you feel you need to show the seriousness of your intentions. Your role is grumpy old coot." Cast to type.

Should we also leave him ammunition? No.

Shawn was waiting – with an arched eyebrow – for his assignment. There was no getting around it; he had to be involved. In fairness, he'd earned a place on the starting team.

"Shawn, it's down to a stakeout now. If Bob will drop us all off up at the parking area, Sally and I will go to the top and you'll stay out of sight near where they'll have to park. I trust you not to shoot the wrong person." With effort I didn't look at Bob.

If the kidnappers showed up we were assuming there'd still be a casual relationship between captors and captees. That would change if the Klansmen felt threatened. But up to this point, the girls might be able to get a little separation.

24

The day was hot and the mosquitoes voracious. We'd forgotten to bring DEET and we weren't going to ask Bob to bring it. We didn't want him bumping into the Klansmen on the road.

We had water, sandwiches – Brenda was getting into her role as quartermaster – and no good place to sit as we waited in the trees 30 yards from the mine entrance. I examined the rifle apprehensively. I'd certainly do better with the rifle than with a pistol, but still . . . Sally would have to be on her game. She explained that the scope was excellent for one target, but slowed re-aiming if there were multiple targets.

"If it comes down to it, I want you to target the goober farthest away from the girls. I'll take out the asshole closest to them."

You'll notice her choice of words: I would 'target,' she would 'take out.' We assumed two Klansmen, three at the most.

At midday there was noise on the path. We both aimed in that direction and, again, Shawn narrowly escaped death by friendly fire.

"What the fuck are you doing up here?"

"I was thinking. Should I follow them up the path so we could saw them up in a crossfire?"

"Christ no, Shawn," said Sally. "We don't want bullets flying around. I'll take the shots. As soon as the lead starts flying, count on these assholes to hold the girls in front of them. Surgical shots, taken at the start. If that doesn't do it, we're screwed."

No, the twins are screwed.

I added, "Patience, Shawn. Wait for the moment. We rely on Sally. Remember, they'll have a lot to do up here. The mine is plugged so they'll have to deal with that. Maybe we can get the girls away from them while they're working on clearing the entrance."

"Do you think they'll be expecting us?"

"They're pretty stupid, but yes, they'll have to expect us at every turn. They must have heard that the FBI was working the case and they've got the missing Rocky to worry about. I'm sure they're not roaring around with their flags flapping anymore. We don't know what their exit strategy is, but it might be to find the treasure and then lie low somewhere, maybe as long as a few years. That was one of the options they were discussing."

Shawn retreated down the path.

"He was just lonely," explained Sally.

We waited. I was behind Sally, who squatted, intently watching the opening to the trail. Since she had that covered, I studied her curvaceous behind. Ten years with her, and she was still the most alluring woman I'd known. There was movement in my pants. A sad realization: I'd come to that point in my life when I regretted not taking advantage of every erection that popped up.

Sally thought she heard a vehicle coming up the road. It turned off at the fork toward the house. Probably Brenda coming back with antibiotics. We tried to ignore the mosquito bites and ate the sandwiches, more to pass the time than to satisfy our hunger.

At two o'clock another vehicle started up the road. This time it continued toward the mine. We tensed. Were we breathing?

No voices on the path. Then the sound of labored panting, and Deputy Sheriff Karl stepped out. He bent forward, placed his hands on his knees, wheezing, and after a minute turned and headed back down.

"Karl's doing a good job. I wonder for whom?"

An hour later there were more sounds of movement on the road. After two false alarms Sally and I were more relaxed. When we heard the crunch of footsteps on the path we picked up the rifles. The sounds stopped and there were whispers. More than one person this time. We trained our rifles at the opening and waited.

More whispers. Whoever was approaching had arrived at the top of the path, but they were unwilling to expose themselves. Then Skeeter pitched forward onto the gravel, as if he'd been pushed.

"You check it out, good buddy. It's like Doreen said, ain't it."

The opposing team had arrived.

Skeeter stood, dusted off his hands and walked up to the blocked mine entrance. "We could really use a track hoe, Boon." He pulled a few medium sized rocks off the entrance.

"We ain't got no track hoe, now, do we Skeeter. I sure rather not blast 'cuz of the noise."

Where were the twins?

Skeeter pulled some more rocks off the plug. No one came out of the concealed path to help him.

Sally and I looked at each other. It was obvious the Klansmen were avoiding direct exposure. That meant diminished chances of separating the twins from them, if the twins were there.

From the path, "Dammit, Boon. Let's stop pussy footin' around and open that cocksucker up. Pardon the language, young ladies."

The twins *were* there.

"C'mon back here, Skeeter. Billy's right. We's just wastin' time."

Skeeter shuffled back to the path entrance and emerged again a minute later holding a stick of dynamite and a lighter. "Where do you want me to stick it?"

This brought a laugh. "Not in yer ass, Skeeter. Not yet, anyway." More laughter. "Shit, Skeeter. I don't know where to put the charge. Put it at the bottom."

Skeeter wedged the brown stick under the bottom-most rocks, lit the fuse, and ran for the path entrance. Sally and I watched, fascinated.

The sound of the explosion wasn't as loud as I'd expected and the results fell short of what the Klansmen had expected. Before the dust had dissipated Boon ran forward, quickly studied the rocks, and ran back.

With new instructions, Skeeter brought another stick of dynamite and placed it midway up the plugged entrance at the side.

Sally and I hadn't expected the Klansmen to stay out of sight, but it made sense. After we crossed paths two nights earlier they realized we could anticipate their movements. The twins had to be figuring out that this was not a chummy bunch of happy-go-lucky treasure hunters. I looked at my wife. She was sweating profusely and her normally steady shooting hand was trembling. My mouth was dry.

Another explosion. This time small stones rained down around us. Something fluttered slowly from the sky and landed in the blackberry bushes. It was the remnants of flowers laid by Bob. Boon ran forward, confirmed that there was a small opening, and again retreated.

"We need more power, there, Skeeter boy. Twist them fuses together and let's see if we can get 'er done."

A minute later Skeeter reappeared and worked two sticks of dynamite into the opening. With an outstretched arm he lit the combined fuse and fled back toward the path.

This time the sound of the explosion was earsplitting. Rocks of all sizes pelted us. The dust was slow to settle and I could only dimly see Boon run forward. "We're in!" He pawed at the rocks, pulling several to the ground, then he worked through the opening.

Skeeter came next, carrying a Coleman lantern and a shovel. He'd gone five yards when Mary and Margaret finally appeared. They were dirty and their clothes torn. Each had a small backpack, each looked frightened, and each was carried close to the chest of a Klansman. A fourth Klansman followed them, glancing apprehensively around at the circle of bristling blackberry bushes. Four of them? Of course. These guys were on the run. They'd want to stay close to their hostages and out of sight. Another one or two might be down watching the cars.

Was this a shot Sally could make? How was she taking the appearance of our children, disheveled and frightened? I looked back at her. My wife was stretched on the ground, a red bruise on her left temple. *Dear God. Don't let her be dead.* It took a few seconds and a lot of self-control to reach for her neck and search for a pulse.

Nothing. Keep looking.

A quiet neck. Keep looking.

Christ! I'd gone straight to the right spot on Rocky. There has to be a pulse. I checked for my own carotid pulse, found it, and checked the same spot on either side of Sally's throat.

Thank you, Lord. The rhythm of her good heart, beating steadily. She was alive, but out of the fight.

I turned back to the clearing in front of the mine. Skeeter had already disappeared into the mine and the man carrying Mary had crawled in and was now pulling Mary behind him. The man who'd been using Margaret as a shield did the same. The fourth kidnapper hunkered down and scanned the surrounding trees and bushes. Were we still concealed after the hail of rocks?

Boon stuck his head through the hole and spoke to the man left behind. "I never know'd a nigger that didn't lie. Len, you keep your guard up. I got a feelin' they's more of 'em around here." Len nodded.

There was only one way to interpret Boon's statement. Shawn had been captured but had maintained he was alone.

A setback, and very bad news for Shawn.

We hadn't bothered to think this through. What would the Knights do next? That was answered when a fifth Klansman came out of the path, carrying two crowbars, another shovel and a metal detector. Len addressed him as James.

You're on your own, Max. Figure this out. The kidnappers had to open the original tunnel, look for buried treasure with the metal detector, and dig it out if they found it. Give them five minutes to open the abandoned tunnel. Another ten to fifteen to sweep the floor with the detector, and, if they got a chirp, an unknown amount of time to dig. They would be wise to hurry. The explosions could easily attract a visit from a landowner or a law enforcement officer checking for blasting permits.

Would Sally come around? Would she awaken quietly or announce our location? Or was she in a coma that might last the rest of her life? She told me that she'd suffered a concussion during boot camp and was out for almost an hour. The saw-bones had assured her that was a good thing – the resting brain was making repairs; she was just sleeping off the concussion. We didn't have an hour.

"Everything quiet down there, James?"

"Quiet as the grave. Heehee."

What's that about? Have they killed Shawn? James retreated back down the path.

I checked my watch. Three seventeen. If they hadn't reappeared by three thirty-seven, there was a good chance they were digging. If they found something, the twins' fate was sealed. Do I shoot Len, the Klansman standing guard, and rush the entrance at three thirty-eight?

Len, perhaps to pass the time, started enlarging the hole. When it was big enough to edge through standing, he stopped and resumed squinting at the trees around the gravel area. I wanted water but was frozen in place. *If the guy would leave I could pour some water on Sally. That works in the movies.*

Rethink this. Assume they find treasure. Also assume the worst and they intend to bury the girls in the tunnel. They won't blow the mine until after they've removed everything they want. They'll tell the guy standing guard they hit the jackpot because they'll need help. Forget the clock and wait for a cry of eureka.

The guard looked the other direction and I poured water on Sally's face. No response. So much for the movies. But her pulse was still good. *Sally, beloved life companion, I'm so very, very glad you're alive. Now I need something more.* She didn't stir.

I checked the time. Three forty. Were they digging?

Three fifty. My knees ached from crouching. When the guard looked the opposite direction I eased onto my stomach and sighted through the scope. With the rifle resting on a solid branch, I could hold him in the crosshairs. Maybe I could make this work. But this was Len, the guy who'd argued against killing the girls. He didn't deserve to die.

At three fifty-five a head appeared from the mine entrance. "Hey, Len. Bring up them bags. We may of found somethin'." Len put down his gun and headed down the path.

No indecision, Max. It's your show now. I could slip through the opening, move quietly down the mineshaft and get the drop on the three Klansmen who were holding Skeeter and the twins captive. They'd be busy, excitedly digging up Beauregard's treasure.

I didn't have a plan for getting out again.

I stood for a few seconds while my knees got used to bearing weight, then ran across the gravel and peered into the mine. There was a distant glow of flashlights, but there seemed to be no one immediately inside the opening. Turning sideways I started to work my way in, rifle pointed down the shaft. I took one glance back toward the path, leaning out through the opening, to see if Len was returning. That slight movement saved my vision and perhaps my life.

The explosion was immense and hurled me out onto the gravel. Stunned, it took a minute to get to my knees. A cloud of dust continued out of the opening, which now seemed larger than before. The ground shook with a low vibration. Then everything was still.

They'd done it. They'd sealed my little girls in the mine. Or buried them under tons of rocks.

25

I got unsteadily to my feet, capable of only one thought: *Kill them. Now.* The ringing in my ears was intense. Could I hear anything?

"God, Cletis. What the fuck happened?" I *could* hear. Len had come back up the path and was speaking to me. I was coated in black dust, clothing torn, and unrecognizable. "Where all chew get that rifle?"

Without a thought, I spun and faced the man five yards in front of me and pulled the trigger. The bullet tore through him and he slowly went over backward, reaching for the right side of his chest, a look of betrayal on his face. I turned and charged the mine entrance.

The swirling dust inside reduced visibility to zero. I could hear coughing in the distance. *Fire blindly? No, that reveals my presence.* Staying close to the left wall of the tunnel I inched along. The abandoned adit would branch off to the left. That's where I'd find the killers. More soft coughing, now closer. I thought I heard footsteps. Then I remembered: the rifle was bolt action. I hadn't rechambered a bullet after I shot Len. It's impossible to operate a bolt action silently, especially in a tunnel. But the blast would have put a dent in everyone's hearing. I slowly worked the bolt. The sound of footsteps stopped.

I froze. Who would move first? Another muffled cough and the shuffling footsteps resumed. How wide was the tunnel? I pressed myself against the left wall; whoever was approaching seemed to be slightly to my right. Could they pass by and be silhouetted against the opening? That was the time to shoot. There would be three of them and I'd need every advantage. I didn't care if they shot back, or shot accurately. I just wanted to be sure that I killed them all.

I held my breath as the footsteps came closer. *I could reach out and grab one of them if I wanted. Wait. Get them all.* Then the footsteps were past and I turned carefully toward the mine's opening. It was possible to just make out movement from the weak light that filtered through. I raised the rifle to my shoulder.

The scope was coated in dust and useless. *Too late to clean it now. Hard to sight around it.* Peering to the left side of the scope, I tried to line up the barrel with a dark shape. *Hope this is a person, and not just a column of dust.* I applied pressure to the trigger, trying to hold the rifle steady. A whispered voice –

"Let's just peek outside. Maybe we'll have to go back in and hide from the other two."

Mary's voice!

"Babies," I wept. I stumbled toward them over the uneven floor and pulled them both to me. "Babies, babies." I was crying and couldn't stop.

"Dad, pull it together." They pushed away. "Where's Mommy?"

I couldn't pull it together. I thought I'd lost everything. Sally unresponsive, the girls buried.

I wiped my eyes with a dust covered sleeve which made my vision worse, but brought back the reality that there were still major problems to be solved. "What about Skeeter and the three men?"

"I think we trapped them. We snuck a stick of dynamite and a lighter out of their box when they were trying to blow up the junk by the mine door. Mary carried it in her backpack." Mary curtsied.

Did they understand what was going on? It's not a school play.

"When the men were all busy digging they told us not to go too far but we went back up where the mineshaft splits into two parts. Mary lit the fuse. I threw the dynamite because I'm a good thrower. Then we ran around the corner into the big tunnel."

Mary added, "It was really loud, Dad!"

Had they killed their uncle Skeeter? "Do you think the roof fell on Skeeter and the men?"

The dust was settling and I could make them out better. They shrugged. Another question: "How many men stayed outside?"

"Two. One stayed down with the man they call Nigger. They tied him up and then tied the rope to the back of their car. They said that could help him get rid of all that black skin."

"Okay, girls, here's the deal. Mommy was hit by a rock. She's unconscious. I shot the man who came up here with you – the one they call Len. I want you to stay with mommy in case she wakes up. I'll go down and see if I can rescue Shawn." Looks of incomprehension. "The nigger."

I'd have to clear that up later.

Our eyes having adjusted to the pitch darkness of the mine, we squinted, half blinded by the light outside. I thought Len showed a little chest movement, but nothing more. Was he bleeding out? Hard to care, even though he was the one who'd opposed killing the girls.

I led the twins over to their mother. Seeing the three of them together undermined me again.

Come on, Sally. Wake up. She was still.

Come on, Max. Shape up!

"Whatever happens. Stay here. Stay with mommy. If she wakes up, help her move a little farther back into the forest."

I started down the path . . . and stopped. *A little planning, here, Max.* The last unaccounted-for Klansman would have heard the gun shot that felled Len. He'd be sure to respond in some way. Worst option: he had immediately come up the path and been watching when the twins and I came out of the mine. Then he'd watched as I left my family behind and now he was reclaiming them as hostages.

I started back up toward the mine, but through the trees. Reaching the edge of the clearing, I crouched. No movement. The minutes passed. Nothing. He wasn't up here. I started down through the brush again. It was slower than going along the path, but the remaining Klansman could be anywhere.

A noise to the right. I froze. A squirrel ran through the branches.

Should I go back to my family and wait this guy out? Bad idea. He could always get in his truck or car and drag Shawn to his death. That would be the logical course for him as soon as he realized that all the other members of his team were either entombed or dying. I pushed down the hill, aware that I was making noise as twigs snapped and dry leaves rustled. The turn-around was ten yards in front of me. Also in front was a tangle of blackberry bushes, each with hundreds of razor-sharp thorns.

I couldn't see Shawn, but I could see a black van, a rope tied to the rear bumper. At the other end of the rope would be one very frightened young man who was regretting his willingness to help us. No sign of the other Klansman.

The only way into the turnaround that didn't require a pain-ful trip through blackberry bushes was back on the path. Curs-ing every twig snap, I returned to the path.

Shawn was bound up with duct tape, the Knights' medium. His face was bathed in sweat, his left eye swollen shut. Taking a quick look around, I knelt beside him and started to peel the tape off. Like everything else, it was a noisy process. First his mouth, but before I'd untied the rope around his legs, twigs snapped behind me. Wheeling, I looked directly into the barrel of a shotgun. I'd put my own gun down to have two hands to free Shawn.

"Well, looky here. Daddy showed up." The one they'd re-ferred to as James surveyed me with a mixture of contempt and satisfaction. "You leave that nigger trussed up just the way he is and let's go up and take us an inventory." He picked up my rifle and motioned up the path.

Think. His shotgun has a pump action. Maybe one second between shots

When we got to the top, my captor examined Len. "Seems like he's still alive, but he ain't in very good shape." James turned to me, "You shouldna' shot Len. He's got a family and his wife's sick most the time."

"I regret it. He didn't belong with you assholes."

"Why chew say that?"

"We've been listening in. He's the one who argued against killing the girls. We've been recording evidence. I wonder what the recordings will tell a court your position was, James? Infanticide? Or were you the voice of compassion?"

"Well now, I ain't too worried 'bout that recordin' stuff. You cried wolf one too many times with that bullshit about having pictures of us blowin' up Skeeter's trailer. Yer bullshittin' again."

I shrugged. "Believe what you want. You probably do understand that your options are limited."

"Well now, I might have to agree with you on that." He backed toward the mine entrance, gun pointed at me. "Don't get no big ideas 'bout nothin' fancy. This 12-gauge puts out a pretty good pattern. I don't need to aim too accurate to bring a man down."

He leaned into the mine and called, "Boon . . . Billy . . . you boys okay?"

No answer.

"You heard the explosion and cave in, James. They're all buried or trapped."

"Well now, they just might be. That bears checkin' don't it." He was thinking about how to handle this situation. Was he the only survivor? He looked around for something to tie me with. The box of dynamite was by the path but contained nothing else of use.

"Let's look at it this way, James. We can save your friend Len but he may not have much time left. Together we carry him down to your van. We untie the Black guy. You take Len to the hospital. There're some cops there you know. You might get off light. Turning yourself in to save the life of a buddy. It'd be a pretty black-hearted judge that would come down hard on a man who put his friend's welfare above his own."

James' brow knotted as he considered the proposal. After a minute he nodded, his expression brightening – not a positive omen.

"Hows about we look at it another way. I put you in the mine and throw in dynamite until the roof caves in. Then I help Len down and take him into town. I jus' bet that the bullet they take out of him come from that rifle of yours. See, this way we both win. No witnesses to say nothin' 'bout me, and you'll be reunited with your daughters." He laughed. He was prepared to plug up the mine where three of his buddies were trapped to simplify ridding himself of me. This was not one of the good guys.

No arguing it; that was a better outcome than turning himself in. James could spin the story whichever way best fit the available facts. He hadn't mentioned Shawn, but that was a problem easily solved. Seal him in the mine with me. March him off into the woods and shoot him with my rifle. Maybe he'd still drag Shawn to his death if there were an easy way to dispose of the body.

This would be a good time for Sheriff Karl to appear, or Sally to come to.

"Put your hands in the air, mister," said a child's voice.

26

A Remington bolt action rifle is 45 inches long. The average height for nine-year old girls is 52 inches.

Mary's left arm was fully extended to reach the forestock and she was having trouble keeping her finger on the trigger. The barrel waved around in enlarging circles. James kept his shotgun trained on me as he studied this new challenge.

"Come to rescue yer daddy? Ain't that precious." He pursed his lips as he studied his new adversary. "Tell me, chew know what a safety is?"

"Put your hands in the air," repeated Mary.

"Yer daddy here thinks I'm pretty dumb but I'm smart about some things. One of them things is I know which way a safety goes. Yer trigger's locked young lady." Mary glanced down at the gun. "Don't believe me? Give 'er a squeeze."

Mary did. James was on her like a cat, ripping the rifle from her hands and pushing his shotgun into the side of her neck.

"Don't nobody try nothin'. Let's just see who else is here."

Mary glanced back at the blackberry bushes. That look was all James needed to herd both her and me in that direction. Clearly visible from the edge of the gravel were Margaret and – a welcome sight – Sally, who'd risen to a sitting position, but looked disoriented.

"Hail, hail. The gang's all here. Come on out ever'body. You'll notice I kinda got the upper hand." Sally stood and immediately sagged back to the ground. After a few seconds she got up again, slowly and unsteadily. She led Margaret around the blackberries and out onto the gravel.

"If it ain't the tire-shooter herself. Shoe's on the other foot, ain't it."

"Max, what's happening?"

"Yeah, Max. Tell yer little wife's what happening."

"I shot that man over there. The other three are trapped behind a cave-in."

"Skeeter?"

"Also in the mine."

"Okay, that there's enough talkin'. You'll have plenty of time to catch up inside the mine. That is, as long as the air holds out. Now, ever'body inside the mine."

He put the two rifles by Len and motioned us toward the mine with his shotgun.

I stepped toward him. "No."

"What the fuck you mean 'no'? Get yer ass in the mine and you women all do the same."

"No. If you want to kill me, do it looking at my face. Not out of sight as you lob sticks of dynamite in."

"Yer pretty stupid for smart-ass Euro-trash. In the mine you got a chance if the roof don't fall directly on you. At this distance this here shotgun'll make a hole 'bout the size of a basketball."

"Max, he's right. We have a chance in the mine."

"Listen to yer wife, Euro-trash. Now move!"

"Here's the deal James. If you shoot me out here with a shotgun, there'll be no doubt it was murder. If we die in the mine you might sell it as a tragic accident. I don't feel like helping you out."

James was thinking about this.

"You want to commit murder, James, you have to be ready to deal with the consequences."

"Ya know, Euro-trash, yer right. Shootin' you with a shotgun'll splash pieces of you all over the place. But shootin' you with a rifle? Cleaner. Thanks for the tip. Heehee." He backed toward Len where he'd laid the two rifles.

He picked up the gun Mary had tried to use and threw the safety over to the armed position. "See there, little girl. That there's how you get a gun ready to fire. Ever'day's a school day, my mother used to say." He chuckled at his own wit.

"Now, let's just shoot ol' dad here and see if we got any other heroes. I can drag bodies into that mine and then blow it up. Ain't a big thing."

I was out of ideas. Where was the cavalry? This loser wasn't going to take my family.

"You folks might want to turn away if you don't want to see this feller's brains come squirtin' out the back of his head." Mary and Margaret started crying. Sally was hissing something unintelligible.

He raised the rifle.

"Don't."

James wheeled toward the voice. Len, still on his back, was trying to hold the other rifle, the rifle I'd shot him with. "Don't do it, James."

"Ah, Len. You always was a pussy." He shook his head sadly. "There ain't no other way."

Len was trying to aim the gun at James but could raise the barrel no higher than a few inches off the ground.

"Shit, Len. He shot you. This is jus' payback."

"Don't," said Len, more faintly.

"I'm afraid yer gonna do somethin' stupid," and he pulled his foot back to kick the rifle Len was limply holding.

An opportunity. I lunged toward his back. James heard the crunch of gravel and started to turn, while trying to keep an eye on Len. By the time he completed the turn I was on him, inside the length of his rifle.

We went backward over Len, the gun fired, and James was on the ground beneath me.

"You dumbass sum-bitch. This ain't gonna change nothing." He was pushing me off his chest. "You can ferget about a painless death cuz . . . " He didn't finish the sentence because I'd freed my right arm. Putting all my strength into the swing, I buried my fist in his throat, the knuckles penetrating cartilage.

James made a gurgling noise and his eyes widened in fright as he tried to get air. I pulled the rifle out of his hand and stood.

A clear small voice came over the sound of James' gasping, "Wow, Dad. Way to go!"

Keeping an eye on James, I knelt beside Len. We'd rolled over the top of him. "Len. Two things: You're one of the finest men I've known and I'm going to make sure that the world hears about it. Second, if you don't make it, your family will be taken care of. I have the money."

Len said nothing. His eyes were closed.

"Sal, we have to mobilize." I patted James' pockets and found the keys to the Klansmen's van. "You take the kids and get back to the house and call 911. These two guys need medical attention now, and we need lots of diggers to try to get Skeeter out."

The twins were slow to move. There might be more action; action-hero dad was putting on a riveting show.

"Move it twerps. Sal, don't forget to unhook Shawn from the bumper." She still looked dazed. "You can unwrap him on your return. I'd better stay here to keep an eye on James."

Len's chest heaved rapidly, then stopped moving. I'd shot him through the right lung. Mouth-to-mouth resuscitation? It didn't seem it would hurt so I started as Sally and the twins disappeared down the path. I tried to keep an eye on James.

Len appeared to be responding to CPR. I pressed on his chest gingerly, aware of the damage I'd done. I was so involved in CPR while monitoring James that I hadn't heard the car coming up the road.

"What the Sam Hill?" Deputy Karl was back. He shook his head, and – his signature move – hitched up his pants. "I just untied a Black fella down there and now I find you two kissing and poor ol' James all messed up." A second look at Len and Karl understood.

Shawn caught up, limping and navigating cautiously with one eye swollen closed.

"Would one of you take over the CPR duties for a minute. I'm pooped."

Shawn was quick to volunteer. I think he relished the image of a Black man giving mouth-to-mouth to a Klansman. There was probably enough homophobia lurking in Karl that he'd be reluctant to help.

"Sheriff, will the radio in your car reach from up here?"

"Of course."

"Four men are trapped down a side passage in that mine. They may be buried. They may be alive. One thing's certain: time is not on their side."

Karl hitched up the back of his pants, again, and scurried down the path to put out the call for help. He'd been gone five minutes when a faint siren could be heard coming up from the south. Then a second siren. Probably ambulances responding to Sally's summons.

Sally emerged from the path, followed by the twins. She was going to keep them close to her. "I see we have company."

Able to talk to each other for the first time, "How are you, babe? You were out a long time."

"Head hurts. When I walk it hurts. When I try to run it really hurts. It hurts."

"I get the picture. Let's get you priority in one of those ambulances. A major concussion's nothing to ignore. Sit tight for a while." Her eyes looked unfocussed.

Shawn was tiring, but Len still had a pulse. James was clearly alive but needed a tracheotomy, or something like it, to clear his airway. He seemed to be getting just enough air to remain conscious. At one point I saw him looking at the guns. I picked them up and threw them to the edge of the blackberries.

The rattle of a gurney coming up the dirt path announced the arrival of the EMTs. "This one first," signaling Len. "He's been shot."

The four EMTs conferred, strapped both wounded men on the gurneys and prepared to leave.

"FYI, the guy with the busted throat tried to kill me and my family. Special handling."

"Don't worry, sir. We'll intubate him. That means sedation. He'll be no trouble." I nodded at Sally.

"I know it's a little thing," she looked embarrassed! "but I was hit by a rock and was unconscious for maybe fifteen minutes."

"What? Fifteen minutes?" the EMT asked incredulously. "You're coming with us."

The gurneys squeaked and rattled down the path. Sally opted to walk carefully behind them, a less jarring trip; Mary and Margaret steadied her. The girls needed a thorough medical check as well as Sally. Shawn didn't volunteer to return to the hospital.

Sheriff Karl returned and watched them go, then turned to me. "Well, as Ricky used to say to Lucy: Mr. Brown, you got a lot of 'splainin' to do."

My mind couldn't focus and my story wandered from this afternoon to overhearing the Klansmen two nights earlier, then back to the present.

Sheriff Karl made no notes. I gathered this was not a formal statement. When I finished, he said, "Let's see if I got this. Like Fred told me, this is one of the mines you thought your daughters might come to. This afternoon you and the missus witnessed your girls being carried into the mine like human shields. It seems like something was found that distracted Boon and them which gave your girls the chance to slip away and set off dynamite in that side shaft. You were so enraged when you thought the blast had killed your children that you shot Len, who seems to have been unarmed. You found your girls alive and left them with their mother. Then James got the jump on you and was fixin' to kill the four of you one way or another. Len tried to intervene and that gave you a chance to disable James." This was said with an implied question mark at the end. I nodded.

"Here's the problem I see, Mr. Brown. The only witnesses you got for your story is the same as them that's wanted for aiding an attempted murder of a police officer in Dahlonega, or they's the people that you and your daughters assaulted. I'm not saying you're lying." This was alarming. What was he saying?

"What I'm saying is that we might hear another story that con- tradicts yours."

"Oh come on, Sheriff." Fred had said he wasn't the quickest bunny in the forest.

"Come on?" He was annoyed. "First, you and your wife are accused of helping Rocco Snyder's wife in an attempt on the life of an officer of the law. Second, you shot and seriously in- jured an unarmed man, who you say mistook you for one of his friends. You shot him with his guard down. Third, you seriously injured another man by breaking his windpipe under circum- stances that might be disputed. In fact," he was getting into it, "someone might make the claim that your little girls are respon- sible for the deaths of four men. Now we don't execute nine- year olds in Georgia, but you see the gravity of the charges that might be brought."

What a nightmare! I thought we were out of it: The Klans- men all trapped or wounded, Sally awake, the girls back with us.

"I'm afraid I'm going to have to take you, the missus, and the colored fella into Dahlonega to the DPD to be formally charged and booked. We'll pick up the ladies at the hospital." He checked his watch. "It's too late in the day for an arraign- ment so bail won't be set before tomorrow morning. You can plan on spending the night enjoying the hospitality of the good folk of Dahlonega. Child Services will have to figure out where to put the little girls."

27

The rumble of more than one large vehicle coming up the road postponed our departure. "Them must be the rescuers I called."

Karl didn't want to miss the rescue attempt.

Ten minutes later a small bucket loader pushed its way up the path and the operator immediately went to work on the rubble in front of the mine entrance. Within less than two minutes the entrance had been widened so the bucket loader could enter the mine. Within less than ten seconds the operator walked back out. "Karl, that place isn't safe. Just driving shakes the ground enough so that stuff is falling." Karl had no thoughts on the matter, but I did. Skeeter was trapped.

"Four men are in there, sir. The shaft you need to open is down about twenty yards and to the left. If you can move the rubble blocking that shaft on the left to the main shaft on the right, it would reduce the amount of driving around you'd have to do."

This didn't seem to be a very persuasive argument, but the man knew he was expected to try to save four lives. Four trapped men would use up the available oxygen quickly.

We heard the bucket loader start up again and move down the tunnel. The familiar changing of sound that machines make when they're lifting and moving signaled that the rubble was being removed from the side adit.

A tracked vehicle came up the path. It looked like an overgrown power drill. "They'll try to drill through the mess and get an air hose in to the fellas," explained Karl. "That'll take some of the time pressure off us."

The bucket loader backed out of the mine and the power drill went in. Karl couldn't help himself; he had to watch and, growing more resolute with each step, he inched into the mine.

Shawn, who'd been doing his best to be inconspicuous, looked at me questioningly. We walked casually toward the path, picking up the rifles as we passed them. When we were out of sight of the rescue crew, we raced down to the parking area. In addition to the sheriff's car there were two dump trucks with flat bed trailers attached. Both trucks had been parked with consideration for others. Our SUV wasn't blocked in.

"Wait," said Shawn. He popped open the hood of the sheriff's car, jerked the positive cable off the battery, twisted it until it broke, and threw the clamp into the weeds. "His car won't move and his radio won't work." I didn't point out that the rescue crew trucks were still there; they could pursue us, and they probably had radios. Shawn had added to his chargesheet for nothing.

As we bounced through the fork to Bob and Brenda's we almost collided with a car coming up from the highway. Dr. Levine, making a house call on Rocky.

"Did you find your daughters?"

"Yes, and they're down at your hospital being checked, along with Sally. But things have gone sideways on us, Doctor. That charge of trying to kill Buzzcut is still standing, we're wanted for aiding Moondance, and that Deputy Sheriff is half convinced that my attempts to rescue my daughters were unprovoked aggression. We're on the run."

"Welcome to my world," said Levine, wearily. Taking notice of Shawn, "What happened to you, Ferguson?" Without waiting for an answer, he opened his bag on the passenger seat, extracted ointment, gauze and a compression bandage, and dressed Shawn's swollen eye. "You're going to have a splendid shiner in the morning, son."

Before returning to his car Levine handed me a card. "This is my home address. My wife will understand when you explain, although, Mr. Brown, you look like you were fired out of a cannon." Easy to forget your appearance when you're on the lam. "After I check on Mr. Snyder I'll try to contact a lawyer." He started to leave, then turned, "Yes, a Jewish lawyer."

From above on the hill we heard the sound of a truck motor starting. Our absence had been noted. Should I drive carefully and not attract police attention? Or should I worry about a dump truck lumbering after us? Worry about the dump truck.

Running two red lights on our way into town, we slid to a stop at Emergency Admitting. No evidence of cops or cop cars.

"A red-haired woman and two girls arrived here thirty minutes ago. Where are they? I need to pick them up. It's an emergency." A strange statement at a place where emergencies are normally dropped off, not picked up.

I saw red hair over the top of a partition and ran in. "Sally. We have to split. Did they check you out?"

"An MRI. I'm waiting for the results."

"We'll have to get them later, babe. We're still wanted and they're piling on the charges. Krazy Karl is even talking about M&M being murderers. He wants to slap you, Shawn, and me in the pokey and turn the kids over to Child Services."

That was enough for Sally. She returned with the girls in an instant – Margaret was still tugging her shirt on and protesting – and we got back in the car.

Shawn was lying on the floor. I handed him Levine's card. "Directions?"

The Levines lived in an upscale community less than a mile from the hospital. No cop cars in the driveway, a driveway which circled up behind the house to the garage. I pulled to the end, out of sight of the street, and turned around, the SUV ready for a quick departure. A matronly woman came out on the back deck and motioned us in.

"You poor dears. Harv called. It's despicable."

Agreed.

"Mrs. Levine, this is so kind of you to let us come here. Did Dr. Levine tell you that we're wanted by a Deputy Sheriff from Union County?"

"He did. I'm afraid this is not an unfamiliar situation, although it rarely involves white gentiles." She had welcome news for us. "Harv told me to tell Mrs. Taylor-Brown that her MRI is normal. His words were: 'That woman has one tough coconut'."

I asked to use the phone and called Fred. "It's good and bad, Fred. We got the girls back, but your idiot sheriff has his teeth into this 'aiding and abetting' thing and he's come up with new charges."

"I know; he called me on someone's radio about ten minutes ago, asking if I knew where you were. Apparently you disabled his car. Homicide might have been a lesser offense. Tell me the full story, but don't tell me where you are. Saves me from having to lie."

I complied, ending, "Now we're trying to find a lawyer. Something's not right about throwing us in the hoosegow on the strength of 'there might be another story'."

"That's just Karl. Like I said before, his heart's in the right place, but he doesn't do well with complex situations. He puts a lot of people in temporary custody until a judge can sort it out."

"Fred, I'm going to have to ring off. I think I just heard the lawyer come in. Keep low. We really appreciate everything you've done. Remember you'll still be up here trying to make a living long after the Taylor-Brown family is gone."

"Appreciate the reminder."

Shawn was already paying a heavy penalty for involving himself with outsiders. Let's keep the collateral career damage down.

The attorney, O'Brien, was not Jewish. His partner was, but the partner wasn't available. After introductions, "Lay it all out, Mr. Brown. Everything you tell me from this point forward is privileged and will not be divulged to anyone." He looked at Mrs. Levine who was slow to realize she should leave the room.

Sally and I took turns. At the conclusion, O'Brien said, "Well, I have to warn you that this could be strung out by these clowns for some time. Bond would be set immediately by any reasonable court. The court would, of course, take your passports. Then you would spend a couple of months in hotels waiting for court dates, having them postponed at the request of your tormentors, and so on."

Sally and I had spare passports under different names; the twins did not.

"Options, Mr. O'Brien?"

"As an officer of the court, I'm bound to advise *against* what has probably already occurred to you: going to the airport before the alarms get any louder and heading back to Switzerland. What I *must* advise is that we go together to Atlanta to a court that's open. You turn yourselves in, enter pleas of innocent, post whatever bond is set, and then try to keep yourselves entertained while the process drags along."

From the emphasis he placed on the words it seemed clear that the attorney was advising us to get out of Dodge.

"For the sake of argument, let's say we did skedaddle. What would be the long-term consequences? Would we never see our native land again?"

O'Brien smiled. He'd gotten his message through. "No. You could all come back when the charges had been dropped. Here a lot hangs on Moondance." Apparently he knew Moondance, or knew of her. "The big issue is the attempt on the life of a policeman. If she'll behave rationally, she should prevail and get that dismissed. The problem is that no one other than Moondance saw – Buzzcut, you called him? – trying to kill Rocco. He could say he went into the room to check on the patient and was savagely attacked from behind."

"Bad news," said Sally. "Moondance seems to be looking for a way to atone for her moral failure. Taking the rap could be it."

O'Brien resumed. "That's why I say a lot hangs on how she behaves. If the charge against her collapses, then the ones against you for aiding also go away. Regarding the charge of murder against the kids, that doesn't pass the laugh test, but courts are humorless so it could drag on for a while. Should the trapped men live, then we're down to endangerment. If the courts had to hear every complaint of a child endangering someone . . . well, you understand.

"The only thing left is shooting Len. I think almost any jury in Georgia – assuming it didn't go to trial in this county – would decide in your favor. When you last saw Len before the shooting, he was armed and he was one of a group of men who'd kidnapped and possibly just murdered your daughters."

Actually I saw Len leave his gun behind before heading down the path. Something to keep to myself.

"The worst-case scenario?" I asked. "Again, for the sake of argument let's say we skipped town."

"Well – Switzerland. Our firm had a client with extradition issues from Switzerland.

"The US has an extradition treaty with Switzerland, but the Swiss have not been very forthcoming about coughing up Americans for trial in the US.

"Let's say it all goes sour. Moondance is convicted and the court issues warrants for your arrests. Add on the shooting of Len. The US would request extradition. All documents have to be translated into French or German, and a Swiss judge will, essentially, try the case and determine whether you would be culpable under Swiss law. That's not a given; they reject many extradition requests where white collar crimes are alleged. Your case as a distraught father is pretty strong.

"If a Swiss judge rules against you, it's not the end. You can appeal. The whole process takes at least one year and some tenacious defendants have dragged it out for ten years."

The sound of an approaching siren seized our attention. Should we hide under the beds? The siren receded.

"Sally and I will have to discuss the options. The morning may also bring more news that weighs on this. Len is in the hospital. Efforts were being made to free the trapped kidnappers and Skeeter. We'll collect information, sleep on it, and try to decide tomorrow."

To my left Shawn cleared his throat. Embarrassing. I'd forgotten about him. He wasn't going to Switzerland. Or maybe he was. Had we adopted him?

O'Brien asked, "Were you part of this?"

"Yes sir. I'm in the same boat as Mrs. Brown." Shawn filled in the details about his own involvement that I'd skipped.

O'Brien was quick to reply. "Your fate also hinges on how Moondance goes on this. But, given that Deputy Karl found you trussed up by the Klansmen and your car had been blown up, you're starting to look more like someone who's trying to protect himself, than someone who's taken the law into his own hands. Venue and jury selection will be all-important." Shawn looked stricken at the prospect of a long and expensive legal process, "But that's only if Moondance takes everyone down the toilet with her."

O'Brien left, handing out business cards, including to two twins, delighted to be part of the drama.

Mrs. Levine came in and avoided eye contact. Eavesdropping. She offered us the guest bedroom and bath. Her look suggested that we'd be more welcome if we were spreading less mine dust throughout the house, so the Taylor-Browns took turns in the shower. Shawn was directed to a basement bathroom to clean up. Separate and unequal.

I proposed showering with Sally to speed the process. There's something about winning a fight that ratchets up the testosterone. Sally demurred. While I was in the shower I could hear her shouting at the twins. She'd gotten beyond relief that they were alive. Should I weigh in and invest some of the rare respect I'd earned from the girls that afternoon? No. Better to bask in it a little longer. They'd be back to viewing me as an artless old fool soon enough. Then I could express my displeasure with their behavior.

When we emerged from the guest room, groomed and sparkling, Dr. Levine had just returned. "Lots of news, lots of news," he called out. Then he disappeared in search of his martini shaker. *And the news, for Christ's sake?* Exasperating.

28

Martinis were prepared for all five adults. Sally dislikes them, but she was disinclined to refuse since that would lead to discussions over what drink would be more suitable, followed by a lengthy search for ingredients and preparing the chosen beverage. Shawn seemed to want to be spared the same process; he eyed his drink – through his one good eye – with no enthusiasm. We wanted to hear the news. We were also uneasy about staying too long in one place.

"Well," said Levine, with a smile, "I wanted us all to have a drink in our hands to toast the good news."

We waited, then realized we were expected to raise our glasses.

"Everyone will live."

"Uncle Skeeter?" asked Mary.

"Yes. Uncle Skeeter. He'll spend the night at the hospital under observation. Len is stable. He'll be okay too, but it'll be slow."

"Were the kidnappers taken into custody?"

Dr. Levine looked surprised by the question. He'd forgotten about that. Is this the result of his occupation? If Hitler recovers and walks out of the hospital under his own power, it's a win?

"I, uh, I guess . . . I don't know."

We looked at him incredulously. Did that mean the Knights were roaming around, looking for revenge?

"Of the four men in the mine, only Thomas Lonegreen, Skeeter, came down to the hospital."

"May I use your phone." I needed to alert Fred.

————————

"Fred. Glad you stayed late. Do you know what happened to Boon and his pals after they were freed from the mine?" As Fred started to answer, his phone was slammed back into its cradle. *Fuck.* Fred was up to speed on the status of the Klansmen.

I dialed the FBI agents' pager. Had they gotten around to fixing their antenna? I left the callback information and hung up. Within a minute the phone rang. Mrs. Levine answered and handed it to me. It was Bernstein.

"Agent Bernstein, one of your fellow federal employees is in deep *kimchi.*" I explained the events of the past two days as economically as I could.

"The kidnapping's over, right, Brown?" I acknowledged that it was. Was she dithering over jurisdiction? She was. "This is really a case for local law enforcement, even if the man is a federal employee."

"Look, it was local law enforcement that just turned three kidnappers loose. The fugitives went straight to a source that could lead back to my family. Where are you now?"

"Driving back to the hotel from the Atlanta airport. Another day of trying to figure out what connects the dots."

"If you'd like to do some actual crime-busting, someone is trying to beat information out of a good man up in Blairsville. The beaters have committed at least one hate crime and kidnapped two children. Any interest in that?" I could hear Malkowitz's indistinct voice. He may have been listening in on the car's speakerphone.

Malkowitz came on. "We'll try to borrow a chopper. The locals here owe us a ton of favors since the gun-running is turning out to be a blip. There's always some asshole trying to demonstrate his second amendment rights the wrong way. We'll call back."

Ten minutes later he did. The Atlanta PD would ferry the two agents up to the Blairsville ranger station in a fast chopper. ETA, about one hour.

I explained the situation to everyone, including two little girls who seemed to be recovering nicely from the dressing down they'd received from their mother.

"It's a good hour from here to Blairsville," said Shawn.

With nothing to lose I called 911. "Please connect me with the Blairsville police. There's a crime in progress."

A minute later a mountain voice announced, "Blairsville police. We're here to protect and serve. How may I help you?"

"I was just on the phone with a ranger at the station west of town. It sounded like he was being threatened, maybe beaten. Could you have someone investigate?"

"I shore could. Please don't hang up." I could hear her speaking into the radio, "Shaughnessy. What's your 10-20?" An unintelligible response. "Could you go down to the ranger station? I got a report of a 10-31." More unintelligible gibberish. "Thanks."

"Now, sir, we got that underway. I need some info from you." I provided her with my name and the Levine's phone number and wondered if we'd later regret that. "Would you like a call-back regarding this incident." Absolutely! We hung up.

Sally was decided. "Max, we have to get out of here, and I mean out of this country. We think we've won, and we're back two spaces."

I agreed.

"Okay. I'll call KLM and change our reservations. First let's keep the line open to see how Fred is."

Five minutes later we got the call. "Mr. Brown. Our officer went down to the ranger offices. He reported there seemed to be signs of some kind of a disturbance in the office of a Ranger Jones, but no one was around . . . Wait a minute . . . The investigating officer is calling in again." This time I could make out some of the gibberish. There was the unmistakable mention of a body. "I'll have to call you later, Mr. Brown," and without waiting for my reply she hung up.

"A cop went to Fred's office. Things were messed up. Fred wasn't there. More news as it becomes available."

I'd promised to call KLM and did so, my mind fixed on the mention of a body. How far out of control had things spun?

The change in reservations went smoothly. All it takes is money to get these things done with the airlines. Then the agent asked, "Is there some kind of legal problem, Dr. Brown?"

"I hope not. Why do you ask?"

"There's a note on your record that the check-in agent should ask for a police release before issuing you a boarding pass."

"Thanks. I'll look into that." I placed the phone back in the cradle with controlled care.

"Fuckity, fuckity, fuck, fuck, fuck!"

"Da-a-ad! Mom, Dad said a no-no word."

"Five times," added her sister.

"So?" from Sally, eyebrow arched.

"Sooo, they've blocked the exits."

The phone rang again. I didn't bother to let our hostess answer.

"Mr. Brown. Tom Malkowitz. I'm calling from Jones' office. There appears to have been an altercation of some sort here. Officer Shaughnessy was the first on the scene and is still here. He said he was preparing to leave when he heard something down the bank behind the building. When he investigated he found Karl, that dimwitted Deputy Sheriff, wrapped up in duct tape, but basically okay. Karl says the three Klansmen took Fred with them in Karl's car."

That's what happens when you relax and allow yourself to think the worst is behind you. Yes, the twins were out of the clutches of the Knights and we were safe in a sanctuary provided by a Jewish physician who'd stepped up repeatedly. On the negative side of the ledger?

- Levine's reward was to become an accessory to possession of an illegal firearm and was now harboring known fugitives.

- Shawn's future looked grimmer. He'd tried to help a pair of clueless honkies and then intervened to save a cop from strangulation. He was faced with the prospect of high legal costs and perhaps incarceration.
- Fred had been a rock from the start, and wound up in serious trouble.

We were really spreading the joy around.

Sally wanted an explanation. "I'm speculating on some of this, babe, but I'm guessing Karl took the three Knights back to Blairsville. They got the drop on him and went looking for Fred. Why Fred? Maybe they think he has a lead on the gold. Fred told Karl which mines to check on and Karl may have told the Klansmen this. Or maybe there's another reason. There might be a history there. I remember Fred saying he 'really wanted to crush those assholes'."

"So, you're wondering about the boundaries of our responsibility, right?" She knew me too well. I also knew Sally; she'd be the last person to abandon someone she'd gotten into trouble. "Let's try to be practical." Sally was better at practical than I was – when she wasn't holding a loaded gun. "As you said, the exits are closed. No skying off to Geneva in the next few days. But, what can we do, Max? The five of us link arms and conduct a manhunt through the forests of north Georgia for Fred?"

The twins looked excited at the prospect. Had they learned nothing? Of course they hadn't. They were adding chapters to the exciting story they'd tell their little buddies in the fall.

I had no ready answers for Sally's questions. The sun was nearing the horizon and habit took over: it was time to put down the day's mental labors and relax. Or maybe it was Levine's martini; my glass was empty. Whatever the reason, I couldn't focus on our problems. Sally was looking at me; some response was expected. "Okay, Sal, let's do what we can for the moment, and think about next steps later." Whatever those next steps might be. Then, something better, although obvious, came through the fog, "It would simplify matters if we could persuade Moondance to back away from an over-principled position."

As we stood to leave, the front doorbell rang. Before answering it, Dr. Levine looked through the curtains. "Dahlonega's finest has arrived. Do you want to try to avoid him?" The tone indicated that was the doctor's strong preference. Five fugitives in his living room?

"Is our SUV blocked in?" Levine shook his head no. "Okay. If you can maneuver this cop away from windows that look out onto the driveway, we'll see if we can slip away." Levine nodded.

I turned to our hardy band: Shawn with one eye swollen shut, Sally recovering from a concussion, and two nine-year olds itching for more drama. "Come on, everyone. Bring your glasses to the kitchen, grab your bags, and let's see if we can stay out of jail."

Shawn gulped down his martini and made a face. Still close enough to his college days that he couldn't allow free booze to go to waste.

While we hastily gathered up our dirty clothes, Mrs. Levine sang out in the direction of the front door, "Coming. Just a minute." She seemed surprisingly natural and nonchalant about this.

As I closed the backdoor behind us I heard the Levines opening their front door and greeting the cop. Dr. Levine was speaking loudly. "A medical emergency, officer? No? Please come in and tell us what we can do for you." The cop's reply was indistinct.

"Okay, everyone. No noise. After you get in, pull the doors toward you, but don't close them. We'll do that further down the street." I put the SUV in neutral and we slowly rolled down the Levines' driveway. After wrestling with power-less steering for a block, I started the engine.

"Jesus, Max. They really do have a dragnet out for us."

"They think we tried to kill a fellow cop. I guess Levine's house was a logical place for them to look since he's been implicated in this. They don't know anything about Bob and Brenda's."

Brenda was sitting on her porch when we arrived, the rifle across her lap. "I thought I should keep watch after somebody snuck in here and took that black van. I was vacuuming and we didn't hear anything until they were already down the road. Bob's up at the mine. He went up there over an hour ago. I think he's worried about Roberta's grave being desecrated."

Over an hour ago? It was now dark. "Brenda, did you hear any traffic on the road to the mine?"

"Lots. The last one was maybe half an hour ago. Someone going up. I figured it for those guys with the machinery."

Sally and I looked anxiously at each other and turned toward Shawn. "Shawn. No arguments, please. The goobers know about this place. Take this pistol and get anyone who will listen into the most secure room in the house. Lock yourselves in, if possible."

"Should we have a password to open the door?"

"Won't you recognize Sally's or my voice?"

"What if you've been captured again?" That put a more dramatic face on it.

"Okay. The passphrase is 'obnoxious son.' If we haven't returned with Bob in thirty minutes, call the pager number on this card. It's the two FBI agents."

In the SUV, Sally asked, "Why would the goobers come back?"

"Easy. They'd just started digging in the shaft for treasure when M&M sealed them in. We should have anticipated this."

"They'll hear us coming up the road."

"Maybe. A chance we have to take. I'll go up the path ahead of you. You follow with your Beretta so you can rescue me like you usually do. Or, they may all be back in the mine, digging away."

Karl's car was in the turnaround. There was no sign of Fred.

"Shit, Sal. They probably have both Fred and Bob." The two dump trucks were gone, but the flatbed trailers had been left in the turnaround area. We guessed the borer and bucket loader were still up at the mine, perhaps for more repair work in the morning.

With the stronger flashlight I headed up the path, Sally trailing me in the dark. It seemed unlikely the Klansmen would fail to post a guard somewhere along the trail. I was hoping that in the darkness the guard wouldn't recognize me and shoot me on the spot.

I called out in an unconvincing falsetto, "Bob . . . oh Bob, honey. Dinner's ready." I heard the sounds of movement on the left. Shining the flashlight in that direction, "Is that you, honey? I was getting worried."

More sounds of movement, then I saw it, rearing up in the flashlight's beam, a mature black bear. More movement at the bear's feet. The flashlight illuminated two cubs. A dangerous combination. The non-confrontational black bear becomes notoriously aggressive when cubs are present.

I started to back away slowly, maintaining eye contact with the bear. Could the animal see me behind the flashlight?

"Hey," came a shout from above the bear. I kept the beam on the bear. It could drop to all fours and charge in an instant. "Hey, down there . . . Lady, do somethin' 'bout that damn bear."

The bear had treed one of the Klansmen. That meant he'd dropped his gun and climbed a tree, which everyone in north Georgia must know provides zero protection from a motivated bear, but that may have been his only remaining option. For her part, mama bear had elected – for the moment – to stay with her children on the ground and lay siege to the tree. I continued to slowly back away. The bear looked up the tree and snorted. *Good, mama bear. Keep your eye on the bad guy. I'm not even a hunter. I carry spiders outside and place them carefully on the ground, for God's sake!* A hand on my shoulder and I jumped. It was Sally.

"Look at that, Sal." She wasn't interested in the animal show.

"Come on, nature boy, let's get out of here before the bear decides we're the bigger threat."

We did. There was no sound of pursuit as we hurried up the path. In the distance, "Hey . . . how 'bout a little help?"

Everything was quiet outside the mine. The bucket loader and borer were parked at the edge of the clearing. The dynamite box was on the seat of the bucket loader. A distant glimmer of light from within the mine and the occasional clank of a shovel or pickaxe were evidence of activity.

"I'll go first this time." The pistol extended in front of her, my darling brave wife slipped into the mine. I was a few feet behind, armed with a rock in each hand. The clanks became louder and we could hear voices.

29

"C'mon' Freddie boy. Put yer back into it. You too Grandpa." The Klansmen had laborers to do the digging. For us that meant they had faster access to their guns, if they weren't, in fact, already holding them. I peered around the corner and looked down the adit. Boon and another Klansmen were seated on rocks on the far side of Fred and Bob; guns were resting in their laps. A hissing Coleman lantern illuminated the scene. I put a hand on Sally's elbow and signaled retreat.

Back outside the mine, "Any ideas how to take them without a gun fight? I can see collateral damage if the lead starts flying. Fred and Bob are in the line of fire."

If one of us knew how to operate the bucket loader we might be able to pile some rubble in front of the entrance which would hold them until help came. Dynamite? Use that to the same effect? Or would that shake things loose in the mine?

"Whatever we're going to do, we'd better do it pretty soon. If they strike pay dirt, Fred and Bob's value will drop to zero."

We could hear voices again and the flickering light emanating from the mine was growing brighter. We ran across the gravel and ducked behind the bucket loader.

"Well, if that don't fuck ever'thing. All that diggin' and all it was was one of Grandpa's kids' toys. A damn ol' tin box with baseball cards."

"Technically speakin', Billy, it wasn't us doin' the diggin'." They were standing behind Bob and Fred who were blocking a clear shot.

"What chew wanna do with these here two now?"

"Well, Fred might still prove useful. He's got some more ideas where to look. Don'cha Fred." Fred didn't respond. "Grandpa's another kettle of fish."

"We ain't killin' him, Boon. Let me put it on the record straight out. Things is gettin' out of hand. Tape him up and let someone find him."

"A fine idea, Billy, 'cept that we used up all our tape on Karl, now didn't we?" Boon gestured over his shoulder. "You know how to run that bucket loader?" They both turned their flashlights in our direction. "Hey, better yet. Ain't that our box of dynamite sitting over there? Fred, you be a good boy and fetch the dynamite. I'll just keep my twelve-gauge pointed straight at your federal neck in case you git any funny ideas about leaping into the bushes." Fred started toward us.

We crouched lower. We couldn't retreat; the bucket loader was backed up to the blackberry bushes. Would Fred see us behind the tractor? Would his reaction give us away? Sally had it figured out. Fred was less likely to mistake her for an enemy and she edged in front of me. As Fred reached for the box of dynamite on the seat, she made a low hissing noise. "What's that noise?" shouted Boon. "Hope there ain't no damn ol' rattler nesting in with the dynamite. You be careful there, Freddie."

Fred the forest ranger knew what sound a rattlesnake makes. As he reached for the box on the seat, he peered behind the tractor. Sally gave him her most reassuring smile. Fred didn't respond.

Watcha doin' there, Freddie. Let's get a move on."

What was he doing? He seemed to be having trouble getting the box off the seat. "If you don't mind, Boon, a little caution. I'd just as soon not stick my hand into a nest of rattlers." Then he took the box and returned to Boon and Billy.

"Okay, Grandpa. Into the mine with you. If I was you I'd go a ways in and put my hands over my ears. Heehee." Bob walked into the mine, his posture better than I'd seen. You had to admire his dignity. No whimpering. "Okay, Fred. It's your show." The two goobers ran into the path before Sally could get off a shot. "Let 'er rip anytime you feel like it."

Fred studied the rubble that had been moved to the left side of the mine entrance. He moved some small stones and wedged a stick well down into the rubble. Did he know what he was doing? Producing a lighter, he ignited the fuse and walked rapidly toward the path.

Another explosion, another rain of pebbles. I turned and checked Sally. She'd survived this one. The entrance appeared to be blocked; perhaps there was a small opening at the top that would admit air for Bob until he could be dug out.

"Fine work, Fred. Yer a credit to yer uniform. Now let's get outa this place."

They headed down the path. A minute later a scream broke the stillness. We exchanged looks and crept cautiously in the direction of the sound, following down the path. Another scream and crashing around in the forest.

"What the hell's going on?" Billy's voice. This was followed by two shots.

"Ah shit, ah shit! Billy, you won't believe this. Ah shit! Cletis been mauled by a bear. It's bad. It's real bad."

The shouting over, we could hear only indistinct conversation. Maybe the distraction would allow us to take these two out. A moving flashlight ahead stopped us and we slipped into the trees. I stuck my less conspicuous head up. Ten yards away Fred was carrying the lifeless form of Cletis over his shoulder. The two surviving Klansmen were on his far side. No shot. Soon they were well down the path.

"Ah shit," that's Sally, picking up the refrain. "They'll see our car. Do you think they'll come back up looking for us?"

"At night? I certainly wouldn't." A minute later we heard four shots and then a car started and headed down the road.

"Do you think they were shooting at the bear?" asked Sally. I knew exactly what the four shots had targeted.

We turned on our flashlights and directed them toward the tree where Cletis had been trapped. No sign of mother bear and her cubs. We apprehensively went down the path to the turnaround, sweeping the flashlights around us constantly.

All four tires on our SUV were flat.

"They would've done it anyway," declared Sally.

I kept my mouth shut.

"Bob," blurted Sally, "I'd completely forgotten about Bob." So had I. "Let's see if we can get him out of the mine."

Back at the mine entrance we pulled a few rocks off the face of the rubble and agreed that was going to be a slow process. I was interested in the bucket loader. How hard could it be? The keys were in the ignition. What guy hasn't wanted to operate heavy machinery? Even the scaled down versions.

"Sal, give me the good flashlight." The penlight was dying. "Maybe I can figure out the controls."

There was a lever that was marked with arrows for lift and lower. Another lever was labeled release. There seemed to be a clutch, accelerator, gear shift, and other controls that I remembered using one summer on a tractor in Idaho. Worth a try. I was about to turn the ignition key when I saw another instruction, faintly visible in the dust on the instrument panel, "Pisgah."

Clever Fred. We knew where he was going in the morning.

I started the bucket loader and after a few miscues was able to move some of the rubble away from the mine entrance. Sally was nervously monitoring this. Like many wives, she didn't trust a man with an oversized power tool. Testosterone, in her view, was not an adequate substitute for knowledge and experience. For my part, as I got the hang of the thing, I considered the pros and cons of a career as a bucket-loader operator: A feeling of accomplishment, a job that didn't follow you home, a variety of challenges. But, the Swiss probably have multiple levels of certification that discourage foreigners from getting prized jobs such as this.

After ten minutes the entrance had been opened enough for Sally to slip through.

"Your turn to stand guard in case those morons surprise us and return." She handed me the pistol with an expression of deep misgiving and went into the mine for Bob. She took the working flashlight, leaving me in the dark where irrational fears took over. Bears. Klansmen. I parked the bucket loader against the blackberry bushes again and crouched behind the bucket. Behind me the thick tangle of thorns provided some protection, but not from a bullet or a bear.

Fears confirmed. A car coming up the road. Two doors slammed. A few minutes later, someone could be heard approaching up the path. Where was Sally? She'd had enough time to locate Bob. I steadied the pistol as best I could on the bucket and pointed it at the top of the path. An indistinct voice. The goobers had decided to come back and finish us off. Had they recruited more troops? Should I start blasting away? Probably. I didn't want them going into the mine; Sally and Bob were unarmed.

My eyes had adjusted to the dark and I could see branches moving at the top of the path. *They must be about to emerge onto the gravel. Wait. Let them come out where I can get off more than one shot before they take cover. Shaking hand. Nothing new there. I really should learn how to shoot. It would come in handy every few years when these situations arise.*

One person came out onto the gravel, flashlight beam sweeping the area. Then a second. They stopped as if they were scouting. Of course, looking for us. The pistol was dancing around more all the time. I had to get a shot off before the damn thing flew out of my hand or I banged it noisily on the bucket. I squeezed the trigger. Nothing. The safety. I threw the safety and the small click made both targets spin toward me. I squeezed the trigger again and got off a shot. Both bodies went down, prone on the gravel. Injured? A bullet ricocheted off the bucket, accompanied by the report of a gun. Shit. I was pinned. Then the bodies rolled away from each other. Not only pinned, but I was about to be flanked. Every time I tried to peer around my protective bucket to aim, another bullet would ping off the thick metal. Giving up on accuracy – if that were ever an option – I held the Beretta above the bucket and, without aiming, fired wildly.

One of my adversaries had been able to work himself back as far as the path entrance. Now out of sight, he could circle around behind me.

Back out through the blackberry bushes? No. The thorns would grab at my clothing and I'd be immobilized. Charge them with the bucket loader? It barely reached walking speed. Not much of a charge.

Dammit. I'd been on a roll all day, peaking when I took out James with a combination of bravado and a knuckle chop to the windpipe. This couldn't be how it ends. Shot to ribbons by goobers who would then do unspeakable things to the woman I was pledged to protect. I almost teared up at thoughts of my failure to Sally. Who would look after the girls? Skeeter?

"FBI. Throw your weapon out and come out with your hands behind your head."

FBI?

"Malkowitz? Is that really you?" No answer. "It's me, Max Brown." I threw the pistol out and then wondered if I'd been tricked.

No trick. FBI presence was confirmed by the snarl of Agent Bernstein, "See what leaving these dummies untethered gets you? Huh? Trying to shoot us in the dark? Huh?" Malkowitz was going to hear about this for a long time.

With both hands compliantly behind my head I stepped out onto the gravel. "I didn't hit you, I hope?" In fact, I hoped I'd nicked Bernstein. Not seriously wounded, just a little scar across her fat ass to remember me by.

"We're fine, Mr. Brown. We assume those were warning shots." *Thank you, Agent Malkowitz, for covering for me. Or does he actually believe no one could be that bad a shot?* "Your friend Shawn called. We got here as soon as possible. He apologizes for not waiting the thirty minutes."

I was sorry he hadn't called them earlier. They might have rounded up the Klansmen and liberated Fred. I briefed them on the situation and realized that Sally was overdue. She must have heard the gunfire. No response? Unlike her.

"Lend me a flashlight. I have to go in after my wife. You might want to watch for the Klansmen and mama bear. You're in possession of all the weaponry, for the moment." Sally was going to get her pistol back, without, I hoped, shedding the blood of a federal agent.

Bernstein looked uncertain, then apparently decided that if she kept her eye on the mine entrance I couldn't slip off and further impede the course of justice.

30

My two prior trips into the mine hadn't allowed time or visibility to look around. Now I could see drawings that Bob's grandchildren had scratched into the walls, remnants of picnics and campfires, and a few toys. It made the death of his granddaughter more poignant, and the survival of my own children the more precious.

"Sa-a-a-a-lle-e-e-e." Nothing.

I continued to the fork where the original tunnel had gone left. There was light down that direction, coming from beyond where the box of baseball cards had been unearthed. "Sally?"

She came up the tunnel. "Bob doesn't want you to see, but I insisted." She led the way back down to where Bob, by the light of a hissing lantern, was digging furiously. The metal detector lay against the wall. A curious level of dedication, given the circumstances.

"Bob, what's the rush?"

Sally explained, "While Bob was waiting to be rescued he decided to conduct his own treasure hunt. The detector let out some significant chirps here."

"If something's down there," gasped Bob between shovelfuls, "I need to get it out before everyone and their dog is in here snooping around."

"Bob, that's nuts." People were being shot at; Fred was in deep trouble; a bear had mauled someone near his house; Bob himself had just been freed from entombment. He's treasure hunting? "Look. By staying in here after you've been freed you're going to attract the wrong kind of attention. There are two FBI agents out there. Do you want them to join you?"

That got his notice and he stopped digging and looked at the shallow hole in the mine floor. He may have been trying to decide if he should refill what he'd worked so hard to create.

"Okay. But not a word to anyone." Before leaving, he checked the site again with the detector. It did indicate metallic material in that area.

We left the mine and told the agents Bob's foot had been pinned under a fallen beam which delayed his exit. "I needed Max's help lifting the beam," explained Sally. Then we all rode back to Bob's and Brenda's house in the Fed's Suburban.

I think the twins were relieved to see us. Mainly, however, they wanted explanations for the explosion and gunfire they'd heard. And they were excited to host two actual G-men, a display of interest that Bernstein responded to with enthusiasm. She showed the twins her badge and gun, and, deepening her voice, described training at Quantico. This was interspersed with questions from the twins regarding entrance requirements, length and rigor of the training, career paths, and pay. I was impressed by the intelligence and practicality of the questions. Had the two pills abandoned treasure hunting and were contemplating careers in law enforcement? We'd read every *Nancy Drew* detective novel on the shelves.

Bernstein was midway through a story about a drug bust in Miami when Malkowitz politely interrupted to suggest the adults share information relevant to the current case. Bernstein's expression suggested she saw no value in a wider conversation; Sally and I couldn't know anything that a trained federal agent hadn't already intuited. She turned to her attentive audience of two and was about to resume.

"They're going to Pisgah Mountain in the morning." I announced quietly. Bernstein rolled her eyes toward the ceiling.

Sally was visibly annoyed at Bernstein's indifference. She'd retrieved the Beretta from Malkowitz. Had she put it away?

"Are you sure?" asked Malkowitz.

"I'm sure it's Fred's intention. He wrote 'Pisgah' in the dust on that tractor."

Bernstein's expression indicated actual interest in this news, but before she could speak the conversation was interrupted by the arrival of Dr. Levine and Skeeter. Levine had come to check on Rocky and to hand off Skeeter, who, I suspected, had morphed into a medical professional; he was probably trying to scrub in on surgeries. For whatever reason, the decision to keep him in the hospital overnight had been reconsidered.

After checking Rocky, Levine returned to the living room with Moondance. "I've made arrangements to move Mr. Snyder to a hospital in Atlanta. We'll check him in under a pseudonym. He's doing okay here, but this is less than ideal."

And an imposition on Brenda for whom the fun of hosting a cops-and-robbers/ER drama was ebbing.

"Can I get some help?" asked Levine.

"Now?" from a startled Moondance. "You're taking him right now?"

"The ambulance is outside. It looks like we have enough manpower to move him."

I, too, was unprepared for the sudden departure of Rocky and Moondance, but they'd be more secure 50 miles to the south registered in a hospital under different names. Levine didn't offer the name of the hospital; I assumed he'd decided to limit distribution of information on Rocky's whereabouts. Malkowitz and Bernstein didn't know yet that Moondance was wanted for the attempted murder of a policeman, but they soon would.

Levine departed – no siren this time – and we put the twins to bed in bunks that had been built for Bob's grandchildren. They resisted more than usual. There was still a lot more that they wanted to know about being a crime fighter.

"We'd better get going too," announced Bernstein. Malkowitz looked surprised. "We have to get back to Atlanta and then pick up tomorrow morning where we left off at Hartsfield airport."

I was surprised too. I'd assumed their presence meant that they were back on the job.

"Um, doesn't the attempt to drag an African American to death violate some federal statute?"

"I'm sure it does, Brown. We'll report that. But we're not free to pick our own cases. We'll have to be assigned."

Malkowitz added, "I intend to raise this forcefully with my boss in the morning. She's not an unreasonable person," he glanced at Bernstein, "and I hope we can join up with local law enforcement in Blue Ridge by mid-morning. Pisgah Mountain's the destination."

Bernstein clearly didn't share Malkowitz's enthusiasm to return to north Georgia, but kept quiet for a refreshing change.

"Don't you need to update the locals about what happened this evening?"

"We do, Mr. Brown. I'll call in to the Union County Sheriff's office before we leave. I'm guessing that taping up Karl and dumping him in a ditch will dispel any doubts about where the Knights' loyalties lie. But I see by your expression that you have a concern?"

"Well, yes. Do you want to give them information that might be passed on to the Klansmen?"

This brought an indulgent smile. "Of course not. I don't plan on telling them we're going to Pisgah Mountain until we meet face-to-face tomorrow and are prepared to head out."

He asked to use the phone and called the Union County Sheriff. After inquiring about the well-being of Karl, he told the Sheriff about the return of Boon and Billy to Three Sisters, the bear attack on Cletis, the attempt to seal Bob in the mine, and the Klansmen's departure in Karl's car with Fred and the injured or dead Cletis.

After some questions and clarifications, the agent asked, "Could you let me know if any of the medical facilities treat a man who's been mauled by a bear?"

. . .

"Thanks. If we're able to get approval, we'll be up there by mid-morning."

Sally winked at me. What was that for? I'd heard nothing entertaining or ironic in Malkowitz's telephone conversation with the sheriff.

As the agents prepared to leave, Bernstein – who'd looked like she'd been holding it in – spun toward me. "I hope you see what your meddling accomplishes. You could have killed a federal agent tonight – something Agent Malkowitz seems willing to overlook. You certainly could have been killed by our return fire. Even the dumbest person should be able to figure this out." Her face was getting red. "Butt the fuck out! If I see you up on Pisgah tomorrow I won't wait for you to shoot first. Capisce?"

Malkowitz placed his hand gently on her arm. "Message delivered, Bernstein. Let's go get some shuteye." Did the training at Quantico include how to handle a nut-job partner?

"Let's do the same, Max. The guest room is ours again." Sally pulled on my arm. I felt our departure was a little abrupt; Bob and Brenda were still perched on the sofa, and Shawn and Skeeter had each just cracked open another beer.

No sooner were we through the door than Sally slammed it shut behind us and had her mouth on my ear. "I am soooo hot for you, Studly." I couldn't believe my good fortune. "I know it's terrible and anti-feminist and everything, but, God, what a *man* you are!" More mouth on ear, tongue exploring it as she worked to release my belt buckle. I helped her.

Are you expecting an explicit description of jungle sex? Forget it. This is where the narrative goes PG; it's tacky to brag about one's sexual prowess. There'll be no quantitative data on duration, number of orgasms, new positions tried, and similar details of which modesty forbids disclosure. But, I was pretty damned good. No, I was better than 'pretty good.' The day's events had brought my libido back with a roar. Plus Sally's ministrations.

––––––––––

The best night's sleep we'd had in a long time. When we awoke the Georgia sun was pouring through the window. I turned toward Sally, wondering if we might squeeze in one more quick encounter. Big answering smile.

These plans were interrupted by a tap on the door. It was just like the twins to come calling at an inopportune time. I opened the door and found Grandpa Bob smiling sheepishly and wringing his bony hands. Perhaps there to announce breakfast?

"Sorry to disturb you, Max, but we can't find the two little girls. Skeeter seems to be gone too. It looks like they must have left early in Mr. Snyder's truck."

From M&M's *Guide to Treasure*

Treasure in Red Bone Cave
How much? Many bars of gold.

What is it? Way back 300 years ago the Spanish
people dug up gold and also took it away from the
Indians. They were carrying this gold to the sea to
put on ships but stopped for the winter and stayed
with some Chickasaw Indians. When the Spanish
were leaving they demanded 100 Indian women to go
with them. The Indians were furious and killed the
Spanish. Then they hid the gold in a cave.

Where is it? Near the Tennessee River where there
are cliffs made of limestone.

Proof it exists. 80 years later a trapper made friends
with the Chickasaw and they finally showed him the
huge treasure, but they blindfolded him so he didn't
know exactly where it was. He and his friends spent
many years trying to find it.

31

"I'm a terrible mother." That's Sally, sitting on the edge of the bed, shoulders slumped. "My first thought was, 'whatever happens to them, they deserve'."

That was close to my own reaction. Back in the nest for a little over twelve hours, and they were already off and in trouble again.

"I'm pissed at them too, babe. I'd tan their little hides if I could get my hands on them right now." Strong language. I'd never raised a hand to either of them, despite years of provocation.

Brenda had been awake when the three adventurers departed so she fixed them a quick breakfast of scrambled eggs and made tuna salad sandwiches to carry for lunch. It never seems to occur to anyone – other than their battle-wise parents – that those two are up to no good.

"Did they say anything about their plans, Brenda?"

"Not that I recall. I think they went back to Bob's tool shed before they left."

Bob went to check his shed and returned to report that the shovels and a pickaxe were missing. This was good news. Our greatest fear had been that they'd switched careers and had charged off to bring the goobers to justice. On the evidence of the digging implements taken they were still treasure hunters.

"Here's something strange." That's Shawn's voice coming through the house, a voice rarely heard at that hour of the morning. "I'm sure I put the two rifles on the porch. They're gone."

Both rifles? This was bad news. The little hoodlums were following dual careers: they were after booty *and* bad guys.

"Breakfast's served," announced Brenda, who still hadn't grasped the gravity of the situation.

We forced scrambled egg into our faces, grabbed two slices of bacon apiece and found Shawn frantically getting dressed.

"No." I said.

"I haven't asked anything," Shawn protested.

"Still no. I'm not taking a Black man, who's wanted by the police, into solid white north Georgia. You'd be a hazard to yourself and to us." Shawn started to say something and I continued. "You do remember what they did to you yesterday? Your eye still isn't fully open." Had Shawn forgotten that he'd come close to being dragged to death? "They may have restocked with duct tape – and rope."

"I've got payback in mind. You owe me that."

"Wrong mission. Sally and I are going after the girls, not the goobers. The girls aren't with the goobers – at least not yet. We hope we find the kids scratching around in the dirt next door in the Three Sisters mine."

"And if you don't?"

"Okay, then we cover the worst case; we go up to Pisgah Mountain. Without you. However, there is something you can do." Shawn curled the corner of his lips. He'd had enough of the minor support roles. "We have mobility problems. Could you contact your employer and have someone replace the tires on the rental SUV?"

"Do I have a choice?" A rhetorical question that we left unanswered. There was little doubt that once the SUV was back in service Shawn would be on his way to Pisgah Mountain.

Bob reluctantly lent us his Toyota Corolla. We left a sulking Shawn on the porch, his hands on his hips, and drove up the access road to the mine. The sedan couldn't negotiate the deep ruts and Sally and I walked the last two hundred yards to the parking area. No sign of Rocky's truck.

"I was so sure they'd be here, Max. Yesterday it seemed the Klansmen had detected something under the mine floor and were digging. I just assumed the twins would follow up on that."

"My thoughts, too. Should we go up to the mine and check just to be sure?"

"I'd rather not. I'm more worried about falling further behind them."

We returned to the car and drove toward Blue Ridge. Sally was studying our now well-creased topographical map for the fastest route to Pisgah Mountain. "Two options. We can park on the east side of the mountain and hike four thousand feet to the mine. Or we can take a long route around to the north, come up a Forest Service road, and park about two thousand feet away from the mine on the west side of the mountain. The contour lines make it look like the slope is about the same on both sides. The map provides no information on snake density."

Which way would Skeeter go? He might try to keep the hiking to a minimum, given his short-legged fellow travelers.

"Let's go around to the side with the shortest hike. The kids are not great hikers and at least one of them will be toting a rifle." I was immediately sorry I'd mentioned the rifle.

The weather, which had been unseasonably dry and pleasant since our arrival in the country, looked like it was going to take a turn. As we crested a hill a wall of dark clouds could be seen to the west. Looking for the silver lining, I hoped that rain would drive the intrepid little explorers back to the truck.

Progress over the rutted roads was slow and it was almost midday before we parked at the end of the Forest Service road. No sign of Rocky's truck.

Sally insisted I check my pistol. It was loaded. On safety. No visible impediments lodged in the barrel. Should I be flattered that she thought these checks were important and I might apply the gun to some useful purpose?

There was no path into the forest, and that's the way the USFS wants it. It emphatically prohibits the public from creating paths through the national forests and seems to frown on the public's use of public lands in general.

There was a deer trail that tended in an easterly direction. We counted ourselves lucky to find it, but here's the difference: a deer can vault over a four-foot obstacle, like a fallen tree, and do it again and again. We bipeds are left searching for the least painful route around the obstacles. It was slow slogging.

Occasionally a break in the trees would grant a glimpse of the peak of Pisgah Mountain and we would correct our course.

We were zigzagging back and forth as we approached what we hoped was the mine. This one had been abandoned for over one hundred years. No road in, no markers, and, according to Fred, a well plugged entrance. He thought dynamite would be needed to open it. Had the Klansmen restocked?

After 30 minutes we stopped, found a large log to sit on and each ate half a sandwich and finished our water. In the far distance thunder could be heard. In the hope that we were getting close to the mine, we spoke in hushed voices as we ate so as not to announce ourselves to the competition.

'Hushed voices' until Sally let out a forest rattling shriek and leapt into the air. A copperhead slithered away.

"I almost forgot about them. It didn't strike you, did it babe?"

"Holy shit! That wasn't two feet away!"

"They do blend in. I guess we need to watch our feet more than the horizon. If it's any comfort, I understand that the bite is almost never lethal." Sally scowled. My expression of concern hadn't risen to the level of her recent scare.

"Let's take a little detour to the north. The going looks faster. Boon and Billy could have heard that yell and may be coming to investigate."

The easy going toward the north lasted only fifty yards and then the forest took over again. We plunged in, trying to keep the noise down. We hadn't gone a hundred yards when Sally grabbed my arm. I jumped. She put a finger to her lips and cocked her head. I could hear nothing but the freshening wind in the trees. Had she picked up the girls' voices?

I hoped she saw my impaired hearing as a badge of honor – along the lines of a dueling scar – and not another sign of impending dodderhood. "Can you make out who it is?"

"Mountain twang. Could be Billy and Boon. Not our FBI buddies." And not the girls.

"Trail me by ten to twenty yards, babe. If the goobers jump me, you can pull off one of your patented rescues." She was good at that, when she was conscious.

After a few minutes of quietly moving branches out of the way and circumnavigating spiky looking bushes, we came to a wall of felled timber, ranging from five to seven feet in height. Sally caught up as I surveyed the obstacle.

"Looks like a small tornado came down through here and piled up timber along its path." Beyond the wall, there was a twenty-yard-wide cleared alley running along the mountainside, populated by short tree stumps. On the far side of the cleared area there was another barrier of scattered timber, lower than the one in front of us.

Thunder boomed; the storm was closing fast.

"There you go, Max. The thunder God will provide sound cover for us . . ." She hadn't finished the sentence when a streak of lightening jumped from cloud to cloud across the sky. We were ready when the thunder started to roll and both grabbed the topmost branch in front of us and pulled. We removed a second branch before the thunder subsided. The barrier was down to three feet in height, but would be noisy to cross.

The storm cooperated. The next lightning flash preceded the thunder by only a few seconds, but I reacted immediately and was able to scramble over the barrier and sprint to the far side of the cleared area, where I crouched. Sally hadn't followed. Feeling exposed, I took the pistol out of my pocket. That only increased my apprehension. At some point I have to learn how to use these things.

Another lightning strike, accompanied by the first large drops of rain, and Sally vaulted the barrier of timber and ran across the clearing. A smaller strike followed and we took advantage of it to clear the second fence of timber and pushed into the foliage toward the mine. Now I could make out the voices.

"Get movin' there, Freddie boy. I shore would like to be warm and dry in that mine." Fred's response was unintelligible.

"Boon?" Billy speaking. "Maybe we could risk using some of that dynamite. What with the thunder and all."

The wind continued to come up; the rustling of branches masked the sounds Sally and I were making and we moved more quickly toward the sound of voices. We halted when Boon shouted, "Ever'body back." Less than ten seconds later there was an ear-splitting explosion and the ground shook beneath our feet. Boon had gone back to doubling the charge.

"Shee-it, Boon. All you done was brought more of the mountain down across the entrance." No answer from Boon, but a minute later a smaller explosion signaled that he'd switched to a more surgical approach.

Sally had taken the lead and was creeping steadily forward. I knew what she was thinking. Are her children here? Abruptly we could see the clearing in front of the abandoned mine. Boon was rooting around in a box, Billy was cradling his rifle, and Fred was slumped against a tree. Fred had been hobbled, a tangle of ropes and tape tying his legs so he could take only short steps. He wouldn't be making a break for it.

No sign of the twins. Boon selected a stick of dynamite and with exaggerated care wedged it into the rubble across the plugged entrance. Another warning shout, another small blast, and another unsatisfactory result.

"She-it, Boon. I'm guessing you wasn't in demolition or nothin' like that in 'Nam." Boon responded with a grunt and returned to the box.

This looked like a satisfactory situation. No twins, Boon and Billy occupied with their fireworks, and law enforcement on the way. A perfect time to withdraw. Crouching, I stepped back slowly. I did so alone. Sally jumped to her feet, "Freeze, ass-wipes!" and she fired into the ground at Billy's feet.

Ah, Sally. What a bad move! All we had to do was slip away, bide our time and wait for reinforcements. I should have seen this coming. There, in front of her, were the two men who'd planned to bury her daughters alive. Sally Taylor-Brown couldn't do anything else.

Something moved under my right foot. Before the significance of this could be processed, the pain in my left ankle eclipsed other thought. A four-foot-long copperhead was attached, to my leg just above the top of the running shoe.

I tried to stamp on the snake with my right foot, but the left leg was already unreliable and I toppled over onto the branches and leaves. The copperhead disengaged from my ankle and turned toward my face. We were at eye level.

32

A shot, and leaves and branches erupted by my side. Sally had shot the thing.

No. She'd missed.

Another shot. The snake continued its untroubled stare at me – no show of concern. Sally Taylor-Brown had missed twice? Unbelievable. The snake's tongue flicked and it started to weave its way toward my head. Venom in the neck might be fatal. I tried to squirm away but couldn't get a purchase on the wet leaves and small branches. The snake was gaining ground.

A third shot and the creature twisted in the air and fell on its back.

A fourth, more distant, shot and Sally fell on me.

She saw my panicked expression. "I don't think I'm hit. I took a dive, but check me over."

No sign of blood, but I couldn't see all of her. She rose to a kneeling position and trained her pistol on the clearing in front of the mine. There was no one there.

"Drop it, lady. We got you surrounded."

Boon and Billy had taken advantage of the distraction caused by the snake and were each ten yards from us on opposite sides. Sally might get off a shot at one of them, but not both.

"I'm gonna count to one, and then I'm gonna put a bullet through that red head." Sally dropped her pistol.

"Now let's have you two lovebirds get up off the ground. Hate to interrupt yer tryst, but we got a mine to open."

Sally helped me up; I leaned heavily on her.

"What's this here?" Billy squinted at me, then saw the dead snake, writhing slowly in the leaves; he recoiled. "Damn. I think Euro-trash got hisself bit by an American copperhead."

Another flash and simultaneous crash of thunder made us all jump. This signaled the start of heavy rain. The advantage tilted further to Boon and Billy whose faces were protected by their caps. Sally and I tried to shield our eyes against the downpour.

Sally inclined her head and whispered, "I don't see Fred." Boon must have noticed my head movement in the direction of the clearing as he looked too.

"Ah shit, Billy. Fred's took off. See if you can run him down." Billy started, reluctantly, in the direction of the clearing, giving the snake a parting glance.

We were down to one adversary. Where was my pistol? Still in my right hand. I'd fallen on it when the snake struck and I'd been oblivious to it since. If I could pass it to Sally she could take out Boon.

My left arm was around her shoulder for support. I reached across my back with my right hand and prodded Sally with the barrel of the gun. She shot me a look of annoyance; I was, I realized, goosing her. I prodded her higher in the back and her expression changed from indignation to recognition, but she made no move to take the gun. Was I supposed to do this myself? A test? Max Brown: backwoods hero, staring down bears, disabling goobers, getting off deadly shots as he toppled to the ground. Would there be another amorous reward at the end of the day? I poked her with the gun again. No response from Sally.

Boon responded. Alerted by the movements of my shoulder, he walked behind us and, without ceremony, took the pistol from my hand. How many opportunities could we afford to squander?

"Thankee very much. Should of thought of that before. Now, why would you two lovebirds be up here? Nature hike? We see assholes up here alla time from Hotlanta, traipsing through the woods, scaring game, singing coom-fuckin'-by-ya." He chuckled. Here was a man who was easily amused and whose own wit reached the standard required. He backed away and examined my pistol. Pursing his lips, "Here's an idea. I'm just thinkin' out loud, mind. Yer lookin' for them two kids. They get away again?"

I detected movement in the direction of the mine; something was tumbling through the air. It was intercepted by a sturdy pine and fell to the ground where it exploded, sending up a shower of dirt and leaves.

"What the fuck was that there?"

It seemed pretty obvious. Fred, when he escaped, had taken the dynamite. Did he understand that dynamite is an indiscriminant weapon? We needed to get separation from Boon. Boon also understood how it worked; he pocketed my pistol and moved closer to us.

"Well, well. I didn't think Fred had it in him. I figgered he'd be halfway back to Blairsville by now. We don't need to worry none. Fred throws like a girl." Boon liked this and chuckled again. He wasn't worried about Fred the bomb thrower.

"But I tell ya' Euro-trash, seems like a father what can't keep his children from runnin' away shouldn't be allowed to have children. That the way they do it where you come from?"

Sally spoke up. "Why do you keep calling my husband Euro-trash. He's an American. He served in Vietnam." Did she assume a strong bond among Vietnam vets? I didn't.

Boon snorted and spat. The 'Nam card having been played, I followed up. "What was your service, Boon. I'll bet you were Navy. Sitting out there in the Tonkin Gulf. Sleeping in a dry bed every night. Three hot meals a day. Never heard a shot fired in anger."

He spat again. "Infantry. I heard plenty of angry shots and I fired most of 'em myself." This was followed by a long silence. His mood had gone from belligerent to reflective; he pulled out my pistol and examined it again.

"Well," continued Sally, "Max was Air Force. Over half the pilots in his squadron were killed or captured."

"Musta been piss poor pilots, that's for sure."

I snapped. The fever from the bite? "Fuck you, Boon! They were excellent pilots who were handed the lousiest job in the war. We got shot to shit and the next day we'd go back out to the planes and fly those same goddamn missions. I don't need to hear any crap from a ground-pounder who should know better."

I could see the alarm on Sally's face. Boon would take this out on us.

Surprise. Boon looked at the ground, the disdain on his face turning into an expression we hadn't seen before.

"Ah man, I shouldna said that." He really was apologizing. "Ever'thing about that whole war makes me say and do shit." More silence. "We coulda won if the pencil-dicks in Washington woulda let us." He looked at the pistol again. After another long minute, "You know they got people down at that Atlanta airport who stand where passengers come out and they clap ever'time someone comes out wearin' a uniform. Nobody never clapped for me. I got cussed at. Hippies was shakin' their fists. Couldn't get a decent job. My own mother seemed to go sour on me."

Boon was withdrawn, lost in his thoughts. I wasn't the one to take advantage of his inattention, wrapped up in my own memories of the open loathing I'd encountered when I returned from Vietnam. An explosion on the far side of the clearing brought us back to the present. This was followed a minute later by Billy, racing across the clearing and vaulting over the fallen trees.

"She-it, Boon. Fred's throwing dynamite at me." He pulled up short as he caught sight of the twitching snake.

"Calm down, Billy. As long as we keep these folks close to us he won't take no chances blowing them up too. But he might set off the alarm. We'd best be movin' back to the van. That mine ain't goin' nowhere."

"That's fine by me. But what we gonna do with these two when we get there? I'll tell you straight out, Boon. I ain't for just killin' 'em."

"Nah, I ain't neither, Billy. This one here was in 'Nam. That's enough for me to let him live. We'll tie 'em up and let someone find 'em later. With the snake bite prob'ly don't even need that."

"There ain't no tape. Fred took the box."

Boon considered this.

"Well . . . if a snake bite's enough to stop one of 'em, should be enough to stop 'em both. We'll just bring that copperhead with us, and then milk a little of that venom into Red here." He grinned. "Where should we inject that poison, Billy?" The grin turned into a leer.

You couldn't sustain positive thoughts about Boon for long.

"I ain't touching the thing."

"No need. Red, pick up that dead snake and bring it along." He pointed his rifle at Sally's mid-section.

Without hesitation she reached down and grabbed the twitching snake. I wish I had her balls. Much as I needed to lean on her for support, I hoped she'd keep the slowly writhing creature on her far side.

"Now let's get a move on. Finding you two up here makes me think they might be others."

We moved out, the rain abating and the thunder retreating to the east. The pain had arrived at my hip. I tried to focus on something other than the throbbing running through my left leg.

"C'mon there, flyboy. Yer slowin' up progress."

I was. I couldn't lift my left leg over even the lowest obstacles; Sally would have to pick up the leg and place it on the far side of every branch or log. Our pace was too slow for the Klansmen.

"We got us a dilemma, Billy. I feel we need to clear out of here right now but gimpy there, he's a regular pimple on the ass of progress."

"We ain't killin' him, Boon."

"Nah, we're leavin' him, though. Don't look like he'll get far on his own. If we keep Red close to us, Fred won't throw no dynamite and then when we don't need her anymore we'll dose her with some of that snake venom. Might be good to squirt some in both legs so she stays put."

"How 'bout where her legs come together? More efficient, doncha think?" They both laughed at this.

"I'm all for efficiency, Billy." They laughed some more. "Okay, Red. Say goodbye to yer flyboy. He's staying here. If ever'one behaves you might be together again pretty soon."

Sally's response was to grip me more firmly around the waist.

"Do what they say, babe. Just a little further and let me down on that log by those small branches."

She looked uncertain, but helped me along another ten yards and then eased me down next to a pile of promising looking branches. I was already checking them to see if one might be converted to a crutch. It occurred to me to also check for the presence of snakes.

"Ta-ta, flyboy. Yer lucky Billy here's a softy. I personally keep goin' back and forth. You was in 'Nam, so you live. You shot Len, so you die. Tough call." This was said over Boon's shoulder as the three headed eastward, Boon leading, Billy trailing, watching the snake. It looked like Sally was stepping on and breaking down small branches along the way to smooth out the rough path.

As soon as Boon and Billy had turned their attention to working through the forest, I started picking up and discarding branches. The best candidate had a decent fork for my armpit, but was a little long. Hoisting myself up on it, I immediately lost my balance and fell. The second attempt was successful, but the excess length of the branch meant the improvised crutch was angled out 30 degrees from my body. The thought of the Klansmen attaching that snake to any part of Sally's body was strong motivation to keep moving, although my left leg was of little use and I almost fell on several occasions, catching myself on a small tree or bush. Every near-fall was accompanied by panic that I'd land on a nest of copperheads. Or —this must have been fever from the bite – where was that rogue bear? Thirty miles to the south last night. How fast can a bear travel? *Forget the bear.* I had to pick up the pace if I was going to help Sally.

There was movement in the bushes to the right of the path. A large animal was approaching.

From M&M's *Guide to Treasure*

The Bear's Silver Mine
How Much? We can't find out.

What is it? A boy named Mundy was with trappers
in 1752. They wounded a bear that went into a cave
and Mundy was sent to pull out the bear because he
was the smallest. In the cave Mundy saw the silver
in the walls. Then he was captured twice by Indians
and finally became partners with a rich man named
Swift. Mundy showed him the bear's cave and the
two of them dug out a lot of silver. Because there
was so much they hid a lot of silver ingots. Swift
visited England but said some things about America
that the English didn't like so they put him in jail
for 15 years. When he got back to America he
learned that Mundy had disappeared while looking
for the mine. Swift was almost blind and couldn't
find it.

Where is it? In eastern Kentucky in Floyd county.

Proof it exists. Swift and Mundy became rich so
everyone believes it was from the silver.

33

"Jesus, Max, what happened to you?" The large animal was a disheveled forest ranger, dynamite sticks bulging out of his pockets.

"Snakebite. Hurts like a mother. You don't look so well either, Fred. Injured?"

"No. Dehydrated, hungry. Boon wouldn't let me have any food or water from the time they jumped me in my office last night. I collected a little water from that rain shower just now. It's helping."

"They have Sally; they plan to inject copperhead venom in her when they reach their car."

"I'm not surprised. Real sweethearts, aren't they?"

I nodded and tried to lurch forward.

"With all due respect, Max, I don't think you're going to move fast enough to be much help. I probably know these woods better than those guys. Maybe I can get ahead of them."

Without waiting for consent or comment, he was off, angling uphill toward, I assumed, a faster route to the parking area.

More lurches. Why was I bothering? Because I had to.

All my life I've been plagued by sick thoughts of the people close to me being harmed. I've learned to turn those thoughts off. Now I turned them on. I pictured Boon trying to stick the snake's fangs into Sally's crotch. The image sustained me for fifty painful yards. Then, with misgivings, I replayed the same tape, this time with Sally's pants removed. That image was too much and almost stopped me. Then I thought of the twins. They could show up at the wrong time and get the snakebite immobilization treatment. Their small bodies couldn't tolerate much venom. That fired more forward progress. I thought about my parents being killed by a backwoods loser, much like Boon and Billy; I thought about a decent cop in Holland who'd been tortured to death; I thought about my graduate assistant in Bangladesh who was skinned alive. I thought about every sick and evil thing I could dredge up in order to not think about the searing pain that had made its way into my left side.

Were these distractions working? How much ground had I covered? Looking back, I could no longer see the place where I'd fashioned the crutch. I struggled forward along the path of broken twigs and branches Sally had made. Still, I was moving at a fraction of the speed of Sally and the Klansmen.

Something was happening to my head. I wanted the rogue bear to appear. I'd mount her and we'd go crashing through the brush after the goobers. The small part of my brain that was still lucid shouted, *it's the venom, Max.* Of course it was. A snake-bite victim is supposed to remain calm and still. Exertion speeds circulation of the poison through the body. Still, I was making a heroic effort. Would this win another night of torrid passion? Maybe that was a positive sign: the part of my brain that thought about sex was still functioning. But something needed to happen to change the equation. I was falling behind and the Klansmen would soon be doing something horrific to Sally.

Distracted by these thoughts, my right – good – foot caught on a branch and I pitched forward. As I hit the ground, a two-part explosion ripped through the forest. I know that explosion:

Part 1: Dynamite.

Part 2: Gas tank.

Fred had beaten Boon and Billy back to their van and foiled their getaway. Back on my feet – foot – I moved more quickly. A little good news – a shift in the odds – can do a lot to revive one's spirits. I was getting the hang of using the crutch and put a handkerchief over the crook to cushion the pressure on my armpit. *Good old Fred. I definitely will not cheat on my taxes this year.*

A break in the trees and a distant ball of black smoke climbed into the sky: the Klansmen's van, giving up the ghost.

I continued, falling repeatedly. Progress was maddeningly slow. This would be a good time for me to show up at the parking area and lend a hand – while the Klansmen were regrouping. But how would they react to the destruction of their ride? More dark thoughts: they'd take it out on Sally. *Move it, Max. I* started fantasizing about riding to the rescue on the bear again. The pain had continued up my left side and my arm was becoming too weak to control the crutch. Five thousand bears in these woods and you can't find a single goddamned one when you need to hitch a lift? My vision was going dark and I felt I was falling slowly through space.

"Man, you really missed something, Max." Fred's eyes were shining with excitement. "You tell him, Sally; it's your story."

I could see Fred's face – viewed from below because he was carrying the top half of me; Sally had my legs around her waist and was leading us through the forest. That arrangement, legs around her waist, brought back memories of the previous night. Waking thoughts of sex? That surprises even me.

"Thank God you're conscious." Sally turned her head to give me a concerned look. "Is the way we're carrying you painful?" She didn't slow her pace as she asked. I gathered if my answer was yes, there weren't good options.

"What's happening? Where are we?" My voice sounded distant and slurred, but Sally's perfect rump was near and comforting.

"We can put you down if you need a break, Max. Your wife immobilized Billy and Boon, but we can't leave them on their own for long." We bounced along in silence. Fred, carrying the greater part of my weight, was tiring and stumbled a few times.

"How much farther do we have to go? Maybe I can walk with my crutch." The crutch was nowhere around and I realized it was an empty offer; my entire left side was unresponsive and the lack of sensation was creeping into my right leg.

"Maybe another two hundred yards," answered Fred. The smell of burning fuel supported that.

I looked up at the green canopy above. I was on Mama Bear, my legs tight around her.

"Say something, Max, please." Sally's tear-stained face was swimming above me. "Fred, his eyes are open. Isn't there any-thing we can do to stop the venom?"

Fred's face swam into view. "Right now this is the best thing. The exertion of following us was the worst for him. Let's just keep him quiet. Someone has to have heard the explosions and will want to take a look."

The world was coming into focus. To my right a blackened van was on its side, windows gone, interior burned. Boon and Billy were tied together at the ankle by the dead copperhead. Probably not a strong medium, but they seemed quiet, almost in a stupor. I looked questioningly at Sally.

"Fred gets all the credit." She obviously wasn't sincere about that; she was wearing the same self-satisfied grin I'd seen in Paris after she disabled a rent-a-thug. "When he lit up the woods with the dynamite, Boon was approaching the van and the blast blew him backwards. Billy was a few steps behind me so I turned and threw the snake at him. I think the head, maybe even the fangs, hit his face and he went over backwards. So I took his gun – and Boon's too since he was flat on his back, and that was it."

"You're leaving out the best part," protested Fred. "Tell him about the snake."

"Let me guess," I offered. "You did to them what they planned for you."

"Yes, but not in the goolies. Ankle bites." Pity. "Boon was easy since he was dazed. Billy put up a fuss until I hit him in the head with the rifle butt." The bruise on Billy's temple was clearly visible. "If they get too active I'll top them up with a booster dose."

Both Klansmen lay still.

"I'm going to signal for help," announced Fred, and he walked down the Forest Service road. A minute later he came sprinting back toward us. "Cover your ears!"

We did, just in time. The ground shook and dust billowed into the sky. When the reverberations stopped Fred looked at us with an expression of satisfaction. "Last three sticks. If no one hears that, they're deaf."

I was feeling groggy again. Is this the way it works? The venom lets you tune in and out? I was obviously tuning out; the last image was Sally's alarmed expression. I think I dreamed about her. Nothing saucy, fortunately, as this untimely and persistent resurgence of libido was unsettling. I always thought I had a normal, healthy interest in sex, but, under any circumstances?

I tuned back in and reached for her beautiful face, stroking her cheek tenderly. "Sweet darling."

"You fucking perv!" Not Sally. Agent Bernstein. My hand had moved on from her face and had settled on her breast. Bernstein sprang back and seemed to be reaching for her gun. What a nut-job.

"Mistaken identity, Bernstein." Sally's voice.

I was disinclined to apologize. "Nice you could make it Agent. Not too tiring a trip, I hope?" This brought sputtering from Bernstein. As always, Malkowitz was the one to talk to.

"You've taken a beating, Mr. Brown, but Fred here assures me that the swelling in your leg will subside over a few days although the effects may linger for a month or more."

"It seems to be a banner day for the copperheads. The two Klansmen were also bitten. They're pretty much out of it. For some reason the snakes gave them a larger shot of venom than you received." Funny thing, that. "I'm guessing your wife shot a snake and then improvised to keep the Klansmen from escaping while waiting for help?"

Neither Sally nor I answered his question. Everything we'd done to protect ourselves up to that point was being used against us. Would Sally's MO be described in court as a sadistic and inhumane attack on two Samaritans who were motivated by only the purest intentions?

"Speaking of help, Agent, what the fuck took you two so long? And where're the County Mounties?" Maybe not a good idea to start berating our rescuers, but, hey, where had they been all day?

"A complicated and tedious story, Mr. Brown. It took us some time to get clear of our assignments in Atlanta and when we got to Blue Ridge we ran into a wall of resistance. That Deputy, Karl, finally showed up and talked sense into the Fannin County people. We were so sick of dealing with them we divided forces. They went to the western side of the mountain, the side you came in on I understand. I expect they'll emerge from the forest fairly soon. They must have heard Ranger Jones' summons."

"We're not waiting for them, I hope. I think I should get to a hospital. Maybe get some anti-venom."

"Your decision to make. One of the complications we ran into was the allegation that your crimes eclipse those of the two cretins over there. Trying to kill a cop, helping the would-be assassin, shooting an unarmed man, breaking the windpipe of another, disabling a sheriff's car – pretty good chargesheet. They may have come up with even more since we last spoke. I gather Mrs. Brown will be locked up instantly, and you as well as soon as you leave the hospital. There are also allegations that your daughters attempted to kill four men."

Will it never fucking end?

Sally joined us; she'd been warily eyeing her captives. "You don't believe any of that bullshit, do you?"

Bernstein was willing to buy into it and started to blurt something as Malkowitz held up his hand. "Of course not, Mrs. Brown. Part of our delay was due to time spent on the phone, checking out these claims. They're looking like fabrications to cover an attempt to silence Rocco Snyder. What is undeniable, however, is that this is hostile territory for the Brown family. What I'd like to do is get you down to Atlanta, if you can make the trip. Our people there will know how to process you through a quick arraignment. You can post bond, although I'm afraid you won't be returning to your home in Switzerland for some time."

"How about some medical attention? I feel I've earned it."

"Of course. I was wondering if a Dr. Levine, with whom we spoke, might meet us somewhere. Perhaps at the home of those retirees from Florida. I assume that's where your children are."

How could I have forgotten the children? Sally's expression betrayed her own guilty realization. Our babies weren't on Pisgah. Where were they?

34

The little shits were at Bob and Brenda's house. They were on the porch with Skeeter who was teaching them how to shoot a rifle that was as long as they were tall. When we pulled up in the feds' Suburban, Mary was massaging her shoulder and warning Margaret of the gun's kick.

"Daddy! Mommy! We were so worried about you. Are you okay?"

Aren't they good? They ran toward the car, arms out-stretched . . . and skidded to a stop when I was helped from the car, ankle visibly swollen, a pastiche of black, green and purpling flesh. I think there was a moment of genuine concern for dear old dad. Then they looked at each other excitedly; their treasure-hunting story was getting new, dramatic chapters.

Sally was not happy. "Where were you two today?" Another exchange of looks.

Skeeter answered. "We went back up to the Three Sisters mine first thing this morning. It was my idea." If only we could believe that. "Didn't anyone tell you?"

"We looked for you there."

"We were probably in the mine . . . oh, you didn't see Rocky's truck. I parked it in that shady hidden area. Seemed the smart thing to do since the ignition lock's busted."

Sally and I looked at each other helplessly. We'd abandoned the search too quickly. The result? A very bad day, numerous brushes with death, and a mighty dose of snake venom working its way through my body.

Before Sally could resume her interrogation of the twins, Shawn appeared, scowling. "So, what'd I miss this time?"

"Snakes and goobers, Shawn. And it was pretty much for nothing. The little stinkers were here."

Shawn wasn't mollified. His rental car company had been occupied dealing with the damage to their office in Dahlonega and had little time or interest in replacing four tires somewhere north of town. Shawn had spent the day pacing the porch.

We got a better reception from Bob and Brenda. Bob remained thrilled to be part of a drama of this magnitude – and to get his car back since he'd been trapped in the house all day; he wanted to resume digging in the mine.

Brenda was coming around. She had news to report. "KLM called twice today to remind you of your reservations for tonight. They also wanted to find out if the police release thing had been taken care of. I think they want to know if they can give your seats to someone else."

Bernstein snorted. "Looks like some lucky Dutchman is going to get on board." Malkowitz again wore the expression of someone who'd slipped into another dimension.

Dr. Levine showed up – I was losing track of time. He spent two minutes examining me and ten minutes explaining that toxicology was a specialization to which he made no claims. He would – in the current emergency – offer opinions and treatment, but could not be held accountable for the outcome, and that I would be well advised to seek out a specialist. Despite these extensive caveats, he had brought antivenom and an industrial-strength antihistamine that had the dual effect of reducing the throbbing in my afflicted left side and making me even drowsier.

Levine was more generous with his time with the FBI agents, describing Rocky's extraction at the hospital in detail. Bernstein played devil's advocate throughout. "So, no one actually witnessed the cop trying to kill Snyder? . . . You did see this Moondance person trying to strangle the police officer, right doctor? . . . I understand you were involved in bringing a banned firearm into the hospital." And so on.

Sally led me to the guestroom to lie down. More reward sex? Why not. I'd put up a game fight all day. Then I glanced at my ankle. Revolting. Reading my mind, she explained, "Not today, tiger. I brought you in here because Malkowitz wants a private word." She left and the FBI agent entered a minute later.

"This whole thing is spinning wildly out of control. It looks like local law enforcement – a term I use loosely – is rallying around a bad cop in Dahlonega. From what I overheard, they've put a hold on your travel? I guess that's consistent." He looked at my exposed ankle and shook his head. "This may be a badge-loser, but I think everyone would be better off if the Browns went home."

"What about Shawn?"

"If we can line up interested people – maybe the minister of a large church, the ACLU – we can make him this year's poster child for overt racism. Deputy Karl is on record that he found him bound up in duct tape and tied to the bumper of a vehicle. His demolished car is another angle. Our forensics people should be able to identify that dynamite as the same that the Klansmen bought in Dawsonville. In short, the kid could become a minor celebrity . . . if we can get our ducks in a row. His problem will be financial support while this is going on. He'd be wise to stay out of sight, when he isn't in court. That means no job."

"I can help with that. I already owe him for his car – the part not covered by insurance. I'll write a bigger check."

How much bigger? Time to start working on a budget.

"That would be very generous, Mr. Brown. Now, can you get your family packed up and ready to go? I have to figure out a way to do this, but as far as you're supposed to know, you're all going to Atlanta to be booked."

Bob had lent me a cane and I followed Malkowitz back to the porch. "Okay team, pack up. We're saying goodbye to our lovely hosts."

This announcement was met by exclamations of dismay from all sides – except, of course, Bernstein. Even Brenda looked disappointed. I suspected she was constantly on the phone to her friends in Florida. Bob had been a trooper, taking his assignments seriously. Shawn? A little surly, but he brightened ten minutes later when I slipped him a check for thirty thousand dollars. Surprisingly, the twins seemed the most taken off guard by the announcement of our departure. They huddled with Skeeter and then the three of them disappeared into the room they'd been using. I was beyond caring. The exhaustion and antihistamine were taking a heavy toll. I returned to the guest bedroom, indifferent whether Sally pounced on me or not. She didn't. Alright; I was a little disappointed.

————————

Three hours later, one hour before our middle-of-the-night flight, the Suburban disgorged the Taylor-Brown family and their FBI escorts at Hartsfield airport. Shawn was entrusted with locating official parking and staying with the vehicle. He seemed to welcome the assignment.

It had been a noisy trip down. Malkowitz had leveled with his partner – a calculated risk. Her response was predictable. "Doesn't your badge mean anything to you? . . . Or mine? . . . You give these fugitives a free pass and you won't be able to get a job as a parking lot attendant. . . . You heard those County Mounties this morning. . . . I don't want to hear that drivel about 'justice' again. That's what we have courts for. We bring 'em in. We don't judge 'em."

It went on like this for the full trip. In a departure from his previous approach to Bernstein, Malkowitz focused on her as if weighing her every word. He wasn't. He'd made it clear to me he didn't have time to fool around with legal processes in north Georgia and he didn't trust them to produce the right outcome.

With every passing minute the conviction grew that Malkowitz had miscalculated Bernstein's response. "You know you're making me an accomplice. I'm going to have to blow the whistle, Malkowitz." This threat elicited a pleading look but no retreat from Bernstein. "Don't do it."

Malkowitz, out of arguments, sighed.

"You leave me no choice." Bernstein huffed. "You take these four through security and that's it."

This was turning out worse than I'd anticipated. Not only were we fugitives, we were now trying to slip out of the country when we should be giving statements in an Atlanta police station. Flight is reflexively interpreted as an admission of guilt.

Malkowitz continued to acknowledge Bernstein, but his responses had become rote, "I understand . . . I take full responsibility . . . You can take a cab back to the hotel and I'll say you were unaware of what I was doing." None of this was working.

We went to the business class check-in to deposit luggage and collect our boarding passes.

"Dr. Brown? There's a hold on your departure, placed by the Dahlonega Police Department. I see it hasn't been removed. Do you have a release signed by a judge or other competent authority?"

Malkowitz stepped forward and flashed his ID with an impressive air of confidence. Being tall helps. "The Bureau is responsible for ensuring these four leave the country. We'd appreciate your cooperation in making their safe departure as discreet and smooth as possible."

The counter agent looked flummoxed. Was this a deportation? Were we dangerous? Malkowitz anticipated the concern. "This family is being helped for their own security." True enough. "Again, discretion will best serve the national interest."

The counter agent scanned our faces and fidgeted. "They don't have anything to do with the gun smuggling that's been going on, do they?" Ah shit. A logical connection for her to make and also a reminder: where had Sally stashed our two handguns? If those were found on us or in our luggage Malkowitz would lose what little control he had over events. And we would be clapped in irons; not only running from the law, *but* doing it with loaded weapons.

Meanwhile, Bernstein had positioned herself further down the check-in counter, from where she shook her head sadly at Malkowitz. When would she pull the rug out from under us?

"No, this is a separate matter from the gun incidents. I wish I could be more informative, but you understand . . ."

A sweet small voice rose up from below the counter. "Daddy? Can we sit next to you and will you tell us a story?"

The counter agent leaned forward to see what was under the piles of red hair. Four beseeching eyes turned away from me toward the agent, who smiled and, without looking away from the twins, handed over the boarding passes. "Have a good flight. And, Dr. Brown? Make it a good story for the little dears," followed by a rapturous exclamation to no one in particular, "Aren't they just precious?"

Hobbling along on my cane, I whispered, "Sally, where are the pistols? We don't want those surfacing at the wrong moment."

"I thought I should keep one handy in case I needed it."

Needed it? Because KLM served the entrée cold? To get a better seat?

"Agent Malkowitz. My wife needs a bathroom. Could we make a short detour?" I gave Sally as hard a look as, in my weakened state, I could muster. I love her so and she's such a wonderful person. Why this? She returned the hard look.

Sally went into the women's room, re-emerging a minute later. I couldn't read her expression. Had she ditched the gun? If she hadn't, we'd find out somewhere along the way. Agent Bernstein now had her hands placed permanently on her hips. The woman needed a pressure relief valve. I thought I saw steam escaping from her ears. The venom working its magic? I felt lousy.

We approached the security checkpoint. A long line of solemn looking travelers snaked back from the conveyor belts and metal detectors. What would go wrong first? The x-ray spots one or more pistols in our carry-on luggage? Bernstein pulls her gun and places her partner and the Taylor-Browns under arrest? A stronger resurgence of the snake venom would be welcome; I could pass out right there and avoid witnessing the whole mess.

"Last warning, Malkowitz," hissed Bernstein. "I'm not kidding around. Someday you might even thank me."

Agent Malkowitz's response was to approach the security supervisor, a towering Atlanta policeman, and flash his badge. The supervisor – I assume he was a supervisor since he was the only one not doing anything – pointed to a glass door on the far side of the fences that herd travelers along the approved path. Malkowitz returned and led us toward the door; the policeman met us from the other side.

I risked a glance at Bernstein who had her hand inside her jacket, probably on her pistol. Who knew Malkowitz would be so pig-headed? Maybe I should say something and back out of this. Or faint, an increasingly likely event.

The policeman opened the door and we went through: Sally, the twins, limping Max, Malkowitz, and Bernstein. The door swung shut behind us and as the lock clicked, Bernstein pulled her pistol from her shoulder holster. "I didn't think it would come to this. Don't ever say I didn't warn you."

I blurted, "I knew it. Prison time for everyone."

35

Let me try to recreate the scene. I have to do this for my own benefit from time to time. I was woozy and ready to drop.

- Agent Bernstein had her gun out, pointed at Agent Malkowitz.
- Sally had put her hand in her purse, a reflex action that could mean only one thing.
- The policeman's expression had turned to one of stark terror.
- Other travelers were exhibiting the full range of possible reactions: from panic to delight at being part of the drama.
- I was leaning more heavily on the cane. Night was descending.
- The twins were surveying the scene with cool detachment.

I was pulled back to full awareness by something pulling on my legs. "Noooo," wailed M&M with one voice. "Don't make our daddy go to prison." Clinging desperately to their daddy, their eyes had filled instantly with tears. Adjusting tactics after a couple of drawn-out sobs, they ran to Bernstein and wrapped their small arms around her substantial waist. "Please, Mrs. Bernstein. He's our daddy. He's been so brave and taken care of us. He saved us and mommy too. You can't send him to jail for that. Not a good person like you."

I was touched. Maybe there was a tear in my eye at that point. I don't remember.

You know how this plays out, right? The twerps always get their way. It's nice to occasionally see them use their powers for good. Bernstein was no match for tear-filled green eyes, and little arms clinging to her. Plus, they were her biggest fans. She lowered her pistol which emboldened the policeman to timidly ask, "What do you want M'am?" What were the options? A flight to Havana?

Bernstein recovered nicely. "This man needs a wheelchair. Can't you see that?"

"Of course, M'am. I would have brought one without the gun. You FBI people need to dial it back."

————————

Then things got much better. Agent Bernstein pushed my wheelchair to the boarding gate. She seemed to be proud of the way she'd turned toward the good side at the last second. Would that feeling last?

The retinue of badge-flashing FBI agents and the sight of my mottled and swollen ankle, now propped up on the wheelchair's extended footrest, earned us an immediate upgrade to first class. Thank you, KLM; we'll remember that. As we settled into the plush seats, Sally sternly instructed the flight attendants to keep a watchful eye on the twins. We were deeply grateful for the way they'd turned things around at security, but we hadn't forgotten who they were.

————————

The plane reached cruising altitude, we were fed a multi-course first class meal, the twins passed out, and I got a second wind. Not welcome, as I was counting on some sleep before navigating the transfer at Schipol airport with a wife who was probably toting a very illegal firearm in her purse.

Perhaps, now that the Klan was behind us, she could be persuaded to abandon it. We had to be on the same page. "Sally, there's something we need to get straight between us."

"There is indeed," she replied with that wonderful grin. "I understand you flyboys have some kind of club we could join." She stood and took my hand. "Want to see how much room there is in these first-class loos?"

Of course I did. A discussion of the whole gun business could wait for another time.

Epilogue

I've tried this twice before – an epilogue – each time expressing the heart-felt hope that life would settle down. A humdrum life. It sounds great.

We returned safely to Switzerland, the girls became more reclusive, but we were unaware of any major trouble they'd gotten into, and I got busy writing up this – I fervently hope last – installment. The most significant loose strands were those we left behind in Georgia. For an update, I can't improve on a letter we received from Agent Malkowitz a week ago.

 United States Department of Justice
Federal Bureau of Investigation
Southeast Region
Miami, FL

29 August 1993

Dear Mr. and Mrs. Brown,

I hope this finds you safely at home and Mr. Brown's ankle mending. I promised to update you on events after your departure. In no particular order:

You will be relieved to know, as was I, that my efforts on your behalf at the airport went unpunished. There were, of course, some lingering questions about how you all got out of the country, but I think someone in the Bureau thinks so little of the Dahlonega PD that there was no interest in sinking resources into a thorough investigation.

I would like to be able to write that my partner turned over a new leaf at the airport and I now work with a kinder, gentler Lois Bernstein. I can't. She had reverted to her old form by the following morning.

As predicted, Rocco Snyder's girlfriend did seem to want to go to prison in atonement for her moral failure, but there were some convoluted behind-the-scenes workings:

1. The DPD cop dropped the charge of attempted homicide against her.

2. Mr. Snyder refused to file a complaint against either the cop who tried to smother him or the men who beat and shot him.

3. I have not heard directly, but I assume this means the charges against you two and Mr. Ferguson were also dropped. However, you should have your attorney check on this before traveling to the US.

4. As you may recall, we left Boon and Billy with the Fannin County Sheriff's office for safe-keeping. Before they could be arraigned they slipped away into the hills, despite the load of venom Mrs. Brown had administered. The mayor used their escape to argue for federal funding for a better jail. Of course he continues to rail against federal interference in local affairs.

Fred Jones, the nice ranger, was transferred to Oklahoma.

We keep in touch with Shawn Ferguson. The ACLU did judge his case sufficiently high profile and agreed to take it on, but with the charges against him evaporating and the culprits slipping out of custody . . . he faded from the public eye. Interestingly, he's applying to the Bureau and asked me for a reference.

I touched base with Karl, the deputy sheriff, primarily to mend fences. He said your uncle had left town. Uncle Skitter (?) stopped by the animal shelter, adopted a brindle-colored puppy, and drove off in a nice red van.

That's it. If anything more comes up, I'll let you know. All the best to you and your charming daughters,

Tom Malkowitz

Senior Special Agent

Epilogue #2

That, to my profound annoyance, is not the end of the story.

I finished writing this all up a week ago and was allowing a little time to pass before I came back to give it a polish. Then, last night . . .

Sally and I were at a *cocktail/reception/someone showing off their expensive home* event. The attendees were, as five months earlier, the parents of the girls' classmates and a smattering of faculty, including the ineluctable Dr. Piaget who cornered me early on.

"Dr. Brown, Dr. Brown, how nice to see you. Still favoring that leg with a cane, I see."

The cane was evident; 'still favoring' suggested he knew some history.

"Ah yes, Dr. Piaget, a souvenir."

Before I could protest, he relieved me of my empty glass and replaced it with a full one – a double martini. It would be churlish to walk away after that kindness. Sally would have to drive us home.

"Quite an adventure you all had!" Piaget was beaming approvingly. Admiration for another man seemed alien to his nature, especially in my case. "And what a *hero* dad turned out to be; facing down a *killer, and* a bear, *and* a venomous snake." Sally had told the twins about the bear and snake, knowing that my natural modesty would preclude my extolling these acts of heroism to the girls. Were the little pills bragging about their foppish old father?

"A happy ending, sir. We're all back, safe and sound."

"But, the talk of the school. Your daughters bring in something different every week to 'show and tell.' They're little spellbinders, I must say. I've had them over to my class even though they've moved up to the next level."

"Well, you might want to take their stories with a barrel of salt, Dr. Piaget. What – I tremble to ask – have they been showing and telling?"

"Fascinating stuff, Dr. Brown – but of course you know. The first week they read to us from their Guide to Treasure, and we were impressed, but we had no idea what was to come. The next week they showed us the maps. Then that fascinating journal the general's assistant kept during your war over slavery. By that time many of us had started to suspect they were building to something very big. But when they started bringing in what they'd found, well, you can imagine!"

"Imagine what?"

"You know. All the different gold coins! So many! They showed us some one-dollar coins and some five-dollar coins, but they must be worth a lot more, being so old and made of pure gold."

"Fake coins, of course. You've been taken in, sir. In your defense, they are tricky little rascals." Was there a slight quaver in my voice?

"Hardly, Dr. Brown. Heavy and soft. I know a little about gold, if I may say. Your family treasure hunt was a splendid success. You must be awfully proud."

"Proud doesn't begin to describe my emotions, Dr. Piaget. If you'll excuse me, I just caught my wife's eye. There's something we need to discuss."

Glossary

Perhaps out of habit, here's a glossary. The first two books included one.

10-20. *The Association of Public-Safety Communications Officials-International* 'Ten codes' were designed to streamline radio communication. The ten was the uniform prefix and came into use for the curious reason that it provided a brief second for the vacuum tube radios – in use when these codes were first adopted – to warm up; cops were not trusted to remember to pause after pressing the microphone button. The real information was the second number. Here, 20 means 'what's your location?'

10-31. Same system. 31 stands for 'crime in progress.'

Adit. This is a horizontal tunnel leading into a mine for access or drainage. A shaft, the commonly – and mistakenly – used term, actually describes vertical holes that provide access to the mine.

APB. All-points bulletin.

Attractive nuisance. Under Georgia law a landowner may be held liable if a child – including teenagers – is harmed by items on their property that are "inherently dangerous instrumentalities" that are attractive to children.

AWOL. Absent without leave.

BATF. The Bureau of Alcohol, Tobacco and Firearms. Initially part of the Treasury Department, later transferred to the Department of Justice. Historically ATF was primarily concerned with collecting taxes on sales of alcohol and tobacco products; consistent with that responsibility, ATF was a part of the IRS. ATF agents were the much despised 'revenooers' that ferreted out illegal stills in the mountains. As time passed ATF became more concerned with violent crime and was moved to the DoJ.

Brig. A prison on a warship or military – especially naval – base.

CDL. Commercial Driver's License. Required to operate larger passenger vehicles and trucks for hire. In Georgia the minimum age for a CDL is 18, but commercial driving privileges are restricted to operating only within the state until the operator reaches 21.

Conversion van. A full-sized van that has been outfitted – usually as an after-sales modification – with the basics for independent living: toilet, sink, stove, refrigerator, beds, etc.

CSA. Confederate States of America.

Deliverance. A 1972 movie that depicted, among other things, how nasty mountain people are (as seen from the lofty moral heights of Hollywood). Four Atlanta businessmen head into the wilderness of northeastern Georgia where they are stalked by some backwoods residents. It gets ugly. Two locals and one of the visitors from the city are killed; another businessman is raped by a mountain man.

Drift. A horizontal or inclined mine passage that follows a mineral vein.

Euro Disney. An amusement park outside Paris, later renamed Disney Paris. It's smaller than its US counterparts, and has been less successful commercially, although that's only when compared to the vast profits Disney operations are expected to rake in.

Grand Dragon. Head of the KKK at the state (realm, in Klanspeak) level.

IDF. Israel Defense Forces. They include ground, air, and sea units.

Kimchi. A Korean spicy pickled dish made from cabbage, or radishes, or cucumbers, or scallions and on and on; there are many variations. An acquired taste; American GIs who served in Korea used the word as synonymous with shit. It's not *that* bad.

KKK. Ku Klux Klan. Formed after the Civil War to oppose reconstruction. Klan members today are most exercised over same-sex marriage, illegal immigration, and full equality for African Americans. Affirmative action sends them into sputtering paroxysms of rage. Although their numerical strength has declined steadily, they continue to be a presence in many towns in the southern and south mid-western United States. Some incarnations have attempted to project a kinder, civic-action face. I'm not buying it.

KOA. Kampgrounds of America. A privately owned chain of campgrounds. They operate around 500 in the US and Canada.

Loo. A Britishism for toilet. It originated, according to legend, in 17th century Paris and London where chamber pots were emptied from upper story windows into the street with the shouted warning, "Garde de l'eau.'' (Watch out for the water.) In England, l'eau morphed into loo and the cry became 'gardyloo.'

Mile High Club. Come on. Surely you know what this is.

MO. *Modus operandi.* Latin for 'method of operating.' The way a person normally does things.

Mutt and Jeff. A comic strip launched in 1907 featuring two loveable losers, one tall (Jeff) and one short (Mutt). Over time it's become a term to refer to any pair that's comically mismatched.

Pager. Testimony to the speed with which telecommunications technology is moving, some reviewers of this book were unfamiliar with pagers. The typical pager could receive a simple message sent to it. For example, many could display ten digits, as in a phone number. The first general use was by physicians in New York. Cellphones have relegated pagers to buggy-whip status.

Speleology. The scientific study or recreational exploration of caves. Also includes recreational exploration of abandoned mines.

Theodicy. This is a long-running theological controversy over why an all-caring and all-powerful God would allow evil to run rampant in his creation. If you read my first book (*How I Made $3.2 Million From My Hobby* – available at remainder counters and yard sales everywhere) you'll see how, when I was younger, the question fascinated me.

Topographical. Topographical maps show the physical features of the landscape; for example, they typically have contour lines so the gradients of slopes can be better interpreted by the map user. Most topo maps also include major man-made features.

USFS. The United States Forest Service administers the country's 155 national forests that sprawl across 193 million acres – about nine percent of the land in the US. There are over 600 Ranger Stations, including the one in Blairsville. The largest item in the budget is for fighting fires. The USFS is frequently the subject of critical scrutiny for: mishandling a forest fire, not doing enough – or doing too much – to mitigate the threat of forest fire, overzealous protection of endangered species, selling logging rights too cheaply, failing to sell timber at all, being too *in*flexible about encroachment on USFS property, being too flexible about the same . . . you get the idea.

USGS. The United States Geological Survey is a scientific agency that does many things, including conducting surveys and publishing maps. It has no regulatory responsibilities and manages no significant resources so is rarely in the public eye.

Zelig. The title character in a Woody Allen film about the fictional Leonard Zelig, a human chameleon, who would adopt the characteristics, attitudes and appearance of those around him. The film's release kicked off a discussion among psychologists whether such a personality disorder was plausible.

About the author

Michael Bernhart lives part-time in northern Georgia among many hard-working fine people.

www.ingramcontent.com/pod-product-compliance
Lightning Source LLC
Chambersburg PA
CBHW050018180626

46810CB00002B/468